ARRIVEDERCI LEOPOLIS

THE LION'S WAR

SAM IVEY & GEORGE PERANTONI

"...man has dominated man to his injury." (Eccl. 8:9)

ARRIVEDERCI LEOPOLIS: THE LION'S WAR

ISBN   978-1-64552-115-0   (Paperback)
ISBN   978-1-64552-116-7   (Digital)

Lettra Press books may be ordered through booksellers or by contacting:

Lettra Press LLC
30 N Gould St. Ste N
Sheridan, WY 82801, USA
3035861431 | info@lettrapress.com
www.lettrapress.com

Set against the background of World War II, this is a story of the 20th century as experienced through the lives of an Italian wine exporter, his family and his friends.

Depicting historical events of the early 20th century, World War I is seen as the precursor to the destruction of the World Trade Center on September 11, 2001.

Literary material registered with
Writers Guild of America, East, Inc.,
as "Leopolis – The Philatelist of Lwów" (2010)
and "Arrivederci Leopolis – The Lion's War" (2011)

Photography and Stamp Collections
courtesy of Vittorio Perantoni

TABLE OF CONTENTS

"I have seen the ruthless, evil man, spreading out like a luxuriant tree in its native soil. But he suddenly passed away and was gone; I kept searching for him, and he could not be found." — Psalm 37: 35, 36 (NWT)

Sic transit gloria mundi.

PROLOGUE

"What time ya' got, Ed?"

Ed Lemanski threw a quick glance at his watch. "Eight forty-five, Charlie."

They had one minute to live.

Vernon Duke's *Autumn in New York,* courtesy of Muzak, hung hauntingly in the office air. Charlie Kroger rose from his desk. "How about some coffee, Ed?"

Fifty-six seconds remained.

Lemanski nodded and smiled. "Yeah, I could go for that."

He organized some papers he was working on and stood. Together they walked across the office.

Forty-four seconds now.

A short walk down a hallway brought them to the employee's lounge. Others were there.

Thirty-two seconds.

Kroger was drawing a cup as Natalie Forrest remarked from her seat, "Gonna be a warm one today, Charlie. I can feel it."

Twenty-one seconds.

"Yeah, you might be right," Kroger replied, casting an appraising glance at the window's bright, glassy expanse. "It's sure a sunny one."

And he walked to where Natalie was sitting. "Did you catch Leno on *The Tonight Show* last night?"

Twelve seconds now.

"No, not last night. I went to bed early. I seldom watch that anyway."

Seven seconds remained.

Lemanski was drawing coffee now and laughing. Over his shoulder he said, "Oh, you should've heard him, Nat. He really had Bush's number. I was . .."

Lemanski suddenly staggered as coffee flew abruptly from his cup. It was 8:46.

In New York's World Trade Center, the 93rd floor of the north tower suddenly trembled; it shuddered as though struck by the very fist of God. In that nanosecond of time their lives ended.

True, that they were still alive; that is, they were still sentient, still breathing. But below them, on the 90th floor, there was limitless wreckage and chaos; there were fire and blood, terror and death beyond conception.

And they were trapped. There was no way down save to fall; an immutable truth, a morbid dread that galvanized everyone in the room.

There were no alarms, and the lights had gone out; there was no power. Everyone stood dumbstruck. From other offices on the floor, cries of helpless panic began to be heard. There was weeping. The awful reality — the unacceptable and inconceivable reality — was being understood by all. Here is where they would die; they would never be seen again.

Ed's cup would never be filled.

CHAPTER I

Three days have passed since the never-to-be-forgotten tragedy in New York City. Friday, the 14th of September 2001, sees a humid evening in Orlando, Florida; unusually humid for this time of the year. Blowing in from off Lake Weston, bringing the smells of autumn and disturbing the air occasionally, is a pleasant, island-like breeze.

Earlier he had strolled across the lakefront lawn lying between his home and that of his father. And now George Perantoni, his crisp white shirt open at the neck, sleeves rolled up, is seated on a deck that extends over the lake's placid water; a deck he and his brother Roberto had built twenty years earlier. It had been a gift to their father upon his retirement, a deck they had promised their father would survive any hurricane … survive even Armageddon!

In company with his 90 year-old father Vittorio, known to his friends as Victor, they have been in animated discussion over a rare Italian stamp.

Understood by knowing philatelists to be a forgery, the stamp bears the likeness of Benito Mussolini, Italy's fascist leader in the early decades of the 20th century.

Using his pet name for an older son, Robert, Victor said, "Have you spoken with Beto?"

George looked up from scanning the stamp with a magnifying glass, as Victor casts a critical eye on a glass of wine he is enjoying.

"Oh, yes; they're on the road, he and Mary; they left Milwaukee this afternoon and expect to arrive here in a couple days. Roberto said not to worry if he's late; he's expecting huge traffic delays. Since that New York thing, half of America is on the road. Nobody's flying." And his attention returned to the stamp.

Victor nodded and swirled the wine gently, noting the cling—the "fingers" on the interior of the glass. "Hmm, not bad; it's nice."

Looking up again from the stamp and glancing at his father, George said, "It's certainly an unusual one, Dad."

Victor shook his graying head and smiled. "No, not the stamp, George, the wine; the *wine* is nice. But you are right; the stamp is unusual." Then after a pause, his lilting accent unmistakably laden with the flavor of Italy, he continued.

"I canna remember … I canna remember when la nostra familia used to make wine like this." Then shaking an admonishing finger at the glass he added, "Better than this." Then reflectively, "But O … that was such a long time ago.

"I canna remember too, evenings like this in Italy, in the summer when it was warm. I would sit as we are sitting now, with your grandfather, and he and I would look at the stamps together." Now he folded his arms and leaned back in his chair. Staring vacantly into space he said, "It was such a good time, George— a really good time."

George laid down the magnifying glass. "And then it all changed, didn't it, Dad."

Silent tears suddenly glistened in Victor's aging eyes. "Yes," he said. "Yes, it all changed: our wine business; la Winiarnia; la mia cara Polonia; even la bella Italia. Tutto—everything!" A sigh and a plaintive whisper as he added, "It all changed."

With the back of a thumbnail, George scratched one of those inexplicable itches on the side of his nose and looked at his father with a skewed expression. "But why, Dad?"

"Ah ha ha ha ha!" A cynical chuckle and an empty smile. And now a sip from his glass before Victor suggested, "You may just as well ask me why the World Trade Center three days ago, George. Who's to know what goes on in the minds of madmen?" A hopeless shake of his head now, and a puckered mouth. "I could give you a lot of examples, but it would only spoil this quiet evening and waste this fine wine. You just enjoy the stamps, George, and let me enjoy the sunset."

He eased his aging frame from his chair now, and went to walk along the water's edge. He walked slowly, hands clasped behind his back, his eyes fixed on the handsome, mossy-green cedars growing on the far side of the lake. Rising up behind them and as though in competition, other trees blazed in regal autumn colors: reds and golds, and burgundies; now and then one in flaming yellow. But such beauty could not ease his troubled mind, a mind unable to divorce the recent brutal attack on New York's twin towers from two similar attacks—altogether as brutal and every bit as sudden—on the two cities of his childhood, attacks he had experienced and which had robbed him of his youth.

So while George's attention remained focused on his father's collection of pre-war Polish stamps, Victor's mind drifted back to those cities, to Lwów in Eastern Poland and to Volargne di Dolcé, in the Valpolicella region of Northern Italy. Happy days they had been. And Lwów in particular had been where he had acquired a great part of the collection that now held his son's rapt attention —a collection that had nearly cost him his life at the outset of World War II in 1939.

By the time of Victor's birth there in 1912, an Italian with Austrian-Hungarian citizenship, later to be Italian and then Polish due to the idiosyncrasies of European administrations following the great war of 1914, Lwów was already a richly multi-cultured city of great antiquity, having at various times been the possession of Germany, Russia, Poland and Austria- Hungary. The city's name, therefore, and according to one's language, had more than one pronunciation. To Ukrainians it was Lviv, only somewhat different. To the Russians it was Lvov. But the meaning in both languages was the same: *Lions*. To Germans and Austrians it became Lemberg, originally Lowenberg, meaning *City of Lions*, while to Italians it was Leopoli, again with the same meaning. If circumstances required that he speak English, Victor preferred to use Elvov, while in Italian, if necessary, he would pronounce it Levov. But however it was pronounced, its name from ancient medieval Latin—Leopolis—was recognized by all who lived there.

And Victor loved his hometown, his birth town, preferring to pronounce its name only in Polish. For it was in this city that he had spent the happiest days of his youth, a city eventually lost to the Nazis in 1939, and later to the Soviets.

The old man had returned to his seat now, and his eyes were bright with more pleasant memories. "As to your question, George," he began, "simple courtesy demands an answer; so just let me say that it all changed because of the second world war. But I don't want to talk about that, not now. Instead, let me take you back ten years before that, back to nineteen twenty-nine. Let me tell you what it was like during those years; the best days of my youth they were.

"True that the stock market had crashed, and the entire world was experiencing a great economic depression, but we didn't feel it because it actually caused our wine sales to increase! Life was so great back then, really great. Even so, I seldom talk of this much because … well, because many of the good memories too often lead to unpleasant ones. But tonight just seems like a good time to share them with you."

He paused now, allowing his eyes to gaze unseeingly out over the lake and while George refilled both wine glasses, closed the case containing the collection, and sat back to listen as Victor went on.

"The world was so much quieter then, and I was seventeen … huh huh, seventeen." And he shook his head, smiling at the memory. "I'd come home to Lwów after completing high school in Italy, in Volargne, and your grandfather, Carlo, introduced me to a client of his, a printer whose name was Frodel, André Frodel.

"Now he was thirty-nine at the time, twenty-two years older than I was, but we became very close friends." A look of curiosity on George's face and Victor responded. "I know, you're probably thinking it was more likely that he should have been your grandfather's friend; and of course he was. But our mutual love of philately, of collecting stamps, and his youthful enthusiasm for such collecting and trading—and this despite his age, or maybe because of it— was the bond between us. It was the beginning of a long friendship, George. You should see the letters I have from him.

"Later, as André introduced me to several members of the Lwów Stamp Club, I learned that these were all very distinguished gentlemen, all prominent associates of Central Europe's philatelic society—'the stamp collectors,' people would call us. And I in turn acquainted him with some philatelist connections I had in Italy, and in Switzerland.

"Now then. I didn't know it, but my life was changing; I was meeting a lot of older men. Because André—like I said, twenty-two years older— now introduced me to the President of the Lwów Stamp Club, a fellow by the name of Covasech; a man whose name, curiously and regrettably, has disappeared from history. And after the introduction, André warned me."

Surprised, George looked sharply at his father. "He warned you? Why?"

A sly smile, one that George knew well, warmed Victor's smoothly weathered face. "Aaah!" he said. "That's a story for later, for another time. But O the times we had together then. Many were the fun-filled evenings we spent together at your grandfather's wine tavern. La Winiarnia Italia Inn it was called. Sometimes dad would join us, along with my older brother, your uncle Luigi, and we'd spend the whole evening trading stamps and playing cards— gambling; and the stamps made up the pot. And we'd eat! Oh, yes! Usually it was pastasciutta, the house specialty. Delicious! And the cooks would prepare it several different ways; all local Italian styles. My personal favorite was always *a la carbonara con pancetta*. And there was red wine. Oh, yes; always there was the wine!

"And the songs! Oh, loud boisterous songs they were; all inspired by Italy's fascist thinking, of course." And he broke into a spontaneous ditty as the words flooded back to his mind. "…Giovinezza … Faccetta Nera … Ciao Biondina … Vincere … Fiamme Nere …" Then smiling sheepishly: "They were all songs of the fascist youth of Italy. And we had no idea; no idea at all of the horrors that lay ahead.

"And there was this Polish fellow, a university student he was. His name was Mrowicki, Franciszek Mrowicki. We just called him Franki for short. Anyway, he was a year older than I was, and through him I met Michele Kolbuch, a Vatican missionary priest that we all called 'Padre,' and who was older than both of us. He was twenty-six. Back then we were all Catholics, of course, and we were all ardent philatelists; André and Padre having been loyal clients at your grandfather's Winiarnia Italia for several years."

Over the next half hour or so, largely in response to George's queries, the old man went on about the family's early years; about his grandfather's wine exporting business and about the winery tavern there in Lwów. It was then inevitable that the pending rise of fascism in Europe would incise its way into the conversation. And it was finally with tears brimming that Victor suddenly lashed out, reviling Hitler and Mussolini, both of whom he charged with costing him the loss of the two beloved cities of his youth.

With acid contempt and his dark eyes snapping he said, "And I can still remember the day that Hitler and Mussolini came to our Winiarnia."

"You met Hitler?" George exclaimed quietly. "Really? Wow! Now that must have been something."

"No," said the old man softly, shaking his head; fingers stroking a lightly whiskered chin. Then the same hand waved about as he said, "Actually it was more like nothing. Because back then it was Mussolini who was the world famous figure; he was the one who got all my attention. Hitler was with him, but he meant nothing to me at the time. Actually he meant little to most people outside Germany. He was not then the infamous Führer; he was not even Germany's chancellor, not yet. What he was, was a copy-cat; he was going to copy Mussolini's way of doing things. Matter of fact, it's been said that in her memoirs, Mussolini's wife, Donna Rachele, wrote that her husband had once called Hitler '*una scimmietta*,' 'a silly little monkey,' as in 'Monkey see, monkey do'."

George smiled at the sarcasm as a yawn distorted Victor's next words. His mouth widening he said, "Oh, how the tables turned years later. But remind me to tell you more about that at another time. It's getting late now. Go home George; give my love to Valerie and go to bed." And he finished his wine.

Indeed, dusk had fallen and fireflies could be seen sparkling in the low shrubbery as George stood. He hugged his father and turned to leave. But even as his son walked away, Victor knew that his own sleep would be troubled. It had happened before, when talk of Mussolini and of Hitler had dredged up too many unpleasant memories.

For as they had spoken he had been reminded of the hatred he had felt for Hitler's Nazism, and his great disappointment in Mussolini's Fascism; this for their having initiated World War II and all the misery and suffering which it produced. He remembered also the miserable conditions of his Ukrainian friends in Lwów and regions of Southeast Poland; social conditions which had sometimes triggered armed attacks on Polish military barracks and police stations. This by irate Ukrainians protesting their oppression.

And he remembers that there had been more than ample reason for such displays of rebellious discontent. Because even before the war, in the early 1930s, thousands of Ukrainians comprising the intelligentsia: the university professors, the writers, poets and playwrights; the musicians and the artists whose loyalties were suspect by the dread *Narodnyy komissariat vnutrennikh del*, or NKVD—the Soviet Secret Police—were arrested and subsequently vanished. It was a period of time that came to be called the *Rozstrilaniy vidrodzhennia*, the "Executed Renaissance" of Ukrainian literature.

Added to that was the memory of Stalin's banning of Ukrainian churches, both Orthodox and Catholic. The Russian Orthodox Church alone was allowed to function. Little wonder then that many

Ukrainians, in and around Lwów, believed there could be nothing worse than Communist Russian slavery. And they consequently, though naively, welcomed the German Army; an Army representative of what they understood to be a cultured nation.

Regrettably, as would later be the situation between Russia and Poland in the 1940s, Ukrainians were unaware that Nazi ideology classified them as *Untermenschen*, that is to say, people less than human. As regards their land—the so-called "Breadbasket of Europe"—the black earth of which is some of the richest agricultural land in the world, it was Hitler's racist design to colonize it with a German population. He had in mind, in fact, as with the Jewish people, the total extermination of the Ukrainians.

Particularly bitter was one memory: that following the Russian-Ukrainian surrender after the Battle of Kiev in 1941, when a total of 665,000 soldiers were captured by the Germans. These men, who had so willingly surrendered, were intentionally starved to death; or they died of exposure in open-air concentration camps during the 1941-1942 winter. And it was but only two weeks after Germany's invasion, when the Nazis began their open persecution of the Ukrainian nation.

On December 16th then, in 1942, it is recorded that Hitler ordered the use of—in his words—the "most brutal means" against guerrilla fighters in Ukraine, "even against women and children." And he recalls that for three years, Ukrainians suffered under the Nazi occupation.

Such thoughts as these would bedevil him through the dark hours. And if he did sleep, they would lace his dreams. It would be an uneasy night.

"I thought it would be a good idea," said Victor, having resumed his story telling on the following evening, "to have monthly meetings at the Winiarnia. I thought it could be good for business."

Sitting with his wife Gina in the patio of George and Valerie's home, the four of them watched a fiery autumn sunset paint the western sky with flamboyant colors. With cold orange juice in glasses, they listened as he began to explain how he had convinced his father, Carlo, that a swap-meet for their philatelic friends might very well prove to be a business advantage. "I had also come to know something about André," he said.

And George remembered. "Does this have anything to do with the warning you mentioned last evening?"

The crafty smile again, the little crow's feet crinkling at the corners of his eyes. "Yes, as a matter of fact, it does. You see, André had told me, confidentially of course, that if I allowed Covasech to trade stamps with me that I'd lose my shirt! And André was right. On that very night, in fact, this Covasech fellow obtained from me the first two series of Italian postage stamps; those of eighteen sixty-three and eighteen seventy-nine."

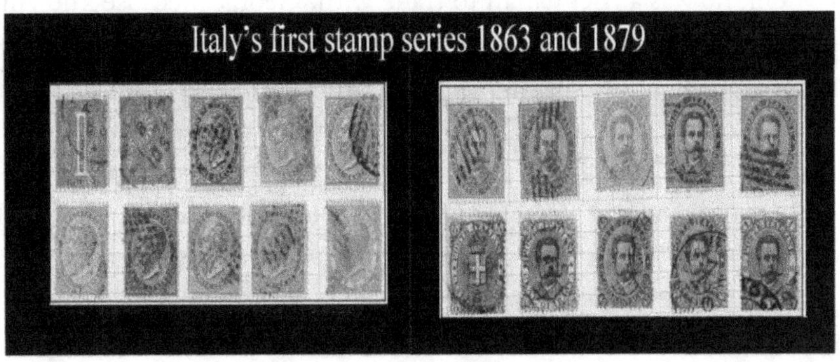

"And you got from him …?"

"Ha ha ha ha. From him I got one complete set of commemorative stamps." A deep sigh before he added, "Which he had made himself!"

"He what?" George exclaimed, the words punctuating a soft laugh. "He made stamps?"

"Yes, and I understand your surprise. But can you just imagine that? Stamps that he made himself! With no authority whatever, he had made commemorative stamps. And on top of that, about five hundred of these were actually mailed and postmarked! And he had some of those also. So now he wanted to trade some of his postmarked envelopes, bearing his stamps, for some old Italian letters that he knew I had, attractive letters, hand written in gorgeous calligraphy; letters that were mailed before there were any postage stamps in Italy. Now that's going back to before eighteen sixty-three.

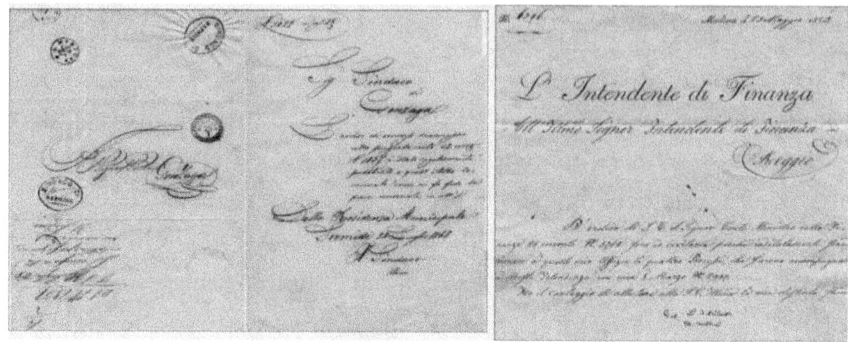

"Oh, he was a tricky man to trade with, George, because knowing that I had several of such letters, he really wanted them. But this time I remembered André's warning, and I refused to trade with him; like I'm a little smarter now; right? WRONG! What a mistake that was!"

"Oh? Why, Dad?"

"Because, my boy, those stamps—those unauthorized stamps which Mr. Covasech had made—have become so very *rare* that modern catalogs don't even list them. Oh, I've been kicking myself in the seat of my pants ever since! Because the last listing of Covasech's stamps was in the German catalog—the *Michel Briefmarken Katalog* of nineteen forty. After that … nothing; it's as if they never existed!"

George's brow now furrowed with confusion. As he refilled his glass with juice he said, "But I don't get it, Dad. Because if the stamps were not official, wouldn't they just be … Could you explain that?"

"Oh, yes. You see, son, Mr. Covasech had been a mail officer in the Austria-Hungarian Army during the Great War—World War One; he had been a lieutenant. Now in October of nineteen seventeen, eighty-four years ago next month, with the war at its height and following the battle of Caporetto, Austria- Hungary had successfully occupied eighteen small towns in Northern Italy. But their army's mail van had been completely destroyed in the battles; it had been burned. So lieutenant Covasech, acting on his own authority as the mail officer in charge, and claiming, of course, to be acting in the interest of soldier morale at a time of a military postal crisis, saw the situation as a prime opportunity to issue provisional stamps—stamps which he knew all along would become a very limited and rare item."

And now it was Valerie, her dark Latin eyes bright with interest, who voiced her confusion. "But it seems to me that if there were no stamps to be had, why couldn't this Covasech fellow have just …"

"Moved mail without any stamps?" Victor interjected.

"Well … yeah!"

"O you're absolutely right, Val." And Victor shook an acknowledging finger toward her. "He could have done just that. But … fanatical philatelist that he was, he seized the opportunity to manufacture his own stamps— *commemorative* stamps. He designed eighteen sets of four stamps each, a complete series of seventy-two stamps to memorialize the eighteen towns they had recently captured."

As with Valerie, George was now virtually consumed with curiosity. "But how, Dad? How did he do it?"

"Oh, he was clever, George, he was *una volpe*—a fox. I swear; between him and André, I don't know who was the better. He used— can you imagine this?— local matchbook tax seals. These were gummed stamp-like seals produced for the Italian matchbook monopoly, and he overprinted them with the Austrian word *Ortspostmarke* in four colors, this to represent four monetary denominations. Then he overprinted the names of the eighteen Italian cities which had been captured by his army, with each city in four denominations, thus making complete sets of seventy-two gummed tax-seal stamps, commemorating their recent eighteen victories. Two days later, when a replacement mail van was furnished, he destroyed all remaining sheets of his provisional stamps; with the exception, that is, of five complete sets. And I am the fortunate owner of one of those very rare sets."

"So why kick yourself in the seat of your pants?"

"Because, George!" And now his excitement grew. "During the first two days after that battle, those encamped Austrian troops sent letters home using Covasech's stamps! And he, Covasech, *personally* postmarked and initialed each letter himself. And those stamps are *extremely* rare, because they were only in circulation for about sixty hours. And though I own a complete mint set ..." He grew wistful now. ". . . it would be really wonderful if I also owned only a few of those postmarked letters to go with my set, and to validate their usage. Fortunately I have that *Briefmarken* catalog, and I can use that to prove the existence and circulation of these very rare stamps."

George refilled their glasses again, and Victor continued.

"But getting back to André: Remember that I said he was a printer? Well, he was also a very talented artist. And that, coupled with his printer's skills, made him a very accomplished counterfeiter!"

"But Dad, that would ..."

"Be illegal? Yes, George; yes it would be illegal. That is, if he had used his skills to defraud the Postal System, or to even cheat stamp collectors. But he was an honest man, and he never defrauded anyone. So, like Covasech, André never did this to deceive. With him it was a ... well, it was a hobby; he made counterfeit stamps as novelties. Why, we even used to award them as door prizes during the Winiarnia's stamp meets."

On he went then, telling of how they had made fancy invitational postcards, each of which bore legal postage, but with a simulated stamp placed at the center. And on that stamp was the face of Benito Mussolini, Italy's dictator—Europe's rising superstar.

The old man grinned now with remembered satisfaction. "You can imagine what a success *they* were! And postal clerks too, enjoyed adding their own touch, putting collector-quality cancellation marks on these mock stamps. Well, they soon became the talk of all Italy—of Europe even, causing a buzz of confusion among collectors in those countries who had never seen a Mussolini stamp.

"However, and rightly so I now realize, my father was outraged. You see, despite his position—Honorary Vice Consul of Italian Affairs in South Eastern Poland—his politics, like those of so many during this time in history, were somewhat confused. His loyalty, he felt, was to the king, Victor Emmanuel the third, Italy's proper king, and not to Mussolini. Actually, I think he named me after King Victor. So to see this stamp—this symbol of fascist youth—along with the Winiarnia's address on his son's invitational postcards; well, it was just not acceptable.

"Even so, the meetings became very popular. So much so that early one morning in nineteen twenty-nine, the Italian Consul in Warsaw called my father. You'll never guess what he said."

There was a long pause before George said anxiously, "So what did he say?"

Spreading his hands as though helpless, waving them about with typical Italian enthusiasm, Victor said, "He told my father that Mussolini—IL Duce himself, along with thirteen others—were flying from Vienna to Warsaw, and that he had decided to make an unscheduled landing in Lwów. Later I found out that one of those in the group was Adolf Hitler, leader of Germany's growing Nazi party."

"Ah hah! So that was when you met Hitler."

"Yes, that was the time, George. But right then transportation was the issue; everybody suddenly needed transportation to the Winiarnia.

And lunch reservations were needed, and these for fourteen people. Furthermore, the Consul had also ordered that the Winiarnia be closed to the public during the visit. So my father doesn't like this, but what can he do? Luigi and I are set to cleaning the hall and getting a menu ready, while your grandfather scuttles about, trying to locate five cars—five *deluxe* cars—to transport fourteen people.

"Well, the cars were had; the lunch was a success; and it turns out that your grandfather was delighted. And afterward? Afterward there were several impromptu stamp presentations and some trading. Even IL Duce got involved. Just imagine—the leader of the Partito Nazionale Fascista! He too was an avid philatelist, and he traded me ten PNF party badges for ten of André's Duce art- stamps with his image. Then came an even greater surprise. Mussolini personally initialed two sheets of André's stamps; one for André and one for me. And as a joke he commissioned me to oversee all of the Fascist party's future stamp printing. And I remember that we all laughed at that."

George refilled his glass yet again. "And what was Hitler doing all this time?"

"Oh, he was enjoying himself. Particularly he seemed to enjoy the lively conversation with the younger ones of the group, about the Great War—that's what everyone called the First World War. Well ... since then we've seen the second, of course, and the word *great* has taken on a different meaning.

"Anyway, as he talked on about how that war was lost, and why it was lost, I noted that Hitler appeared to take great pleasure in assigning blame. While granting that the so-called Central Powers had lost the war—he had no choice, of course—he insisted it was not the fault of the *people* of Germany and Austria, nor of their soldiers. Oh, no! No, he put the blame on the Hungarians; he blamed the Bulgarians; he blamed the Turks of the old Ottoman Empire. And it shouldn't surprise you that he blamed the entire Jewish race.

"O he was quite boisterous about it. In fact, he said Germany and Austria could have won the war all by themselves if these others hadn't been involved— and if the Jews hadn't owned the wealth which governed the economy … on both sides, that is. Oh! And though he had claimed that the German people were faultless, he strongly attacked the decisions of the German leadership. Kaiser Wilhelm was wrong; Paul Von Hindenburg was wrong; and for Franz Joseph the first, of Austria, he had nothing but utter contempt!

"And when it came to the Treaty of Versailles, he really started ranting away; blaming those leaders for having accepted the burdens of that Treaty. He literally shouted, 'The Germanic people of Deutschland and Austria did NOT lose the war!' Or something like that; that was the gist of it anyway. No, it was the leaders and their allies, he insisted."

And now Victor shook his head. "Well, we all looked at him, of course, but Hitler wasn't the star of the show back then. No, it would be another four years before he'd even be Germany's chancellor. And besides, this wasn't Germany, this was Poland. And it was Mussolini— IL Duce and his closest companions—who were seen as the really important ones."

Now he grinned, took a deep draft of his juice, and wiped his mouth with a knuckled finger. "Interestingly though, there was a point in the afternoon when Hitler hinted that I should ask André to make an imitation stamp with his picture also. I say it was interesting because this man, this fascist leader, wanted *me* to make the request! So why didn't he do it himself? But I didn't take him seriously. Because after all, who was he? A German politician with a jail record; in this country he would've been a gangster. And Mussolini? Well, he just ignored him. Personally, I felt that IL Duce may have been somewhat annoyed by Hitler, who was arrogantly blowing the Germanic trumpet about how the war was lost; and this in Mussolini's presence, ignoring altogether that Mussolini himself had served in that war, but on the opposite side! We didn't know then, of course, what a monster this Hitler would turn out to be.

"So now your grandfather, dear man that he was, thought it would be nice to have a picture of all of us together. So he got out his camera, an old Ziess Ikon Ikonta with an automatic shutter. And since I loved photography and I was pretty good at it, he asked me to arrange the group and to take the picture.

"So I set up the chairs in our courtyard and mounted the camera on a tripod. Then inviting all the guests to take their places, I made sure that IL Duce sat in the center, the place of honor, right next to your grandpa Carlo. I didn't know what to do with Hitler, however, because the pastel plaid suit he was wearing made him look out of place. So I asked him to stand in the middle, flanked by the other taller guests in dark suits. And I still have that camera.

"When everybody was in position, I set the timed shutter and ran to the back of the group. And there I stood, on a wine box and next to Italy's fascist flag, while the shutter went off. I still have that photo."

"You do?" Valerie said perkily, expressing her surprise. "Could we see it?" Victor looked at her and grinned.

When he returned from the house he was holding a box. Seated now, the box on his lap, he said, "Now there's an interesting story behind this photo. In fact, it just may be one of the rarest, certainly the most controversial, ever taken of Hitler."

As Victor removed the cover from the box, George said, "Oh, really! Why is that?"

The old man looked up from beginning to finger through the treasured collection of photos that meant so much to him. Twisting around to see his son, standing just behind his shoulder, he said, "Because many people won't believe it's true. You see, the history books say that Hitler and Mussolini had never met before nineteen thirty-four, and that was in Venice. June fourteenth, they say, and the history books are very specific about that. But …"

And now he took a black envelope from the pile.

"Keep in mind a couple of things. First: that this is a genuine photograph! This picture was taken when there was no computer; and nobody … no one would have even *imagined* manufacturing a picture; you know, putting people in places where they never were, or altering the faces, such as they can and do with digital photography today.

"The second thing to remember—and many forget this or never knew—is that Hitler had great respect, great admiration for Mussolini, but it was not mutual. He also knew that IL Duce was open to meeting with political leaders, and especially with young aspiring fascists who were sympathetic of the Blackshirt movement; and he did this often. So Hitler tried more than once to meet with Mussolini formally; and every time he was refused. Why? This was quite out of character for Benito Mussolini, who was promoting worldwide fascism. Now there had to be a reason for Mussolini's contempt and his refusals, and it may well have originated from a previous introduction, such as at our Winiarnia Italia in nineteen twenty-nine.

"Also, Hitler had been a stumping politician about then. He's one year out of prison, and he's doing a lot of traveling, building up a following that would, and that did, elect him chancellor of Germany four years later. So Hitler may have been anywhere about that time, even in places of which no one made any record. Considering that the Italian Consul had ordered that the Winiarnia be closed during the Mussolini lunch, then maybe even that Vienna to Warsaw flight was off the record too. So for Hitler to be on a plane with Mussolini, coming from Vienna, Austria, and in the company of other young aspiring fascists, would not have been at all unusual.

"But four years later, in nineteen thirty-three, after his appointment as Chancellor of Germany, Hitler had stated: 'Now that I'm a head of state he'll have to meet with me.' But still Mussolini kept him waiting—another eighteen months, until June of 'thirty-four, when he finally agreed to meet with the man. But … when they did meet *officially*—in nineteen thirty-four as is publicly recorded—it was not to be in Rome. Oh, no! There would be no meeting at the capitol, in the heart of Italy. Instead, Mussolini would meet him in an *anteroom* to Italy, Venice! A city renowned for *tourism*! And following an unfortunate suggestion made by Ulrich von Hassel, Germany's ambassador in Rome, Hitler regrettably arrived dressed in civilian clothes. Well! Next to IL Duce, in full military regalia as the world's leader of fascism, Hitler *looked* like a tourist!

"But that meeting was staged; it got worldwide media coverage; there was a large military parade; it was for the public! And it was orchestrated to show Fascist Italy's superiority over Nazi Germany, and IL Duce's dominance over Hitler … or maybe his disdain, for that too was noticeable."

"Now then …" And he took the picture from its envelope.

CHAPTER II

Wrapped in impermeable wax paper, and tied with string. It was old; a 6½ x 9-inch sepia tone photograph of 16 men arranged somewhat formally.

Mounted on an 8" x 11" decorated cardboard, with a semi-transparent glassine protector, it had been assembled in a photography shop in Lwów where the photo had been developed, and where the worker had crimped his seal on both the photo and the glassine cover.

As he lifted and folded back the protector Victor said, "Keep in mind, also, that this picture is quite obviously not a digital product, and as such it can be easily tested for image alterations or other graphic tampering … and it can be carbon dated too, it being a genuine old photograph of the highest quality."

Valerie had moved to Victor's left, and was now looking over his shoulder. "Do you remember any of those people, Dad?"

"Sure I do." Victor grinned like a conspirator. "That's me standing in the back of the group; and there's my father seated in the front center, and my mother and Aunt Corinna are there too."

"What?" said Valerie. "Where do you see women?"

"Look hard, Valerie; use your big brown eyes." Some few seconds later he put his finger on the courtyard window behind the group. Amusedly he said, "There they are, looking out from their kitchen window!"

"Well, look at that!" Valerie exclaimed. "This is almost a family photo."

"Wow," said George, chuckling softly and leaning in, focusing with everybody else. "So then, who are these *friends of the family*? I recognize Adolf Hitler. Is that Mussolini, sitting next to Grandfather Carlo? And these others? Do you recognize them? "

"Yes, that's Mussolini. But don't call them *friends of the family*, wise guy!" Serious again he said, "I recognize a few, but only a few. It's been over seventy years, you know, and I never really knew the majority of them."

A brief silence now, wherein history lay before their eyes and while he struggled to remember names. Then he pointed to the man sitting at the left end of the front row.

"Him," he said. "Him I remember. That man is … or he was, Von Schleicher; Kurt Von Schleicher. Before Hitler, he had been chancellor of the Weimar Republic." Now he shook his head. "Came to a bad end, though; I remember him being murdered by the SS back in 'thirty-four, during what was called 'The Night of the Long Knives.'

"And this fellow here …" He pointed now to the man sitting on the opposite side, next to his father Carlo, and paused. "This was aah … Oh, yes! This was Von Hassel, the one who five years later would give Hitler the wrong advice about what to wear in Venice. Ulrich

Von Hassel," and he bobbed his head. "He was Berlin's ambassador to Rome. Very fitting he should be on that flight. Later, however, he was implicated in the nineteen forty-four plot to kill Hitler, and he was left to die a slow death by hanging from a piano wire. Nevertheless, after the war he was recognized as one of Germany's renowned Valkyrie Heroes.

"Now this man here … " and again he pointed ". . . standing third from the left in the back row, this was Rosenberg, Alfred Rosenberg. About ten years after this photo was taken he became Hitler's minister of the German-Occupied Eastern Territories, which, ironically, would include Lwów. He was tried in Nuremberg as a war criminal in nineteen forty-six, and then hung for Nazi war crimes committed by his authority, many of which were committed in Galicia and Lwów."

"And that's Hitler." Valerie was pointing now to the man in the center.

Victor turned to look up at his daughter-in-law. Beaming he said, "Thank you, Valerie. I'm glad you agree. Because if it isn't, then my name's not Vittorio Perantoni." They laughed together now, and he added, "And I challenge anyone to prove … to *prove*, that it's not Adolf Hitler, or to *prove* that isn't Benito Mussolini sitting next to your Grandfather Carlo."

"Have people tried?"

George had taken the photo from his father and was looking at it closely.

"Not yet, son. I haven't shown it to anybody since our leaving Poland in nineteen thirty-nine. It belongs with my other collections, and you know how personal and dear those are to me. However, someday you and Robert may want to make it public, as you will with my collections too. And then, without doubt, someone will challenge you or try to discredit the authenticity of this photo."

His eyes snapped now with the fires of indignant challenge. "When that time comes, just remember, it won't be for you to prove that the photo is real, because there it is! It will be for others to prove that it's *not* real! Because if that's not Hitler …" and he pointed now to the photo in George's hand. . . "then that's not me standing at the back of the group!" And now George handed the photo back to his father.

As Victor returned the treasure to its envelope he said, "So around three o'clock that afternoon, these men resumed their trip to Warsaw.

Now that evening, with IL Duce still fresh in our minds, your grandfather called me and Luigi into his study. And there, for the first time, he explained to us his concern—his deep concern—about the direction in which fascism was taking the world. He said also that he was concerned about us, that we, his sons, were following blindly, without really thinking. And he quoted the Bible to us; that I'll never forget. Because when he did he emphasized this point: that men can dominate men to nothing but their own injury; that's the way he put it. He read it from the Bible. Years later I would know how true that was.

"You see, my father—your grandfather—was a smart man, George; he knew: human government would never work; that only a government ruled by God himself can solve mankind's problems; can provide a true peace and lasting security.

"Well, I remember now that Luigi was pretty impressed that evening." And here he shook his head. "But me? I didn't understand what Dad was telling us. And then your grandfather gave each of us a Bible, a protestant Bible he called it. And I'd never seen one before."

As his conversation with the family went on, the shadows in the patio growing longer, Victor told of how his father had related to him and his brother, things that most people didn't fully understand— things that they seldom if ever thought about.

"Your grandfather explained to us, for example, that the world had changed dramatically since times before the Great War. He had no ecclesiastical training, of course—he'd never been to no cemetery, and he was … "

"Dad."

"What is it George?"

"I think you mean seminary, Dad."

"What? Isn't that what I said?"

"No, you said cemetery."

"Huh. Well," and he smirked sarcastically, "those places might just as well be cemeteries for all that comes from them. Anyway, your grandfather was certainly no priest! But he understood, George. He told us that in May of nineteen ten, when he was about twenty-eight—two years before I was born— that he'd been in Warsaw; and along with about twenty or so others he'd gone to a meeting there. Well, there had been this man from Pittsburgh—some Bible student who'd spent a lot of time explaining to them that nineteen fourteen was going to be a bad year; it was going to be like … like the end of the world."

It should be noted here that had Carlo known it at the time, he could have told Victor and Luigi that for more than 60 years previously there had been, on the part of some few, rising interest in the year 1914, several knowledgeable men setting forth sound reasonings. For example, he could have referenced the year 1844. For in that year, a certain E. B. Elliott, a British clergyman, had focused a spotlight on 1914, highlighting it as a possible date for the end of the "seven times" referred to in chapter 4 of the Bible book of Daniel. Although the man authored at least two books, one of which was titled *The Time of the End … by a Congregationalist*, Elliott was, needless to say, largely ignored; and he evidently failed to successfully promulgate his understanding. Five years later, in 1849, a Mr. Robert Seeley of London, England, had also dealt with the year 1914 in a similar manner.

Some twenty years then passed before, in the United States and in a publication edited in about 1870, Joseph Seiss had cited the year 1914 as a significant date in Bible chronology. And again in the United States, in 1875, a Mr. Nelson Barbour had written categorically in his magazine, *Herald of the Morning*, that 1914 did indeed mark the end of a period that Jesus had called "the appointed times of the nations."

In every case, these were men who understood that the prophet Daniel's "seven times" were a calculable 2,520 years. Those yers spanned the centuries between Jerusalem's fall to the Babylonians and its subsequent desolating about October of 607 B.C.E., and the restoration of theocratic rule in the earth in October of 1914 C.E. But Carlo had been unaware of these persons.

He had, however, been very much aware of the imposing man from Pittsburgh. But it had not been due to any flamboyancy on the man's part—the man had been no showman. It may accurately be said that the man's impressiveness had lain primarily in the fact that he was not ostensibly impressive. A quiet man; an unobtrusive man; a man whose incisive presence was largely embodied in his clear and affirmative explanation of Scriptural matters; a man whom Carlo could never forget.

"And that," said Victor, "was when your grandfather first began to understand the Bible." And now he closed his eyes as though to say that the conversation was at an end.

But the family's curiosity was aroused, and it was George who persisted. "So what happened with this … this … man from Pittsburgh?"

Victor squinted at his son, looking at him with a dismissive scowl and out of the top of his eyes. "You're not going to give up, are you George." And he smiled as the others chuckled and while he went on. "Well, that might have been the end of it. But then dad learned that this man was going to visit Lwów in March of the next year, in nineteen eleven, and … well, you can only imagine his excitement. And this was no little thing! You see this fellow was touring Europe! I mean he was giving lectures— he was giving a *series* of lectures—in many of the major cities there.

"Now in Lwów there was a large hall called the People's House, and it had been rented for this event. And let me tell all of you; dad said that posters went up all over town. And the newspapers—seven of them—carried nine advertisements. Everybody was invited to hear that man's talk. And it was free! And that's when your grandfather learned the man's name—from the posters: Charles Russell."

"Aaah, ha, ha, ha" George chuckled. "Now there's a familiar name! And what was this talk to be about?"

"Ah! Something far different from what you'd hear these days. You see the general understanding then was that a number of Bible prophecies applied specifically to the natural Jews; that God was somehow going to favor Israel, gradually restoring them to Palestine. He was going to open their understanding to the truth about Jesus as their Ransomer and Messianic King; and then using them—the Jews—as an agency, God would extend blessings to all the nations. So the talk was entitled: 'Zionism in Prophecy'."

"Humm. Great news for the Jewish people of Lwów." Valerie ventured her observation.

Victor turned to look at her in that way of his. Head down and looking infinitely wise he said, "You'd have thought so, Val, but it turned out quite differently. Anyway, Russell—we call him Brother Russell now—arrived by train, and using an interpreter it was planned that he was to deliver this talk twice that day. What Carlo and others in Lwów didn't know, however, was that a lot of ill feeling was building against this man right here in this country, the U.S. of A. So what happens? A Jewish Zionist rabbi from New York City, fiercely opposed to Russell and his teaching, sent a cable message to his Zionist associates in Lwów. In it he denounced Russell and anyone associated with him, inciting the opposers to a mob mentality, intent on preventing Russell's message from being heard. So now what?

"Well! The hall was packed that afternoon—interest was very high—but the opposers, in their ignorance, were determined that the talk would not be delivered; I mean they were *determined*! The way a local newspaper put it, the *Wiek Nowy*, was that when the interpreter said his first few words, the Zionists raised a clamor. I mean they screamed and shouted; and they whistled. They simply were not going to permit Russell to speak. Finally he had to leave the stage. And the demonstration was even noisier at the talk scheduled for eight o'clock that evening."

Valerie shook her head in disbelief. "So was the talk ever delivered?"

"No, it never was, although there were many who wanted to hear what Russell had to say. And there were many who requested literature. As a matter of fact, this was when Carlo acquired those two Bibles I mentioned before, the ones he gave to me and Luigi at the Winiarnia, our first Bibles. Actually brother Russell commented on this visit later. He said that only God knew what his providence was in connection with such experiences; that the Jews' excitement over the subject might even lead some to a deeper investigation, even deeper than if they had heard the talk in a decent and orderly manner. So, although there was no immediate response to the message, the seeds of truth about nineteen fourteen had been sown. And many groups of Bible students were formed later, not only in Lwów, but also in other nearby cities."

And what sort of a man was this Charles Russell whom Carlo had met? George Swetnam, an ordained Presbyterian minister and long time columnist for *The Pittsburgh Press* newspaper, was once regarded as the foremost historian of the Pittsburgh and Western Pennsylvania areas. Regarding Charles T. Russell he once wrote:

"It is an amazing thing that no Pittsburgh history has ever even so much as contained the name of C.T. Russell, since his influence has easily been the widest of any man who ever lived in the city … including Andrew Carnegie."

Nearly 6 feet tall, well built and with piercing gray eyes, Russell's manner was always calm. He stressed argument rather than emotion, logic rather than loquacity, sometimes adding a touch of humor. In later life he was snowy haired and white bearded. "Almost saintly in appearance," Swetnam had said.

A pioneer in the Chain Store concept, the Motion Picture Industry, and other important ventures, Russell was one of the most prolific and widely read authors of his day, writing numerous books and a newspaper column carried by more than 1500 newspapers.

Perpetually interested in religion, as a youth he chalked Bible verses on sidewalks. As a boy, quick and alert, his father took him into partnership in his general store. At the time he was only 11; at 15 he was sent out as a buyer.

Troubled in mind over his church's doctrine of predestination, he was unable to accept religion and equally unable to let it go. Thus in 1869, as a successful but skeptical businessman of 18, he stepped into a basement to see if the handful who met there had anything more sensible than Christendom's creeds. What he heard changed his life.

He subsequently rented a hall, started a Bible School, and lectured there for 5 years. Convinced of the Bible's truth, he did a remarkable thing. At the age of 26 and with no formal theological education, he invited all the ministers in Pittsburgh to a meeting. After explaining his beliefs, he urged them to unite with him. And while their acceptance of his invitation evidenced their respect for him, yet after hearing what he had to say they declined his offers.

Rebuffed by Christendom and unable to accept its irrational doctrines, he turned to a life of evangelism. And disinterested now in business, he soon closed his haberdashery store.

"In 1914," wrote Mr. Swetnam, "he completed work on the first epic motion picture, '*The Photo Drama of Creation*' 15 years before any other sound pictures were produced. It ran for eight hours and was viewed by some eight million people!"

Late in life he put his entire fortune, well over a million dollars at the time, into a trust fund for an organization dedicated to teaching Bible Truth. The result was that he made many close friends and many bitter enemies, becoming the target of false stories, all of which had little if any basis in fact.

This then was the man who had so impressed Carlo Perantoni in 1910.

"So your grandfather," said Victor, "came to understand quite clearly some of the Bible's prophecies; prophecies that explain how and why the world has changed; prophecies that even deal with the precise timing of the changes, and the Scriptural significance of the year nineteen fourteen.

"Oh, he described to us, in great detail, how life in general was altogether different before that year. And he knew, my dear ones; he knew in the same way that I know what life was like back in the thirties. He knew. Because by nineteen fourteen he had lived thirty-two of those years! He understood that before Archduke Ferdinand was assassinated in June of that year, there in Sarajevo, in Bosnia, that a war in Europe was not believed to be possible. And he provided us with firsthand accounts, along with his observations and experiences. Yes, he understood things recounted in the Bible, things which, to this very day, explain the frightening transformation of the world's society; things that even explain what happened last Tuesday in New York—September eleventh."

It was nearly dark now, and the old man leaned back in his chair. Closing his eyes again, he breathed a deep sigh. "And that, my inquisitive children, is more than enough for tonight. I feel tired."

He stood now and tucked the box of photos under his arm. Taking his wife's hand he said, "I think Gina and I will go home now. I'm ready for bed."

And George watched attentively as his aged parents slowly made their way across the lakefront lawn.

Victor, like so many elderly persons, was up early. It was only 4:47, yet the Florida air on this September morning was already velvety warm. Given another two hours, Orlando would see the sunrise. It was a quiet time, a good time to think.

Having warmed a cup of his think-drink in the microwave, that is to say yesterday's coffee, he opened the sliding door leading to the patio. Outside, and moving with ultragenarian leisure, he seated himself comfortably. After taking a satisfying draft of his dark brew, he allowed his thoughts to drift back over the things he and others of the family had talked about in the course of the last two days. It had been an interesting discourse, his mind dredging up memories both fond and unpleasant.

He thought this morning of that one particular thing he had mentioned last evening—the destruction of New York's World Trade Center. Only four days ago, and already it was archival history; four days during which he had watched again and again, with tear-filled eyes, the video portrayal of that wretchedly tragic moment. As he reflected on it, he could see clearly the similarity between it and Germany's lightning-like invasion on September 1st of 1939, preceded by the sudden shelling and bombings on his homeland—of Poland.

It was September now, and he recalled that it had been nearing September then. It had been August 25th, in 1939. He had been 27, but it didn't seem that long ago. War winds were astir on Poland's western borders; the German juggernaut was poised to spread its murderous terror and chaos to the east; and the curtain would soon rise on World War II, the second act, as it were, of the escalating crescendo of the Great War.

In the forbidding shadow of what was about to happen, the Italian Consulate in Warsaw had ordered that all Italian nationals were to evacuate Poland without delay. And he remembered the message having reached the Winiarnia Italia, requesting that Carlo Perantoni relay the order to the Italian community in Lwów and in Galicia, and that he was to help expedite the matter with urgency prior to the end of August.

He remembered also that his friends, André and Franki, were determined that there should be no leaving without a party. And so party there was, and a fitting one too; a rollicking goodbye wine bash, a dance party in honor of him and of Luigi; a party given by friends—friends he would have to leave, but whom he hoped to see again soon.

He reflected this morning on the fact that several of his girlfriends had been there, wanting very much to share his affection before he would be gone.

He saw them now in his mind's eye, so clearly as to be virtually present. Among them had been the beautiful Larisa Doroshenka, a brown haired Ukrainian girl whom everyone called Lari. She had been about 23 at the time. Her father, Ivan, had often been Carlo's hunting companion.

Daniela Rabinowitz—Dani to her friends—had been there as well. About the same age as Lari, she was an attractive, gypsy-like Jewish girl who worked as a shopkeeper where he had bought his own Zeiss Ikonta camera.

Surprisingly, even Stasi had been there—beautiful, talented, 21 year-old Stasia Alexiniska, the classy ballet student—the aspiring prima donna. And he smiled as he remembered: *Her parents would allow her to date me, but never inside the winery.* Inside the winery was anathema. And such had been her obedience until that August day. But with him and his family preparing to leave, and she not knowing when she would see him again, she had dared to break her father's strict rule; she had entered the Winiarnia Italia for the first time.

The following day, the whole family was scrambling to put everything in order for the unexpected departure. They were leaving, yes, but all were of a mind that they would return, soon hopefully, but if not then, at least eventually. So everyone was endeavoring to dismiss the ominous nature of the warning, a warning that all money and valuables, jewelry and the like—anything and everything exceeding 100 Zlotys in value—would be confiscated at the border.

And he recalls this morning that the family had put their entire collective savings—a total of some 40,000 gold-backed Zlotys (more than $100,000 in U.S. currency)—into a joint account in a Polish bank.

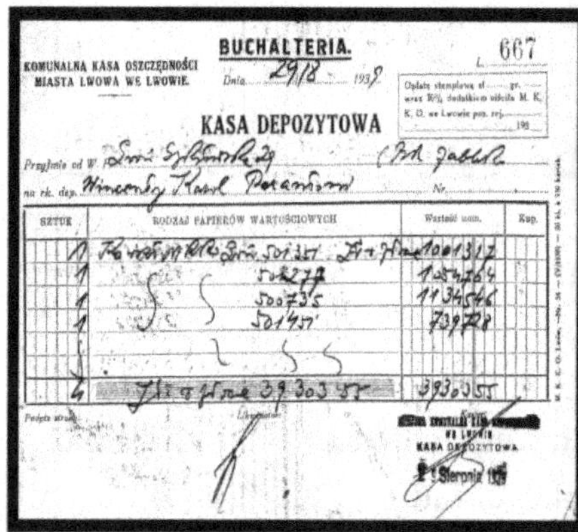

This bank deposit receipt, from Carlo Perantoni's Lwów bank, is dated 29 August 1939. It contains four separate deposit entries: one for the Winiarnia business, one for Carlo with his wife, Romana, one for Luigi, and one for Victor. This deposit was the last thing the family did prior to evacuating Lwów. The money was never recovered.

He remembered Carlo giving the keys to André, those of the winery and those of the apartments as well. A second set was given to the priest, "Padre" Michele Kolbuch.

"I'll stay in the apartment," André had said. "That way I can keep an eye on the winery until you're …"

"Dad. Dad!"

"Wha … What …?

George had come out of his house and into his yard; had walked down toward the water, and glancing to his right had noticed his father sitting quietly, unmoving in his patio. Concerned, he had walked over, and now his hand was on his father's shoulder. Startled, the old man looked up at him.

"You were asleep, Dad." With some anxiety he added, "How long have you been out here like this?"

Victor looked at his watch. Daylight was breaking; the empty coffee cup sat on a table beside the chair and it was 6:50.

"I aah … I must have fallen asleep. I was dreaming, George. Our family was leaving Lwów, and I was telling … aah, telling … Oh, you wouldn't know him anyway. But I was saying that … Oh André! That was his name. I was telling André that I had decided to try smuggling my stamps out of Poland. I knew it would be dangerous—that I might possibly get caught at the border. And …" A soft smile now as the occasion came back to his mind. "And as I recall it now, I almost was caught!

"But I don't want to talk about it now. I'll tell you about it later." Glancing again at his watch he added, "Right now I think I'd like some breakfast."

CHAPTER III

It begins—again. To many, the war being remembered by Victor Perantoni on those warm autumn evenings in Orlando, had begun in 1939. More correctly, however, Victor would tell you it had all begun in 1914—that the events of 1939 were merely another chapter in a bloody and violent horror story, the beginning of which had been 25 years earlier.

Were one to ask him why he felt that way, he would suggest that one remember the Treaty of Versailles, signed on June 28 in 1919 and ostensibly ending the war between Germany and the Allies. That signing had been exactly five years to the day after the assassination of Austria's Archduke Franz Ferdinand. Was there some symbolism in the choice of that date? It would appear so. The Great War was being kept alive!

Recall as well that Germans of all political leanings criticized the Treaty, this for its blaming Germany for having started the war. Such implication was seen as an insult to the nation's reputation. *"The Diktat"* they called it, its terms having been offered as a "This-is-all-you-get" proposal.

In response to what he considered to be overtly high-handed diplomacy, Philipp Scheidemann, Germany's first democratically elected Chancellor, had stood before the National Assembly in March of 1919, and personally vilified the Treaty as a "murderous plan," which—to again use his words—"put us in chains." He said, less caustically,

"The Treaty is unacceptable." Thereafter, he elected to resign rather than sign the document.

In retrospect also, it is generally conceded that the severe conditions imposed on Germany, both politically and economically by the Treaty, fertilized the ground from which, a decade later, would grow the Nazi State and Hitler's rise to power. Sans the shooting, The Great War was still in progress.

Perhaps it may be said that in the mind of Adolf Hitler there had *never* been an armistice. For in June of 1940, when the French government wished to negotiate a Franco-German armistice following Germany's victory in the Battle of France, it was Hitler who chose a site for the event: Compiègne Forest in France, close by the town of the same name. And why that location? Because that had been the site of the 1918 Armistice signing, an armistice that had heaped humiliation on Germany. And here, Hitler decided, he would avenge himself— would avenge Germany—and this at the expense of France's pride. For him it was to be a supreme moment. 1918 was not over; the Great War was not over.

Then to complete the charade, to exacerbate France's absolute ignominy and despite the fact that the object of his desire was in a French museum, Hitler elected to have the 1940 armistice signed in the very same rail carriage where the Germans had signed the 1918 Armistice. Therefore was the carriage removed from the museum and placed at the very spot where it had been in 1918. World War I was being revisited.

Hitler then sat gloatingly in the very same chair which Marshal Ferdinand Foch had occupied in 1918, when he had faced the defeated German representatives. And to further demean the French, after listening to the reading of the preamble, Hitler left the carriage, leaving the lesser negotiations to General Wilhelm Keitel, his Oberkommando der Wehrmacht.

Three days later, and again at Hitler's order, the Armistice site was demolished. The carriage itself was taken to Berlin as a war trophy. A trophy of the First World War, acquired in 1940! The Great War was not over. And with it went pieces of what had been a large stone tablet bearing an inscription. In French it read, *"Ici Sur le 11 novembre 1918 Succombé La Fierté Criminelle De L'allemand Reich. Vaincu Par Les Peuplades Libres Qu'Il A Essayé d'Asservirench."* In English one would read: "Here On The Eleventh Of November 1918 Succumbed The Criminal Pride Of The German Reich. Vanquished By The Free Peoples Which It Tried To Enslave."

Powerful words; dynamic words indeed. But more than that. For whatever may have been the intention of the inscribers, it must be conceded even by neutral observers that the words have an unmistakably inflammatory character.

The Alsace-Lorraine Monument, depicting a German eagle impaled by a sword, was destroyed, the site being obliterated thereafter with the singular exception of a statue of Marshal Foch. This, Hitler intentionally ordered to be left, that it should be honoring only a wasteland. The Great War continued.

In 1945, when Germany could perceive the war of that time to be lost, Hitler had the railway carriage at issue taken to Crawinkel in Thuringia. There it was destroyed by SS troops, its remains then buried, that it might not be used a third time for a second German surrender. Thus there would freshly remain the memory of the French surrender.

Following the war, themselves unwilling to let matters rest, the French used German POWs to restore the Armistice site. And rather than make a new one, pieces of the broken stone tablet were recovered and then reassembled; a replica of the railway carriage was also crafted and placed at the restored site. The Alsace-Lorraine monument and its memorials were rebuilt from scratch. Taking five years to complete, it was finally re-dedicated in 1950. The French had redeemed their 1918 victory.

In light of all this, it is easily seen that neither the Germans nor the French were, or are, of a disposition to forget the Great War; nor seemingly is anyone else, there appearing to be a *raison immortelle* that it continue. Thus do others see history as did Victor.

And such was his feeling because, and without any doubt, it may be said that in 1914 of our common era war truly came into its own. In that cardinal year, peace was taken away from the earth. For this was to be no European war; nor was this to be a war in Asia or in Africa, or in the Middle East. This was to be war on a colossal scale—a scale never before even conceived. Indeed, had they but seen it, the Caesars, Genghis Khan, Hannibal and others of their sort would have stood in stunned amazement. For that which had been called war in previous centuries, suddenly paled to the level of a street brawl when compared with the staggering volume of brutality, butchery and bloodletting that was The Great War, World War I.

Not only was the capacity for killing elevated to new and terrible levels, but there was now introduced the ability to kill with less compunction than ever before, or with none whatever. From the fertile womb of bellicosity there came the warplane; there came the tank and the machine gun, affording ones the ability to kill from a remote distance; to kill without ever even seeing one's enemy. In the warriors' mind, murder in the name of nationalism was being sophisticated; war was being sanitized.

And perhaps we should reflect seriously on the words of columnist Joe Chapman. Writing about The Great War, in *The Spectator* of Hamilton, Ontario, he said: "How innocent, how mercifully ignorant, was the world of August, 1914! And yet, in many ways, the First World War, in a macabre sense at least, may well deserve the title 'great.' It was the first war which could, with justification, be called a world conflict, involving nearly every important nation, with campaigns fought on many fronts, from Arctic wastes to steaming jungles.

"It was the first 'total' war, in which entire nations became deeply involved, with the complete apparatus of civilian life becoming an integral part of the war effort."

Mr. Chapman commented also to the effect that, "the war was a turning point in more than a military and technological sense. It was a social and cultural revolution and the old way of life was shattered utterly."

Then after reflecting on the state of the ante-1914 world, and the changes since then, he said regarding the impact of World War I on society: "Not even the Second World War, to which the Nazis added new dimensions of brutality, and the atomic bomb slaughter, seems to have had such an effect upon us as did the First World War.

"Somehow, we had become conditioned to the idea of total war and numbed, or desensitized by history, and not even Hiroshima or Dresden had the same impact as the first carnage, the awful carnage of the great war's Western Front.

"Perhaps that is why the veterans of the earlier struggle seemed men set apart, much less able to adjust to the new world than those from 1945. Nothing in their lives had prepared them for the reality of the trenches, and nothing since has equaled their experiences."

Even so, despite its sanguinary scope—its total dead can never be accurately counted—and despite the destruction of property, the value of which is likewise incalculable; the priceless lesson—penned in sacred blood across the pages of world history—was lost. Sanity had been lost. For now the world of mankind had been set on a path that would inevitably lead to its own demise. It would never recover. True, that throughout the world revolts and coups would continue; there would be elections, and successions within monarchies; but the reins of the war chariot were now in the hands of madmen. Witness 1939.

With a global society not yet fully healed; with governments still bleeding—still reeling under the economic and social impact of the events of twenty-one years previous, Europe's own particular madman, Adolf Hitler, sent the German killing machine rolling eastward. In Asia, Japan was engaged in bloody combat with China. In 1941, the United States of America would become an active belligerent in the second of those wars to be described as global—World War II.

And now, in 2001, over eighty-seven years removed from the events of 1914 -1918, what may be said as to the possibility for a global peace? What progress has truly been made so that humanity is more secure? The rational mind is left with no other reply: Precious little!

And so may similar circumstances suddenly appeared to 28 year-old Franki Mrowicki on September 1, 1939. His summer classes at the University of Lwów have been completed, and he has reported for duty at the Gdansk post office on that fateful morning. It is nearing 10:00 o'clock, and he is bewildered to find jackbooted Nazi soldiers filling the Hevelius Platz, the city's square. Cannon are also present. He watches for several minutes before he finally approaches a bystander.

"Good morning. I hope you'll excuse me. My name is Mrowicki." Then pointing across the street he explained. "I was scheduled to start work there at the post office this morning, and now I find this. What's happened?"

"Well," said the stranger, turning and granting Mrowicki a dour expression, "it doesn't look as though you'll work today. Actually, I fear that it looks more like war! I understand that some … *Dutchman,*" he said with contempt; some German general by the name of Brauchitsch, from what I hear, brought his troops down from the Westerplatte this morning. Our people tried to make a stand there, I'm told, but they were overwhelmed."

Staggered by the news, Franki said, "Uh huh. I see. But what's going on here?"

"Oh, it's the postal workers. They've been here since around four this morning, I hear. It's said that they're nearly sixty in number and that they've armed themselves quite heavily. They say they're holding the building as a show of resistance to what they expect to be an invasion."

"They're what?" Franki exclaimed. "*Sixty? They're sixty?*" He could not believe what he had just heard. "They must be joking; they must be out of their minds! I mean, just look at them, man!" Gesturing toward the mass of battle- helmeted troops he said, "There are … what? Eighty; a hundred? And who knows how many other hundreds there are?"

"O I agree, sir. But I understand that the building's curator is inside, along with his ten year-old daughter and his wife, and they too refuse to leave."

Mrowicki shook his head. "Well, I must conclude then that they're all mad as hatters. How long have you been here?"

The man glanced at his watch. "About half an hour; just watching."

Franki said, "Uh huh! Well, it's obvious that I can't work. So I think I'll do the same." And he turned away to walk to a nearby restaurant where he ordered coffee.

Left with nothing to actually do, time passed slowly and he ordered yet a second cup. Outside in the street, amid a great deal of noise and confusion, he could hear German officers barking orders. Tensions were growing.

Then suddenly, at 11:00 o'clock, an explosion of small arms and cannon fire announced the German's resurgent efforts to capture the building. Amid the resulting clamor, others came rushing and crowding into the restaurant, seeking security, seeking shelter from the sheer pandemonium that now filled the street. Then watching from the window, he and the others saw bits of masonry fly and glass shatter as bullets and artillery shells riddled the building's facade. As the air continued to reverberate with gunfire and screams, shouting and death, he waited anxiously, hoping for any sort of a lull in the appalling mayhem. When it finally did occur, and brief though it was, he found the opportunity to bolt from the restaurant and escape, running for all he was worth away from the chaos.

Perhaps it was a good thing that he never heard the ear-splitting roar, when a 1,320 pound explosive device was detonated at 5:00 o'clock that afternoon; that he never saw the walls of the post office building collapse, disintegrating in a noisy welter of smoke and dust; that he didn't know of the basement later being flooded with gasoline, and of five of his fellow Poles being burned to death.

But he would never forget the scene that was now indelibly emblazoned in his memory. The firefight with the Germans had shown him brutality and carnage such as he could have never envisioned. For now he had personally seen Europe's first armed resistance to Nazism. He had seen a portion of the opening salvos of the Second World War. And when, finally, he had made his way back to Lwów two days later, there to take up residence at the Winiarnia's apartments along with André and Lari, Dani and Stasi, he learned that the 38 postal worker survivors of the assault had all been executed.

And now it was Tuesday morning. It was September 12th. Eleven days had passed since the mind-numbing slaughter at Gdansk; almost two weeks since many hundreds of German nationals and sympathizers had lined the curbs to watch the grand parade; since the officer-laden staff cars and the swaggering, goose-stepping soldiers had passed beneath the welcoming banner that had been raised to span the street.

Among other obvious changes was the fact that the city was now called Danzig. Its former German name having been restored, German flags were now everywhere. The banner therefore had read; *"Danzig grüpt feinen Führer!"*— "Danzig welcomes the Führer!" And indeed the city's German population, woefully naive and grossly unaware of what was to follow, was largely of that mind.

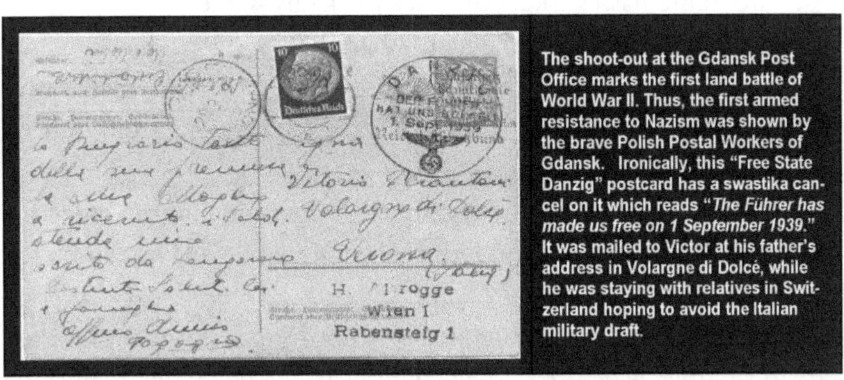

The shoot-out at the Gdansk Post Office marks the first land battle of World War II. Thus, the first armed resistance to Nazism was shown by the brave Polish Postal Workers of Gdansk. Ironically, this "Free State Danzig" postcard has a swastika cancel on it which reads *"The Führer has made us free on 1 September 1939."* It was mailed to Victor at his father's address in Volargne di Dolcé, while he was staying with relatives in Switzerland hoping to avoid the Italian military draft.

Some four hundred and fifty miles to the southeast, at the Winiarnia's apartment in Lwów that same morning, André, Franki and the girls were still sick at heart over the conscienceless massacre of the Gdansk postal workers, as well as similarly depressing news from other parts of the country. Sharing a breakfast of sausage and cheese, of bread and coffee, they chattered excitedly together; speculating as to what these affairs might mean regarding their own futures. Then abruptly the conversation stopped. For while they were yet speaking they had begun to hear them coming. Almost subliminal at first, it was an ominous droning sound, a pre-mortum dirge that drew ever closer. The Stukas!

"Bombers!"André said quietly, and the five of them scrambled for whatever cover was at hand.

As the German aircraft then came overhead, as individual planes began to angle downward to deliver their message of destruction and annihilation, they could hear the sound of their acceleration, the piercing whine of their engines. And then the bombs—their whistling screams heralding their own imminent destruction; and the explosions that followed, one after another across the city. Lwów had fallen prey to Marshall Göring's Luftwaffe.

Then as from out the midst of the ongoing devastation, from amid the swirling dust of pulverized buildings that was suddenly filling the air, Padre Michele came bolting into the Winiarnia.

Wire-frame glasses askew, his black frock dust-smudged; gasping and laboring to get his breath he shouted, "O Lord, they're gone, they're gone!"

"Gone? Who's gone?" André's response as he rose from under a table where he had taken shelter, Franki and the girls crawling from under a bed in the adjoining room.

"The other priests!" Padre exclaimed. "My companions! One of the bombs just hit the church and four of them were killed. The church too is gone! It's nothing but ..."

His next words were obliterated by a nearby explosion that set their ears to ringing. When next they could hear he said, "There's nothing left but rubble. And the orphanage: it too is damaged; it's no longer a safe place. But there are two hundred ..."

Another blast, even closer now, and they felt the whole building tremble. Amid the dull roar that followed, Padre said, "Lord, that was close! I'd started to say that there are orphans back there, André; over two hundred of them!" He gestured back over his shoulder. "Two hundred and three children that need to be cared for now—immediately. And there's also another problem. Father Lantini—he's an associate priest from Rome; he arrived just recently from Warsaw—tells me that the orphans, especially those who are Jewish, are in extreme danger from all this Nazi madness. Now I don't know exactly what all of that means, but it can't be good."

"Yes, yes; I agree," André murmured. And rubbing a thought-wrinkled brow he added, "Let me just think for a moment."

"Bring them over here!" Franki exclaimed, throwing an impromptu solution into the stalled conversation. "It's the only reasonable thing to do. We've got plenty of room; we've got two empty apartments; we've got food and water; and between the six of us and Father Lantini, we can care for them … for a while at any rate."

It was decided. Braving their own destruction and beneath the continuous roar of aircraft overhead; against a backdrop of intermittent explosions, the bombs falling with callously indifferent randomness, the group made their way to the smoking shell of the building that had once been the church. There, from amid the shattered brickwork and splintered timbers, from among crackling flames licking at heaps of burning debris, they gathered the children. And over a path strewn with broken bricks, crumbled plaster and great chunks of shattered masonry, they made their perilous way back to the Winiarnia.

Now arrived, they gave the children some food and calmed their fears to some extent. And there now began no small amount of discussion as to what to do next. It was readily evident that the children could not remain indefinitely. And while sheer fortune, along with his presence of mind, had moved Padre to bring the children's papers from the files of the orphanage, such fortune also made it clear that travel would be dangerous if not impossible.

"If we could only get them to Rome," Padre said anxiously. "At least they'd be safe there. But many of these little ones are Jewish, and there are borders to cross, borders now controlled by the Germans. They've taken Austria and Czechoslovakia already, of course. But if we could make our way south into Hungary, to Bucharest and then into Yugoslavia, our next stop could be Venice. But it's the papers that are the real problem."

Franki looked meaningfully at André. Fully aware of his companion's craft as a printer, cognizant also of his inordinate skill as a counterfeiter, he said, "Can you do anything about that, André?"

André thought for but a moment. Then nodding he said, "I can try, but we don't have much time."

Skilled artist that he was, and over the next several days, André, along with other talented friends from the Lwów Stamp Club, worked at modifying some of the documents, falsifying others and generating new ones where necessary. In the end, by the morning of the 15th, he had eliminated all traces of Jewish ancestry from the children's papers. More than that, all of them were now Roman Catholics.

"And I've done something else," he announced on that same morning. "I've forged a Vatican Travel Order that will …"

"You've what?" Lantini exclaimed. "You couldn't possibly!"

André turned to look at the priest, his eyes sparkling with mischievous wisdom. "Oh, yes," he said. "I could possibly, and I did." And with that he handed the paper to Lantini.

Looking at the document now in his hand, and not believing it possible, the priest said, "But this is … this … It's incredible! The pope could not have done it as well!"

There followed a burst of quiet laughter; and as the amusement subsided, André pointed at the paper Lantini was holding. "That document," he said, "will serve to get two priests and your two hundred children past any European border en route to the Vatican."

And now both of the clergy looked at André, their eyes bright with appreciation and tears. "We … we don't know quite what to say," Padre began.

"Then say nothing," André replied.

There was an emotion-filled silence that followed before Franki said quietly, "I've something to offer as well." As they listened, he went on.

"I want you all to know that I've been to the local post office. Now, by using what postal authority I have from Gdansk, I've sent a telegram to Carlo in Volargne. I told him that we were going to need some assistance with the children's travel from the Brenner Pass. I said that …"

Lantini interrupted. "But we're not going through the Brenner …"

"Yes, I know," Franki interjected, "and so does Carlo. But the Germans don't."

"But how could you … and who is Carlo?"

"Because I've confused them, and Carlo is Victor's father," Franki explained, satisfying Lantini's curiosity, his eyes sparkling with his own cleverness. "Using hints such as Victor and I once used on the potluck stamp packages we sold at the Winiarnia stamp club meetings, I told Carlo that while Padre was en route he would purchase a complete mint set of commemorative stamps, those memorializing Ceferiada's seventieth anniversary this year, and that he would have them ..."

"The what?" said Lantini, fully confused by what Franki was saying.

Franki looked at him hard. "The Ceferiada," he explained, mildly impatient, "the celebration of the opening of Romania's first railroad station in eighteen sixty-nine. But that's beside the point. The point is that Padre is to have them postmarked by the issuing post office. Well now, Carlo knows that the issuing post office was Bucharest. And while Bucharest will be your route, it is not en route to the Brenner Pass."

Lantini smiled now. "Oh," he said, understanding clearly now. "Well and good. But how do we know that this Carlo understands that ..."

"So when Carlo replied," was Franki's interruption, holding up a hand, "he confirmed his understanding by suggesting that Padre also pick up some other stamps: a mint corner block commemorating Hitler's fiftieth birthday, and have it also postmarked by its issuing post office. Now Carlo knows very well that this stamp was issued in Braunau, Austria."

The two priests sat down as Franki went on. "Now there's nothing sophisticated about any of this; it's childishly simple; it's dirt simple. And there are very few who know these things except stamp collectors. And here's the part I really like: even if a smart Gestapo stamp collector were to read the telegrams, what would he think? Probably that a couple of beginners were talking way over their heads.

"So Carlo knows that Padre and the children will be arriving in Italy on an Innsbruck train connection, and not from the Brenner Pass. Carlo has also confused things further by saying that, '*buses will be provided when Padre Michele calls him by phone from the Pass.*' He goes on then in his answer to tell us that more Zlotys are to found under a floorboard in Luigi's bedroom, and that these are to be given to you, Padre."

It was the last thing needed.

There were smiles all around and it was finally Padre who said, "I've got to hand it to you Franki; you and André are really a pair!"

The following day pulsed with hopeful activity as they prepared for their journey to Rome. The girls focused principally on things of a maternal nature, while the men looked to the heavier work and the hard core of organization. But overlaying all was an ominous pall of anxiety. Being keenly aware that Polish partisans were poised in Lwów, preparing to fend off an invasion by Germany's Wehrmacht, the urgent matter of getting out of Poland had become of paramount importance. But what came as a total shock was Padre's announcement on the 17th.

"Really!" was André's surprised response as Franki walked in to join him and Padre in the room. "When did you learn that?"

"Learn what?" Franki queried.

André looked at him with concern. "Russia invaded Poland this morning.

Padre just told me."

Franki was stunned, puzzled. "That can't be true," he murmured, his countenance a mirror of his disbelief. "How … ? They can't do that! We've already been invaded by the Germans, so how … ? There's been no declaration of war with Russia, and … and what about the Germans?"

"What indeed!" Padre replied, his cynicism beyond masking. "It seems that back in late August Mr. Molotov and Mr. Ribbentrop, the Russian and the German foreign ministers, got together." He folded his arms now, pursed his mouth and looked at the ceiling. Nodding philosophically he said, "It appears that the Russians and the Germans are planning to split up Northern and Eastern Europe among themselves."

"Well then," André observed reflectively, "we have enemies on both flanks, do we not?" Then looking at Padre he said, "Best you and your friends get moving as quickly as possible. We have no idea of what these Russians are up to."

Padre nodded soberly. "Yes, you're right. And since I've never liked long good byes, André, I'll say mine now. And Franki … you and the girls take good care. I'll hope to see all of you down the road somewhere."

They had money now, thanks to the generosity of Carlo's family, and with it they bought a team of horses. Along with the horses they bought a covered, double-trailer hay wagon. Then after distributing the remainder of the money among the children, some 5,600 Zlotys, this so that not all of it might be lost, damaged or confiscated in one fell swoop, they began their trek to the west.

It would take them two weeks, and they would pass numerous checkpoints manned by Nazi soldiers. But never once would André's clever counterfeit Vatican travel orders fail their purpose. Upon reaching Bucharest, they would board a train to Innsbruck. From there, another train would take them to Rome.

Left Photo: Padre wrote on back telling Carlo that he has placed the remaining children in ten other residences throughout Italy

It is reported to have been Aeschylus, a 6th century Greek playwright from the Hellenic city of Eleusis, who coined the phrase, "In war, truth is the first casualty." Whether that be an ironclad fact or not, the observation stands immutable. It is politically and strategically unavoidable that information exchanged among nations be self-serving in nature, that national securities be maintained at all costs.

"National security?" an oxymoronic catchphrase—an operation, or operations, by means of which all manner of devious machinations and falsehoods may be, and are, perpetrated. Pacts and concordats are repeatedly seen to mean nothing—witness the "winning of the West" in America's earlier years. A treaty becomes, in actuality, nothing but a treatise; naught but a formally drafted account dealing with whatever subject happens to be at issue. There is, therefore, no "National security," nor can there be. As for the 1939 non- aggression pact entered into by Germany and Russia, the touchstone of time would prove it to be no different.

Doubtlessly, Premier Joseph Stalin himself had sensed the fragility of the matter. For when Germany's Foreign Minister to Russia, Joachim Von Ribbentrop, had initially offered Hitler's proposal that Germany and Russia enter into such a pact, a non-aggression pact, it had been suggested that it be binding for a hundred years. Stalin had responded to the effect that people would think them foolish for even considering such a thing, and had then suggested a ten-year period. Ribbentrop had said he would need Hitler's approval for the change; and after a trip to Berlin and after returning it was agreed.

Stalin himself had been present when the signing had taken place. With him, and actually putting their names to the paper, were his minister, Vyacheslav Molotov, and of course, Von Ribbentrop. And due to those few seemingly innocuous strokes of the pens, things were made to move very rapidly for la familia Perantoni and their friends.

Europe was beginning to burn.

No sooner had the Germans occupied Poland from the west, than they ceded half of the country to communist forces from Russia in the east. Thus, in conformity with the Molotov-Ribbentrop agreement, Lwów had been made an outright gift to the Soviet State. And now—at least for the present—it was the sickle and hammer that flew over the city. Russian troops now occupied Lwów.

Using a time-tested method of social disruption, an operation at least as old as Syria's invasion of Samaria in the 9th century B.C.E., a machination designed to infuse political and military impotency into an enemy, Russian authorities proceeded to set about relocating families in Poland. Much was made of it in the newsreels of the day; that after suffering in basements under German domination, these abused Polish families would now be living in what the press—ever politically discreet—deceptively called "fine new apartments."

Should truth be known however, the Russians were moving them to apartments already occupied by as many as twelve other families. Among the many hundreds of thousands uprooted in this fashion, each of whom would be irretrievably scarred by the tragedy of those war-shattered years, was Victor Perantoni's theater-oriented girlfriend, the ballerina Stasia Alexiniska. And as it was with each of those pitiable individuals, hers too was felt to be a crushing burden.

It was a cool afternoon in late September of 1939. Stasia, her head down and tears streaming from eyes grown far too weary to cry, sat with her friend, Larisa Doroshenka, on the porch of a state-owned farmhouse. But unlike Stasia, Ukrainian-born Larisa from a neighboring farm, was a girl altogether familiar with the rural life.

"I understand," Lari was saying, her voice tender and a comforting arm around her friend's shoulder. "But you can get through this, Stasi; you will get through this. We all will—somehow."

Stasia shook her head in hopeless despondency. "I'm not sure," she said. Then looking up at Lari: "I don't know if I can handle this. I'm … I'm no farmer's daughter, Lari; I'm a ballerina. My family are not farmers; we never have been. I've always lived in a town. My life is music and the theater. And this … this matter of working on a farm, a Soviet farm; more than that even, an army farm, is … is such a radical change. Oh Lari, Lari! I am so very unhappy; so absolutely miserable!" And she bowed her head as the sobbing resumed.

"O my dear Stasi; you poor dear girl. Would that I could change things for you, indeed for all of us." Then patting Stasi's shoulders,

Lari looked about at their bleakly austere surroundings, the stark countryside. "But there's something you need to remember; something we all need to remember about being happy; something that's very easy to forget."Again Stasia looked up.

"My grandmother once told me," Lari went on, "that happiness doesn't depend upon where you live or where you are. It doesn't depend on your circumstances." She paused thoughtfully and then said, "Think about the Perantonis. Now they're a wealthy family, or that is to say they were. But now Carlo and Luigi are in Volargne, along with the rest of the family, and Victor is with relatives in Switzerland. They'd all like to be at home; but they're having to put up with the same difficulties that we are. So happiness obviously doesn't come from having a great deal of money. No, 'Happiness,' my grandmother said, 'is a city in the state called Mind.' That's the way she put it. 'A city in the state called Mind.' Call it ... call it an attitude, Stasi; and ... " She looked intently into her friend's eyes ... "it's an attitude we both must cultivate. We have no choice."

As the tear-filled weeks became months, as they struggled at maintaining the attitude Lari had described, it became a time in which Stasi would find relative comfort in Lari's companionship, a time when a strong bond would form between them. She was also able to experience a much needed sense of accomplishment, as she involved herself in sharing with Lari some of the aspects of ballet. Lari, on the other hand, continued to encourage her friend, helping her to eke out at least some measure of contentment from her unfamiliar bucolic surroundings. Even so, there proved to be many occasions when Lari too found ample reason to weep.

CHAPTER IV

"And I remember when nineteen forty came. Would you pass the bread please, Roberto?"

It was Tuesday, September 18th. With George's older brother Robert having arrived yesterday from Milwaukee, along with his wife Mary, the entire family had gathered at Victor's home for dinner.

"It's not that anything was different—thank you Roberto. The Almighty knows how I wanted things to be different—everyone did." Victor broke a piece of bread onto his plate. "But snow was on the ground now; the Russians were still in Poland and I was still in Switzerland, in Berne. I'd made all kinds of ..."

"Dad." George quietly interrupted the story.

"What now, George?"

"Excuse me Dad, but might this be a good time to tell us what happened while you were *on your way* to Switzerland? You had mentioned something last Sunday morning; something you said you'd tell me about later. You remember: out there in the patio; about smuggling your stamps?"

"Oh, yes." Victor's sharp-as-ever mind remembered immediately. "Yes I do remember that, George. And yes, I suppose this is probably as good a time as any."

"Oh? What's this all about, Dad?" Valerie's curiosity coming to the fore as Robert chimed in with, "Yes, George, what have you and dad been talking about?"

"Oh, dad had mentioned something to me about smuggling some stamps out of Poland, but he said he'd tell me about it later."

Valerie turned to smile at her husband and said, "Well now, I think we might all like to hear about that." Then turning back to Victor: "How about it, Dad?"

Tableware lapsed into quietude, gradually becoming silent as they all waited. And Victor took time to butter his bread as he began.

"I was aah … I was on the train, a couple hours west of Krakow—it would become a Jewish ghetto later, as some of you may remember— and the train had stopped at a border station in Czechoslovakia." He paused now, as though wanting to forget something.

Then he continued. "As I looked out of the train's window, there they were—the Gestapo, strutting about with their usual 'I-own-the-world' attitude. I mean they were everywhere, along with the soldiers! Well, these agents then boarded the train, and then ordered that all the passengers should take their passports, or whatever identification papers they had, and assemble on the station's platform. But no luggage! Luggage was to be left on the train. And there the soldiers would inspect it, looking for … (he shrugged) whatever they were after, and probably also taking whatever they wanted.

"So now we're all standing on the platform, and the interviews begin. Now as this went on, German nationals and other diplomats— ones whom the Nazis considered to be *friendly*—were allowed to re-board the train. The rest of the passengers, myself included, were given the opportunity to voluntarily declare any contraband in our luggage or that we might be carrying on our person. Well, for me this was a major problem! Because, you see, under my clothes I'm carrying my valuable collection of stamps, and also a large sum of money—Polish Zloty!

"Now you may remember me telling you that when grandfather Carlo and the family left the Winiarnia, and when I headed for Switzerland, any amount of money over one hundred Zloty was considered to be contraband, and it was to be confiscated at the border. So now here I am, at the border, and I'm carrying *fifteen thousand* Zloty … in large banknotes!

"Now then. Those who failed to declare anything were ordered into the station's waiting room; there they were to be strip-searched before they could re- board the train."

Valerie was effervescing with curiosity. "So what happened, Dad?"

"Patience, my daughter. I'm getting to it; I'm getting to it."

A bite of bread now, and a sip of his wine before he went on. "Now I had traveled that same train route before; numerous times in fact, while conducting the family's wine business. And I had never experienced, nor expected, such an intensive or severe search as was conducted upon my leaving Poland that day. But this was August of nineteen thirty-nine—the thirty-first actually. And while I didn't know it then, it was one day before the invasion of Poland would occur.

"The Wehrmacht had already occupied what was then Czechoslovakia, and of course the Czech border was now being manned by German soldiers. So now the women were all made to line up facing the ladies restroom, and all the men were herded into another long line headed for the men's room."

Victor paused now, permitted himself another sip of his wine, and allowed the scene he had just painted to become near reality in the minds of his curiosity-saturated listeners. Then he resumed.

"Now while I'm waiting in this line—waiting to be strip-searched—you can just imagine that my feeling of anxiety had risen to … well, it was at a level I'd never in my life experienced! And, I would add, one that I never want to experience again! Even now I have a pretty good idea of how a person might feel on the way to their execution.

"Anyway, about the time I got to where the line curved around a corner, around to the men's room, I learned something. I saw that after being searched, the men leaving the restroom went into another line, one waiting to re-board the train. You see the soldiers were still searching the luggage on board."

Again he paused, a long pause now. Then stretching his shoulders he said, "Oh, cari figli miei—Oh, my dear children. Would you mind if I finished this story another time?"

"Yes, I would!" George replied promptly, smiling at his father. "Speaking for myself, I've been waiting since last Sunday, Dad, and I'd really like to hear the end of this story; if that's okay."

Robert nodded. "If it's not too much, I agree with George. Please, Dad?"

The old man smiled and sighed. Then using that pet name for his oldest son he said, "I suppose, Beto, that it does have a kind of … kind of a drama about it, doesn't it."

"Oh, Dad!" Valerie exclaimed quietly. "You're so dismissive about yourself at times! It's *more* than drama; it's … well, it's real! I mean this is *you*, Dad, going through all this. For us it's like you're a … like you're a hero in an espionage movie, or something."

Old Victor allowed himself a sly smirk. "Well forget the hero part, Val. Because I will confess to you, and without any shame, that back then I felt more like a scared rabbit. So now getting back to the story— at your husband's insistence—and like I was saying: as I looked over to my right, over to where the men were emerging from the restroom, I saw they were forming this other line.

"Now ahead of me there sat this German SS officer. Oh, and didn't he think that he was a splendid looking fellow: him in his black uniform with its red swastika armband; with his polished black boots; and he was seated at a field table unfolded and set up in front of the restroom entrance.

"As each passenger approached he would call them over, one at a time, to check their identification papers. And he asked each man, once again, if he had any contraband to declare prior to entering the restroom where he would be stripped naked and searched. Oooh, the dread and tension I was feeling is indescribable. And right then I knew that I had to do *something*, and I had to do it right now; even something desperate.

"You see, the Germans considered all valuable art and collectibles to be verboten—forbidden, that is. Consequently even a single collectible stamp was considered to be contraband. And there I was, carrying about *five hundred stamps*, strapped to each leg inside my baggy knickerbockers! So …"

And there was that pause again; Victor was a storyteller.

"So …?" said Valerie.

"So I stepped out of the line."

"You *what*!" she blurted. "You might have been killed!"

"Well I didn't think that would happen, Val; I didn't think they'd start shooting inside the station. Actually, I didn't know what would happen. But there are times when you just have to face the Devil, and face him down.

"So I walked over to this officer. Now try to visualize this: there he was intently examining another passenger's passport … he's bent over this document-magnifying machine … and when he looks up, there I am, flashing my PNF party badge in his face. And then I spoke to him in Italian—*l-o-u-d* Italian—and I backed it up with gestures. Oh, I mean gestures; forceful ones! You know how we Italians can be. I told him I was an official of the Italian Consulate's Blackshirts in Warsaw; that I was the son of the Honorary Consul for the Fascio in Eastern Poland and the Galicia region; and that I was expected to attend an emergency meeting of the Blackshirts in Rome.

"Well, the man was speechless! So I went on. I explained that this delay was going to cause me to miss my Vienna connection, and that Mussolini—*his* Duce—would not, when he heard about it—and I'd see that he did—look with any measure of kindness upon this grievous inconvenience!"

"*Dad*!" Robert exclaimed.

"That's what I told him. O I had the bull by the horns, Beto! So now I concluded. Again in loud Italian, I demanded that the train be re-boarded now; and that it depart for Vienna immediately. And you know … looking back now, I think I said all of that in virtually one humongous breath of hot air!"

While the family chuckled at his last remark, he said, "So now it was the officer's turn. So up he gets, pushes his desk and the other passenger aside, and steps up to me. I mean we're almost making physical contact. Standing about twelve inches taller, he shouted down onto my scalp a long string of nasty German words. One or two I could understand, but believe me, there was no need for translation. Then pointing with an outstretched arm he barked, '*Holen Sie!*' something or other. I didn't understand that either. But I remember that he showered me with spit as he hollered, and his meaning was clear: something like, 'Get back in line, or else!'

"However, the line he was *pointing* to was the one waiting to re-board the train! He had evidently assumed, incorrectly of course, that I had approached the desk from that line; that maybe I'd become annoyed while waiting for the re- boarding. But I'd made my point now, so who was I to argue? So now I became very polite, very compliant, and having sidestepped the strip-search altogether, I cooperatively made myself part of the re-boarding line." A mischievous grin and he paused briefly before adding, "By the way, the train did not depart immediately."

Again the laughter at his last remark, and he smiled now. It was the smile of an old man who had done something foxy. He made a typical Italian gesture, shaking his hand with its fingers grouped together.

"But I got away with it, Beto!" An emphatic swing of his head as he repeated, "I got away with it. Oh!" And his eyebrows went up. "Just now I'm reminded of another story, one that happened on that same trip, but in Vienna. But that's for later, not for now."

In all truth, Victor did get away with it, but it could indeed have cost him his life. As the days went by, and in order to avoid being drafted into the Italian military service, he continued on his way to Switzerland. There he would spend the larger part of two years with others of the family. Luigi, on the other hand, who was ineligible for the draft, had traveled with Carlo and his mother to Volargne, in Northern Italy. There they would wait together, hoping to reunite with Victor in Lwów before the year's end. It was an aspiration destined not to occur.

Three days have now passed since aging Victor had left the family in a state of keen anticipation, a thing he took some secret pleasure in doing. And on this balmy Friday evening, with the family again gathered in George's patio, with snacks and drinks all around, they were eager that he resume his storytelling from where he had left off on Tuesday; that he relate to them the "other story" he had mentioned.

It was then not without repeated promptings that he raised his hands as if in surrender and said, "All right, all right! I'll tell you the story." A pause then, his mischievous eyes darting from one to another of his small audience; as though he were Claudio Abaddo, about to conduct the RAI National Orchestra. Then he began.

"Now as I recall I was explaining about my efforts to get back to Lwów, and the difficulty I was …"

"No, not that, Dad." Mary was quick to remind him. "You'd started to tell us about that, but then George raised a question about something that happened at the Czech border. So you told us about that, about the strip search, and then you said there was another story—something you were going to tell George later; something about what happened in Vienna."

"Vienna?" Victor's countenance was one of confusion. "Something in Vienna?"

"Yes, Dad," Robert prompted. "You were on your way to Switzerland; you'd outfoxed the strip search at the Czech border; and then you said that …"

"Oh! Now I remember. *That* Vienna! The thing with the Brownshirt punks."

"I guess so," Robert conceded with a shrug. "You hadn't told us anything about it."

"Well then, let me do just that." And again he kept them waiting while he contented his palate with a sip of some better-than-average Beaujolais.

"As I said, it was in Vienna, and I was at the train station, waiting for my Zurich connection. And here was this group of young Italian fascists. They were all in their mid-twenties or so, about my age, and all of them were proudly wearing their PNF party badges on their jacket lapels. O they were really something, they thought. From what was said I gathered that they were returning to Italy from somewhere abroad—I don't remember where—and even then I wondered why they were coming home. Because more than likely they'd promptly be drafted into Italy's Army. But maybe that's what they wanted; I don't know.

"Anyway, there was the usual crowd in the station, and of this group there were about seven, as I remember, myself not included. So there we were, just loitering around this typical little stand-up coffee bar while they smoked cigarettes and told jokes, and sipped on espresso coffees. The three boldest of the bunch were drinking tall mugs of some kind of strong Austrian brew.

"And as I think back on it now, they were somewhat rowdy, I guess, as they relived their adventures. But the biggest problem was that in one way or another their conversation, especially their jokes, related to IL Duce and to what all of us saw as the exciting times of fascism.

"So here now came these Austrian youths, about the same ages; and they're wearing their Nazi Brownshirt uniforms and patrolling the train station, swaggering about in groups of two as if they were the SS themselves. Well, they took note of these noisy Italians; and in a friendly gesture they saluted toward the group with a sharp 'Heil Hitler.' Well, of course I said nothing, But these Italians—somewhat lazily actually—returned the salute with their traditional, 'Duce a noi!' meaning: 'Duce to us!'

"Now I have no doubt that their obvious impertinence was seen by those Nazis as the prideful superiority of Italy and Fascism over Hitler and Nazism. And their more-than-apparent insolence was further revealed moments later, when their derisive salutes were followed by their loud chuckling and even some raucous laughter.

"Well that did it! Because annoyed by this obvious rudeness, these two Austrian youths left and then returned in the company of two other Brownshirt teams. So now there were six of them. And without any pretense at salutations this time, they arrogantly asked these Italians if any of them were carrying concealed weapons.

"When the boldest of the Italians, and the biggest I might add— probably feeling that the answer was none of the Nazi's business—replied with a surly 'No,' the tallest of the Brownshirts, and completely lacking any courtesy, began to frisk him—patting him down and demanding that he loosen his knickerbockers and raise them above his knees.

"And suddenly it's like I'm back at the Czech border again, which had been only eight hours earlier, and my anxiety started climbing. You see I really loved wearing those knickerbockers. Wide and loose they were; comfortable. And the wider the better. Because, as you know by now, that was where I kept most of my contraband hidden."

He went on then to explain how his stamp collection, as well as his small fortune in Polish bank notes, had been carefully packed in linen bags. These had then been strapped to his legs, inside his voluminously baggy pants. As long as he was not physically searched and as long as he kept his composure, all was well.

But now he became frightfully aware that his new companions, however brief their relationship, were going to spell trouble for him. And he saw himself faced with the pressing need to find some way to escape, or at least to distance himself from the group. Whatever the solution, it needed to be fast, and done without attracting attention.

"So there I was, wishing I were somewhere else—most anywhere else—when the opportunity I so very desperately needed came along. And it was none of my doing!

"You see, the Italian being frisked suddenly yelled at the Nazi Brownshirt, the one who was now bent over and patting down his knickers, and he said, 'I have weapons up here.' When the Nazi looked up, the Italian shook his two fists and said, 'Do these qualify?' And then, instead of raising his knickers as he'd been ordered, he kicked the Austrian over and a fistfight broke out.

"Well, the other Nazis joined in; of course that was to be expected, and the other Italians as well. And immediately the commotion had the attention of virtually everyone within earshot. And when that happened, I just slowly stepped backwards into the crowd of curiosity seekers and very quietly slipped away. Then I kept myself hidden in a toilet stall of a public restroom until it was time to board my train for Zurich."

It was now George who said, "Dad, that was quite an experience. And I have to say this: I sometimes think it's a wonder that you survived. But what I'd like you to do now is to go back to what you were starting to tell us before; before we asked to hear about that matter at the Czech border. You were saying that you remembered nineteen forty, and that you were having problems with the mail—that you couldn't contact anyone in Lwów."

Victor leaned back in his chair. "Yes, that's the way it was, George. I'd made all kinds of efforts to communicate with the friends in Lwów, but I never had any success. To this day, in fact, I aah … I have no idea of what was happening with the mails. But I do remember that after more than a year I was becoming more and more anxious to go home."

He looked at the family now, gathered there in the patio; at his wife, Gina, sitting at his right. And as though explaining what he had just said, he remarked, "I missed everybody. Just like I would miss all of you."

Another sip of the Beaujolais. Then with resolve, and a shrug of his shoulders he said, "But that's the way it was; and the months drug on while I made … Oh I don't know how many efforts to get a travel visa. So what do I get?" And there was that Italian gesture again. "I get *nada*; nothing. Oh, the Swiss authorities, they were okay, but not the Russians. Oh no, not the Russians! But I did learn that bad things were happening back in Lwów. Atrocities were being committed there, and the Russians were arresting Polish men and forcing them into the Russian army. And when I heard of that going on, I right away thought about André and Franki. It wasn't till later, though, that I learned it had happened to them also."

To a large degree, to Valerie and to the others there in the patio, this was all new; it was a vicarious journey into the family's past. And as she began collecting some of the dishes she asked, "So when did you finally get a visa to return to Lwów?"

"I never did, mio amore. The rest of the year—all of nineteen forty—went by, and I never got a visa!"

"So how were you finally able to get back home?" said George.

Old Victor smiled that knowing smile, asked for a refill of his wine and said, "I suppose you could say it was because the inevitable happened.

"You see none of us—certainly no one in their right mind—ever expected the thing with the Russians and the Germans to work out.

I can guarantee that your grandfather Carlo didn't! Stalin and Hitler? Pshew! To him, and to many others, they were like two dogs fightin' over a bone.

"So in June of 'forty-one, about the twenty-second I think it was, the Germans began their second march on Lwów. Only now there were two enemies: the Poles and the Russians. And Molotov's and Von Ribbentrop's so-called *non-aggression pact* went into the trash." Another sarcastic snort and then: "Like it hadn't already been there."

And now Robert, elbows on the table, leaned forward. "And how did that change things for you and the family?"

A sigh. "Oh, Beto," he said. "Let an old man rest." He smiled broadly as he patted a full stomach and said, "You know, Valerie, for a *Wannabe*, you make a nice patio snack. And you also cook some pretty good pastasciutta, like we had for dinner. But I think I've eaten too much. I'm tired too. Besides, I've got some Bible reading I want to do."

George turned to look at his father. "What do you mean, *Wannabe*? How is Valerie a *Wannabe*?"

Victor heaved a sigh of mock exasperation and threw his son that knowing look. "Oh, George," he said smiling, "I've told you before; you've got to remember: the world is made up of two kinds of people— those who are Italian, and those who … "

And three laughing men said, "*Wannabe*."

Amid the communal burst of laughter that followed, Valerie hugged her father-in-law. "Thanks, Dad. I'm tryin'."

The weekend had passed, and it was Monday the 24th. Dew still clung to the grass and the sun was just rising at 7:10. As he had so often done before, Victor made his way across the back yard to George's patio door. Inside, at her kitchen table, Valerie sat with coffee and the newspaper, the *Orlando Sentinel*.

Opening the door and stepping inside he said, "So what's in the paper this morning?"

Surprised, she looked up. "Oh! Good morning, Dad. You startled me. I wasn't expecting you; I wasn't expecting anybody, not at this hour. But as to what's in the paper, there's just the usual; no good news. Coffee?" She started to rise.

He shook his head and raised a restraining hand. "Don't get up, dear; I'll get it."

At the coffeemaker now and pouring, he offered his laconic observation. "Regarding what you said about the paper ... it's to be expected."

And then he was seated, coffee steaming in his cup as Valerie asked, "How's mom this morning?"

"Like me, I suppose; she's as good as might be expected from old folks. I'm kidding. Actually she's fine. I left her still sleeping."

Folding the paper in quarters, laying it aside and picking up her coffee, she looked across the table at her father-in-law. "What you were telling us about a couple nights ago was fascinating, Dad."

He blew on his cup and nodded. "Umm. Fascinating now; terrifying then."

"Yes, I can well imagine that it was." Her head bobbed in agreement. Then leaning forward, "But how *did* you get back to Lwów? You left all of us in suspense last Friday evening."

He smiled. "Yes, I guess I did. So ... so this is to be *our* secret, eh?"

"Oh, Dad!" she chuckled. "You can tell the boys later, but I really do want to know."

"Well, okay," he said, dragging out the words and then taking a draft from his cup. "It was in June of 'forty-one—late in the month it was—and the Germans began what they called Operation Barbarossa—*Operation Cruel*, because it was to be so bloody. Oh, it was really something, Val." He shook his head. "The Germans had committed almost four million men—*four million*! That's over seventeen times the population of this entire city of Orlando. And they were fighting along a border that ran from Finland in the north, down to Romania in the south.

"Now to get ready for this ... this *operation*, they had reoccupied Lwów and had made it one of their staging areas. The Underground Home Army, that's to say the Polish partisans, who began fighting the

Germans, and then the Russians, now had to fight the Germans *again*. From Berne, in Switzerland, I reasoned that the Russians were no longer an issue as far as I was concerned.

"They were no longer controlling the borders. So, a couple of weeks after I got the news of all this, in early July, I figured that maybe now I could get back home— that it might be easier to deal with the Nazis."

"Oh? Why was that?"

"Well, because of Hitler's relationship with Mussolini, and me being a member of Mussolini's fascist youth. You see, Hitler really admired IL Duce, and it was generally assumed, therefore, that all Italians and Germans were supposed to be friends; though in actuality nothing could have been further from the truth. And by now, of course, German checkpoints were everywhere. So I used everything I had in my possession—everything in the way of fascist material, that is—to get past the German checkpoints. I used identification papers and badges, whatever it took. And when that wasn't enough, I'd tell them, in no uncertain terms and faking the authority along with a mild hint of threat; that I was a friend—a *personal* friend—of Benito Mussolini."

"You *didn't!*" Valerie exclaimed quietly, a skeptical smirk lighting her face. "That would have been dangerous, Dad!"

He cocked his head and looked at her wisely. "Oh, but I did. And you're right; it was dangerous. You see, Mussolini had once said, jokingly of course, that I was to oversee all future printing of fascist stamps. So with the memory of that day giving me the idea, and with some small measure of courage, and carrying my camera and tripod over my shoulder, I'd tell them I was on a mission to arrange for postage stamp opportunities—opportunities that were to commemorate the advancement of Germany's one thousand year Reich. Well, as you might expect, most of them loved that idea! And that usually got me through."

Valerie was sipping on her coffee now, and her eyes met those of Victor over the top of her cup. In those eyes he could see the question waiting to be asked—to be answered; the question raised by the expression, "usually got me through."

"There were times, however," and he continued, "when that wasn't quite enough. And that's when I'd play what I called my trump card."

"And that was …?"

"I had a corner block of André's ingenious but phony Mussolini stamps. Oh, they were beautiful, Valerie! And these were not just the regular fake stamps. These had been marked personally with IL Duce's distinctive initial— the letter 'M'—his authentic monogram initial. And these I carried in a glassine envelope." And now a smile of remembered success. "It was my *sine qua non*, as we have it in my native Latin—*that without which I would have failed*—without which I may have been arrested or even shot. But that always got me through. So I guess you could say that I bluffed my way back to Lwów."

Valerie looked at her father-in-law with unmasked admiration. "You crafty old rascal, you. You're really quite a man, Dad."

He drank the last of his coffee, leaned back and folded his arms. Grinning and looking away at nothing in particular he said, "Well, maybe …" And his eyes returned to her face as he added, "Or perhaps I was just young and stupid."

In the course of those bygone weeks, during which Victor was making his deception-laced journey eastward from Switzerland to Poland, the Russians, now under heavy attack by their former ally, were in the process of using conscripted Polish prisoners to form a Polish-manned Soviet Army group. As it occurred, most of the men being from Lwów, André and Franki were among them. Thus in late July of 1941, they found themselves in the Russian village of Totskoye. And there, on a particular day, a Russian officer addressed the assembled mass of prisoners.

Ignoring that he too was a transgressing invader, he said, "Germany has taken your land from you. They have taken your homes and your families; your farms, crops and cattle. But now we Russians are giving you an opportunity to fight back! You will be formed into a unit of the Russian Army!" And those were words that struck a chord.

As a ragged cheer went up from the disheartened prisoners; as they were being offered the chance to do something that appeared positive, Franki grasped André's arm.

Remembering the destruction and slaughter he had seen take place at the post office in Gdansk, and above the shouting that was going on, he exclaimed with a grin, "Did you hear that, André? We're going to be able to fight the Germans!"

Older, wiser, and of a cooler disposition, André replied cautiously, "Well, we'll just have to see how this turns out. But perhaps it's better than doing nothing."

Fortune would have its way, however, and the two men would be parted; a fact they would learn a few days later. Over what passed for dinner on that evening, André broke the news.

"They tell me I'm too old," he said. "So along with others, I'm being sent to a gulag—to a work camp in Siberia."

"Oh, my dear friend," Franki sighed. "To think that it's come to this." "Yes, I know. But it'll not be forever, Franki. And as soon as I can, I'll join you. I have my pens and my inks; I have my papers. Nothing is going to stop me, Franki. Nothing."

It was as though a vow.

Lwów is a city destroyed. Not physically, although there was a great measure of that as well. But it was a city destroyed in every other way; its heart was gone—a city of atrocities; of squalor, depression and decay. As Victor walks its littered streets, he is nearly overwhelmed with the reek of corruption and death.

The city has become a world unto itself. It is now a landscape nearly as foreign to him as would be the surface of a planet in another solar system; and the stench is as that of a charnel house.

What terrible crimes were theirs? he wonders, passing here and there persons hung by their necks in trees. On city light posts as well, murdered citizens of Lwów have been hung in a similar fashion, their corpses now rotting in the heat of an early August afternoon. On the sidewalks and in the streets themselves, putrefying bodies of dead animals, fly-covered and larvae-infested, lie composting and ignored. Had he been asked at some time in the past to imagine the scene, it would have been impossible. For it was beyond imagination; it transcended human reasoning.

Here now in Poland, in Lwów, as had been the case for over a year, was the prototype. Victor was not altogether aware of it at the time, nor perhaps were most of the others who saw it. But here was the precursor of that which would earmark the Nazi presence throughout Europe until the mid-1940s.

He walked then to the Winiarnia, there to be staggered by the absolute purity of its desolation. As he wandered through the empty buildings, the Inn and the apartments where he recalled saying goodbye to his family, to André, Franki, and to Padre—and to his girlfriends, he remembered André having said, "In that way I can keep an eye on the winery until you're …"

But they never did return. They had, although unknowingly, said goodby to Lwów and to the Winiarnia. They had said, "Arriverderci Leopolis." It was all empty now. Ransacked and looted, it had become a place of nothing but gloom and sad shadows. The wine; the laughter; the cheese; and the unforgettable pasta with its tangy sauces—all were gone now. Only the echoes remained.

And he cried.

Then wiping his eyes on a sleeve, he went to what had been Luigi's bedroom. And there, having viewed its stark emptiness he was about to turn away. But then he stopped. It seemed unbelievable, but there it was: the secret floorboard was untouched.

He knelt now and removed the board, eager to know if anything of importance might have been left by any of the friends—a message perhaps. Maybe the ravagers had missed something, something that he might well hold to be nothing short of a treasure.

And there in the recess, illuminated now by the watery summer sun that filtered in through a multitude of broken windows and other fractured openings, was a package. And in André's inimitable handwriting he read the name, "Victor." And thus it did prove to be a treasure. Indeed, more than a treasure.

As though he were a surgeon, his trembling fingers opened the package with great care. Glancing over his shoulder more than once, fearful now of being discovered, he gingerly sorted through the priceless contents. Yes! Yes, it all appeared to be intact. And a thrill went through him as he thought of André's own hands carefully packaging these irreplaceable gems. For here, undisturbed, were André's and Franki's entire collections of stamps. They had been found as André had intended. But there was more; there was a letter. And Victor set himself to reading it.

As he read, digesting every word, every thought, it became difficult for him to see. Tears welled again in his eyes, and he paused often to wipe them away with a knuckled finger. For he looked upon a message of ponderous sadness. André had recorded with him in mind—hopeful that he would be the one to find it—the terrible and frightening events that had occurred in Lwów following his having left for Switzerland.

André had written also of his assumption—one that proved prophetic— that he and Franki would soon be arrested and transported to Russia. Reflective of André's anticipation, he reads the words that implore him to safeguard their stamp collections until they can meet again. So on the moment, at least until that happy day in which they could be reunited, Victor determined that he would look after them on behalf of his two missing friends.

He had reached the end of the letter now, and he is puzzled. Reading portions yet again he notes that his friend has made no mention of the girls he had left behind: Dani, Stasi and Lari have apparently disappeared. No indication is given as to where they might be. Painfully aware now of what has happened here, it is a matter that both saddens and frightens him.

CHAPTER V

It is a Wednesday evening in Orlando, September the 26th. As the two brothers drive Victor east along Mosher, George brings up one of Victor's favorite topics: motor racing—Formula 1.

"So, what did you think of this year's Indy Five Hundred, Dad; particularly there having been a lady in the race — Sarah Fisher?"

"Ah yes, Miss Fisher," Victor intoned, sounding as though something sacred had been violated. "Well, I suppose it had to come to that eventually; women making their mark in so many fields now." Then dryly philosophic he added, "I suppose that perhaps we ought to pray for the rest of the drivers."

And as they laughed together, Robert leaned over the back of the front seat. "Actually, I'd had my eye on the two Brazilians: Bruno Junqueira for example. Had a good car. Qualified at two twenty-four point two; and Castroneves, right behind him at just a whisker under. Either one was a threat. Turns out, as you know, Castroneves took it. Anyway, it feels good to get out of the house. Any place special you'd like to go, Dad?"

They turned right onto Satel, and Robert settled back as Victor replied. "No. I just thought a drive down by Lake Fairview, down along Fairview Shores would be nice. I haven't been there for a while and I like to see how things change."

And now Grand Prix racing and the weather occupied their conversation for a while. As they drove along Edgewater, grandfather Carlo's acquaintance with Italy's famous racing greats, Tazio Nuvolari and Achille Varzi, became a focus of their chatter.

"Your grandfather Carlo loved inviting Italian celebrities to the Winiarnia, especially sports personalities. That's how I got started in photography. He'd lend me his camera and I'd photograph him with the stars. There'd be drivers like Nuvolari and Varzi, Olympic athletes and …"

"Did you say Nuvolari?" Robert interrupted. "Tazio Nuvolari, and Varzi?

"I mean … talk about auto racing! Those two champs put auto racing in the dictionary!

"Wow! Nuvolari and Varzi. They're the icons of the sport! When I think of Ferrari, Alfa Romeo and Maserati, or even tire companies like Pirelli, they owe their *names* to these two famous rival aces. And Grandpa knew them?"

"Oh, yes," replied Victor, equally as excited. "Celebrities of all sorts have been hosted at the Winiarnia Italia Inn. Bicycle racers, singers and others. Why, the entire A/C Milan Soccer Team ate and drank there on one occasion. And your grandfather always wanted to be photographed with his famous guests. And he always wanted me to shoot the pictures!

"And Nuvolari, by the way, was not only a friend, but also a neighbor when we lived in Mantua." Victor grinned as he remembered a particular occasion. "I'll never forget the night we took a Lancia Astura Cabriolet over to Nuvolari's

A/C Milan. (Carlo is 4th from left)

place." And he chuckled. "We needed to hide it from the Germans."

"Oh?" Robert exclaimed quietly. "What was that all about?"

"Aah, that's a story for another time, Beto. It'd take too long to tell it now."

Changing the subject, George said, "Speaking of telling stories, that was quite a tale you shared with Val a few days back; about how you bluffed your way back to Lwów. She told us all about it."

"Aah ha ha ha," he laughed. "Oh, she did, eh? Well, I hope she didn't exaggerate too much."

"C'mon, Dad! That story doesn't need exaggerating. But what did happen after you found that everything was gone, home, friends, and all?"

"Ah, that. Well, around the middle of August the Italians came, an Italian division. Since the Germans now needed all their troops on their eastern front, very few were left in Lwów; they'd left the Italians to care for that."

"And what was that like?" They are approaching Fairview Shores now.

"Well," and he paused thoughtfully. "It was better than the Russians and the Germans. Actually most anything would have been better than either of those; I think the Devil himself would have been better." As they laughed together he said, "But I have to say that the Italians demonstrated a lot more compassion for the people. And we now spoke the same language, which was good. So again I started searching for Stasi and Dani. I had a couple of photos, including the one of me and the girls in our swimsuits, and I'd show people the pictures and ask if they had seen them. But the answer was always no.

"So I decided to hitch-hike out to the farm, Ivan Doroshenko's farm, hoping to find his daughter Lari there. But on the way I was picked up by an Italian Army patrol."

"And how did that go?" Robert's question as they turned right onto Fairview Shores.

"It could've been worse," Victor replied philosophically. "I told them I was an Italian, and that I was a wine importer living in Lwów. But they arrested me anyway. Then it was off to Lwów's Italian Military Police headquarters, where I was interviewed by a field commander. I explained to him there that I had a dual citizenship with Poland, and that I had the legal right to be in Lwów."

"And … ?" said George.

Chuckling as he replied he said, "And I began to feel a little like the apostle Paul. Remember, George, when he had to explain to a Roman centurion that he, although Jewish, had Roman citizenship? Well, like Paul's Roman officer, this commander too was puzzled. So he called for advice from Division Headquarters. And when he did that, the division commander somehow got involved. And for whatever reason he took an interest in me, asking that I be sent to him, to Division Headquarters, for more interviews.

"So now I'm at the Division Headquarters; I've been searched; and I'm still trying to explain that my dual citizenship allows me to remain in Lwów. Then the issue of my draft status came up, and by now I was getting pretty frustrated. I even tried to make a deal with them. I said I'd put on the Italian uniform if I were allowed to serve in Lwów."

"And how did that work?" George asked.

"It didn't. The division commander stepped in and said I couldn't join the Army without a proper induction, and without being trained in Italy. He also said that he was obligated to send me there for military training regardless of my dual citizenship."

Again Robert leaned forward over the seats. "And why was that?"

"In the words of the commander: 'Because there isn't any Poland.' That's what he said: 'There *isn't* any Poland.' And I tell you, Roberto; those words, coming as they did, were like a knife in my heart! Suddenly I realized that what he had just said was true: Poland *didn't* exist! There *was* no Lwów. Not any more. I was just a draft-dodging Italian citizen in a Nazi-occupied territory under control of the General Government of the one thousand year Reich. And that's all there was to it. There was no Perantoni wine business, there was no Winiarnia; it didn't exist any more; my girlfriends were nowhere to be found; and André and Franki were gone. Not only was everything changed, everything was *gone*!" A whispered echo: "Everything was gone."

Victor grew silent for a moment. That of the car and the neighborhood now being the only sounds. And then he said, "And right then … right then and there I just wanted to break down and cry. Well, I guess the way I felt was pretty evident to the commander. Because now he invited me into his office where he offered me a deal."

"Oh really!" said George, taking his eyes from the road briefly.

"Oh, yes. You see, like me the commander too was an avid stamp collector. And he had come by one of those nineteen twenty nine Winiarnia invitation postcards, the ones with the fake Mussolini stamp, you'll remember. He told me that he'd obtained it at a trade fair in Naples; said it had been a hot item and that he didn't get it cheap! So he explained that since he was now stationed in Lwów, that he'd become determined to look up the Winiarnia, hoping to find me or André; better yet both of us. And when I heard that, I suddenly understood why he'd taken an interest in me—why he knew my name and why he had allegedly *overheard* of my arrest.

"Then he reached into his briefcase and took out one of those famous postcards. When I explained to him that the stamp featured in the middle of the card was only fake art, he laughed and said that he already knew that; but that it was beautiful; that it was desirable; and that it promoted IL Duce's face on a stamp—one that didn't exist at the time but was admired by all who saw it. Then he said to me, 'Are you ready to trade?' And now I was surprised. He said that if I could give him a full sheet of André's phony Mussolini stamps, that he would assign me to the new Italian military post office for six months before sending me off for training. Well, I didn't have any of my stamps with me, of course. I had them secured away at the place where I was staying, along with André's and Franki's collections."

They were nearly back home now and about to turn onto the Shasta Drive cul-de-sac. Victor was concluding his story.

"Then the commander said, 'And who knows? The war might be over in six months.' Well, the way that the war had been escalating, I was sure that wasn't going to happen. Even so, I felt like a dead man resurrected! So I told the commander that I'd do even better than what he proposed. I showed him the corner block of those special fake stamps personally initialed by IL Duce; the one which I kept in my wallet in a glassine envelope and which had got me past so many borders and checkpoints. When I offered it to the commander, he snatched it up and sealed the deal with a great big smile and a warm, friendly handshake.

"So as we both ended up happy, I asked the commander where the Italian military post office was located. And he said they didn't have one yet, but that the field postal van was parked outside and that the first mail delivery was scheduled to arrive the next day. So then he asked me, 'Do you have any suggestion as to where we should locate the post office?' And I told him yes, you bet I do! At the Winiarnia Italia!"

They had pulled into the driveway now to find that Valerie, Gina and Mary were in the yard. Roberto was opening the car door as Gina said, "You're back just in time. Dinner's almost ready."

As matters worked out, the commander was pleased with Victor's suggestion, and soldiers were assigned to help. As the war moved into its third year, the days passed with Victor directing the restoration of the winery hall, converting it into a functional military post office. During the next few months, wherein Victor busied himself in serving as something of a postmaster, the atmosphere in the town began to resume some of the characteristics of normalcy.

While Operation Barbarossa was bogging down deep in Russia—Hitler's blitzkrieg, his *"Lightning War"*, proving to be less blitz than krieg—the citizens of Lwów were welcoming a respite from the brutality they had experienced during the German and Russian occupations. Gradually, ever so slowly at first, shops were reopening; some of the restaurants and even some entertainments were starting to offer evening service, it being directed primarily to the Italian soldiers. It was not much, but it was a start.

As August and September passed, even the Italian soldiers, with their love of good food, good wine and good times, gave a needed positive atmosphere to a city which had endured numberless murders. Vicious and unspeakable atrocities had been committed over the two previous years. But with Italian soldiers having largely replaced the Germans, it was as if a plate of raw sauerkraut had been exchanged for one of pasta al dente, with tangy meat sauce and Parmesan cheese.

And now it was October. The post office, operating under Victor's successful oversight, is now commissioned to sort and process the German's mail as well, delivering it to the to the few German troops still remaining stationed in and around the Lwów area; their presence being most evident at the railroad station and at the War Operations Staging and Deployment Center. Victor is also charged with the responsibility of processing inbound and outbound mail to various Nazi units in Western Russia.

But despite the visually deceptive atmosphere of the town, a conscience- jarring anomaly now constitutes a new and ominous presence in Lwów—the Janowska labor camp. For here is where Jews and other political prisoners are being kept. German troops are also busy preparing a ghetto in the city, a restricted area wherein additional incoming Jews would be confined and processed before deportation to other camps—to death camps. It is patently clear: although the Germans are now fewer in number, they still constitute a disturbing authority.

"Signore Perantoni, I have an idea."

It is November now, and the Italian Division commander has approached Victor in the Winiarnia post office. Standing in the vast hall, turning about and spreading his arms in an expansive gesture, he said, "Victor, this place is much too large for a post office, I think. And on that I believe we will agree. That being so, I'd like to offer a suggestion."

"Of course, Signore Commandante. After all, you are the commandante. And that suggestion would be …?"

"Well, the holidays will soon be upon us, and my men, being a long way from home, would enjoy having a place where they could … well, you know, celebrate. Why could we not relocate the post office to the adjacent apartment's front room, and then redecorate the winery to be like it once was? This could then be a club for the soldiers."

Victor nodded and looked casually thoughtful. But inside he was trembling with excitement. Pulsing as did Vesuvius before Pompeii's destruction, he visualized the Winiarnia as an inn, a tavern once again.

"Si," he said, "Si, I think it a fine idea, Signore Commandante!"

"And the ground floor apartment across the courtyard," the commander went on, "could easily be modified to serve as an officer's club. What do you think?"

"Oh, Si! Si, Signore Commandante! An excellent idea! I have no doubt that my father, Carlo, would be more than pleased with such a thing!"

And now the commander looked at Victor more soberly. Referring to Lwów by its Italian name he said, "Do you suppose—that is if the army were to provide the transportation from Verona to Leopoli—that your father would be willing to give us a good deal on the wine?"

Victor is ecstatic. He could not have imagined such a happening. Even in the midst of the war, Carlo and Luigi are to resume exporting wine from Valpolicella. And he and the Italian quartermaster are to import that fine Italian wine to Lwów. The Winiarnia Italia is to be back in the wine business. But even as the old times come to his mind, he cannot help but think about his friends, Franki and André. *Where are they now?* he wonders.

Far to the east in Buzuluk, Russia, 630 miles northwest of Moscow, it is Franki Mrowicki who can also but wonder about his friend Victor. Far from experiencing Victor's recent exuberance and pleasure, he is enduring the military hardship of having been transferred to this remote location. Here he is receiving additional training as a member of General Wladislaw Anders' new Polish Army. It is the plan of the Russian military to prepare this unit for deployment to Iran, via the Persian corridor, and that they should later form the Polish 2nd Corps in the Middle East, thereafter to join with the British allies in Egypt.

André Frodel, meanwhile, is on a train bound for Siberia. But it is not his intention that he should stay there long. For even as he travels he is applying his paper and ink skill in doing what few others could have done: he is preparing a new identification for himself, new documents which he carefully inks in whenever the train is delayed or halted.

When he finally arrived at the Siberian gulag, a work camp in Kolyma, he learned of bitter news. Less than 600 of the Polish prisoners, of whom he is one, are still alive. Originally estimated to have been 12,000 in number, a full ninety- five percent have perished! He then discovered also that the youngest and strongest of his group are scheduled to depart on a return trip, this for the purpose of induction into General Anders' new Polish Armed Forces of the East. The return trip will depart in two days.

Pressed then for time as perhaps never before, André hurriedly but carefully completed his forged documents. Suddenly he is 39 years old instead of 51, and he now has a new craft. For in addition to making himself younger he has wisely forged a new and different work title. Aware of the military's needs, he has chosen to designate himself as a master tentmaker and a multilingual translator. Thus identified, and inwardly amused at the thought that some unfortunate Russian officer may well be broken in rank for having sent such irreplaceable skill to Siberia, it was with little effort that he arranged to have himself redirected back to the new Polish Army. He was then like a new man as he anticipated meeting up again with Franki. He can but hope that he too is still alive.

Robert and Mary have gone to visit a friend; Victor and Gina are spending the evening next door at George and Valerie's home; and the television pulses brightly with CNN's coverage of the day's events in the Middle East.

"Is it never going to end?" said Valerie, her exasperation so very evident. "I can't remember a single year in my life that was a year of peace; not one."

"Nor will you, I'm afraid," said Gina quietly, looking at her daughter-in- law over the rim of her coffee cup. "There will be no peace; not until this system ends. It's God's decree."

"She's right," Victor agreed. "It is God's decree." He paused reflectively and then said, "Maybe you've never thought of it Val, but when Jesus was … No, let me start in a different way.

"Some months ago a friend of mine became curious about his birth. No special reason, but he got to wondering on which day of the week he was born back in nineteen twenty-nine. So he went looking. Researching the Internet, he found the front page of an August, nineteen twenty-nine newspaper. While learning that the twenty-fourth of the month had been on a Saturday, his date of birth, he was also impressed additionally with the headlines of the times. Guess what was going on in the Middle East."

"I have no idea," said Valerie.

"War! said Victor. "The Jews and the Arabs were at it hammer and tong. So now here we are, in two thousand one, and have they settled anything? Nope! Any indication that they ever will? Nope!

"Over seventy years, Val. *Seventy years*, and nothing has been resolved. Now then, getting back to Jesus. As I started to say concerning him, when he was on trial before Roman governor Pilate, and when Pilate suggested that he be released—that he could find no fault with the man—he was saying that the Roman government wanted no responsibility in the matter. But the fact, of course, was that *somebody* was responsible!

"So the religious leaders who were there responded by saying—and this is a quote—'His blood come upon us and upon our children.' It's in the Bible, in Matthew's Gospel; and I can't change that. Look it up: chapter twenty-seven, verse twenty-five. And so with those words, that religious hierarchy accepted on behalf of themselves and their children—their descendents—the responsibility for the killing of God's son."

"But Dad!" Valerie exclaimed. "All that was done in the heat of the moment. Did those men really understand what a serious thing they …"

"Aah! Good question, Valerie. And a fair one too. Did they understand the responsibility they were taking on? And the answer: of course they did; their own fellows had written it years before in a rabbinical collection of rules of conduct. In what's called the *Babylonian Talmud*, Sanhedrin, 37a, such responsibility had been clearly spelled out. It says there—now I can't quote it so I'll paraphrase—that in legal cases involving the life of one falsely accused and *convicted*, that his blood, and the blood of all those destined to be born from him —his descendants, are held against anyone having falsely testified in the matter; and this to the end of time. And *these* men, of all persons, had to know this."

Victor chuckled softly now. "Aah ha,ha,ha, and I can see the question in your eyes, Val. You're asking how do I know this, right? And the answer is simple: I once looked it up.

"So now … God has but allowed their request. And what people are seeing in the Middle East today, particularly in Palestine, in Israel, is but the outworking of that thoughtless, murderous assumption of guilt. And as Gina said, it won't end until what most people call *the end of the world* occurs, the end of this present world system of things."

Valerie reflected on his words. "Well," she said, plaintively quiet, "I wish it would hurry."

Victor nodded and could have responded immediately; and he was moved to do so. But the scenes and words that suddenly exploded in his mind disallowed for that. Much rather it was the reason for mankind's circumstances that precluded his prompt reply, matters that his father, Carlo, had explained to him long ago.

Indeed, at that moment the whole panoply of human empires recited itself in his memory; from the time of Egypt's day in the sun until the rise of the League of Nations and its successor the United Nations, and the subsequent Cold War. They were all there in vivid scenarios.

There in graphic imagery was the fallen tree of Nebuchadnezzar's disturbing dream, recorded by Daniel in chapter 4 of the Bible book bearing his name; there it lay, signifying Nebuchadnezzar's temporary insanity and his synchronous fall from rulership. And by extension, it signified also the destruction of God's representative sovereignty in the lineage of the Davidic kings.

Daniel's own dream, recorded by him in chapter 7 and portraying with colorful animal pageantry the parade of world powers, was itself not unlike a television program.

And yet again in Daniel, in chapter 8, the overthrow of the Medo-Persian dynasty by Alexander the Great at the battle of Gaugamela in 331 B.C.E., and the subsequent dividing of Alexander's Grecian empire among 4 successors. How clearly and how dramatically it had all been outlined; and all of this hundreds of years in advance by God's prophets—by God's own hand as it were.

And still before Victor replied, the Revelation written by John at the close of the first century C.E.. For there an angel had reminded John, in chapter 17, that five of such world powers had already fallen: Egypt, Assyria, Babylon, Medo-Persia and Greece. He then said that one was, namely Rome; and that the seventh had not yet arrived: the Anglo-American power of the 20th century. For that world power, rising from out the wreckage and madness and bloodletting of the Great War, was to be the last of such human global sovereignties.

Oh, it was all there; a blatant, blood-smeared history, staring the whole of mankind in the face yet recognized and understood by virtually no one. Because the next kingdom, the next government to exercise global dominance, would be one of God's own making—his

Kingdom; the one for which multitudes have prayed: "Thy Kingdom come," though with little or no comprehension.

All of this was so familiar to Victor, and to Valerie as well. There was then no need to rehearse the record. And now he replied.

Smiling and patient he said simply, "Yes, I know, dear. You and millions of others." Then pointing toward the television screen he said, "And what you're seeing there is no different from what was happening back in nineteen forty-one; from what was going on in my home country."

Valerie reached for the remote control and turned down the volume. "What was it like then, Dad?"

Leaning his head back and emitting a sigh he said, "I remember … I remember December of that year. Yes, December. I remember it especially because Germany's bloody *Barbarossa* campaign had come to a stunning halt at Moscow. You see, it had been Stalin's determination that Moscow should not fall. I remember it too because we'd received news of this country having joined the war on the seventh of that month, yes, because of Japan's sudden and shocking attack at Pearl Harbor. Back then, *twelve-seven* was like *nine-eleven* this year. Of course the U.S. had always been in the war actually. Oh, their hands were as bloody as anyone else's—selling weapons to anyone who would buy them; usually to the highest bidder. Only now it was official.

"Especially I can recall the two weeks before Christmas. There in Lwów, at the Winiarnia, work on the soldier's club and the officer's club had been completed. And in preparation for the holiday parties, both clubs had been well stocked with wine and decorated in the usual fashion. But on my mind, primarily, were the girls—Lari and Stasi, and of course, Dani. My intended trip to the Doroshenko farm had ended with my arrest back in August. But now I had some advantage: I knew the commander! So I explained to him what I wanted to do and asked for a two-day furlough. But it couldn't be had. There was a problem."

"Transportation?" Valerie suggested.

"No, that wasn't it. The problem, as the commander explained, was that furloughs were never granted in enemy territories."

"Oh, I see. So now what?"

"Well, typical of him, he was the one to offer a solution; he knew what that furlough would have meant to me. So right out of the blue he changed the subject. He gave me a crafty smile and asked if the post office had sufficient equipment; things like rubber stamps, ink pads; things of that sort. Then he asked if I knew of any local sources for such things. Well, I understood where he was going with that! So I played along. In the end he granted me a 12-hour day- trip to look for what *he* had suggested was a much needed *custom-made* postal stamping kit, one with interchangeable lettering for special mail forwarding, a kit which just *might* be found *locally*. What a shrewd old bird that commander was; but not so tough as he appeared.

"So then, hoping at least to find Lari, I wrapped four bottles of wine as presents. And since you mentioned transportation, let me say that this time I didn't have to hitch a ride."

Valerie laughed quietly. "You had a car?"

"Oh, no. But the commander assigned me a car from the division's Motor Vehicle Section, and then offered a driver to help with the search, and also to get me back quickly, I suppose. Anyway, the wonderful thing was—the *really* wonderful thing—I found both Lari and Staci! And O how we cried! I thought we'd never stop. We were all over each other like … like hormone-driven teenagers. It had been two years, Val—*two years*! And it seemed like it had been … like it had been centuries.

"I learned too that a lot had happened, bad things. Dani's parents, for example, had been murdered during a Nazi pogrom against Jews, implemented in July; and that the last they knew about Dani herself was that she had been in the Janowska labor camp since September.

"They told me also that a few weeks ago the Germans had begun transferring all the Jewish prisoners from Janowska to Lwów's new ghetto, and that deportations there were taking place daily."

And now, with the old man's eyes glistening with tears of emotion, Valerie said, "Oh, Dad. How awful. How terrible. Could that mean that …"

"Oh, yes; and it *did* mean—that Dani might well be on her way to a death camp; there were now six of them in Poland. But you know, Val, as sad as that made me, it also made me angry."

He stood now and walked to the window. Peering out into the deepening darkness he said, "I couldn't recall, and I don't recall even now, any time in my entire life when I had ever felt that much anger. And out of that anger, that rage when I returned to Lwów, grew my resolve to find her, and to rescue her as soon as possible."

A long silence now, wherein only the muted sound of the television was heard, while neither of them looked at the screen and while George entered the room with his coffee and sat next to his wife. Uncertain as to the cause for the strained silence, he said nothing. Finally Valerie spoke.

"But how, Dad? How would you go about … I mean … I wouldn't know where to start."

"Exactly. And that was my problem; where to start."

"Start what?" George said, seeking now to understand the conversation.

"We've been talking about Victor's efforts to find the girls, and now especially to find Dani," Gina explained.

"Aah, I see! So what was happening?"

Victor was returning to his seat as he explained. "For a while, nothing, And then I got to thinking of what I might learn from the Germans' mail. And why not? Since I had access to all of it, I started steaming open letters written by the ghetto guards, as well as letters written to them." A playful wink now as he remarked, "And Oooh! I'm learning some steamy things!" Then serious again: "But I was really looking for something big, anything; any kind of information that might help me get favors from them. And I did learn of such things, useful information that I could even use to bribe some of the guards. But I needed something *really* good! It had to be a charge that would really stick, that would stick like *mmm*-elted *mmm*-ozzarella on *mmm*-anicotti!"

"Then one week before Christmas, while I was still digging away with my hot iron and steam rag, I finally struck gold. Primo paydirt!"

"And that was …?" said George.

"A confirmed love affair; a scandalous affair which would've been of the nastiest kind in the eyes of the SS Reichsführer Heinrich Himmler!

This was between—are you ready for this?" He paused and then said, "Between an SS lieutenant, one appointed over the Lwów ghetto guards, and … and *his lover*, an SS infantry captain who'd recently been reassigned to the Russian front and was due to leave soon."

George spilled his coffee and Valerie was speechless.

"You mean …" George was standing now, brushing coffee droplets from his lap. ". . . that these two *officers* were …"

"*Esattamente!*" Victor snapped. "Egg-zactly! Oi! You should've seen the lieutenant's letter! Even Gina and I never used such mushy, schmaltzy words with each other; not even before our marriage."

"Really! What kind of mushy words?" asked Valerie.

"Yeah, what did he write, Dad?" George was laughing now, a sarcastic laughter.

"Well, my German was rusty, but better than when I was in Vienna back in 'thirty-nine. So I'll never forget his opening lines. He started out by saying, three or four times, '*Ich vermisse dich,*' which means 'I miss you.' And this captain hasn't even left yet! Then, '*Ich brauche dich zu berühren,*' which means 'I need to touch you,' and '*Ich brauche deine Berührung*' translates to 'I need your touch.' After that he wrote that he'd never loved any man more than he loved the Führer, and then he said, 'but then I met you!'"

"Oh please!" said George pleadingly, feeling somewhat nauseous about the matter as the others laughed derisively. When composure returned, he said, "What else Dad; what else did he write?" He and Valerie were fascinated by the obsessively passionate and sleazy character of the lieutenant's love letter.

"Some of the expressions I remember are the words that were the thrust of the lieutenant's sentiments for his lover captain. He used words like, '*Ich liebe dich,*' meaning, 'I love you.' Oh, that was in almost every other line. Then there were things like, '*In gedanken dort. Hast du an mich gedacht?*' which meant, 'I always think of you, have you thought of me?' And then, '*ewig dein, hast du mich lieb?*' or, 'I'm yours forever, do you love me?'"

When the satirical laughter subsided, Victor explained, "Now you can say what you want about Hitler; he was a monster—but a peculiar monster! He couldn't tolerate the use of tobacco, and would forbid smoking in his presence or even under the same roof. He abstained from alcohol, didn't tolerate the slightest drunkenness, and he *despised* homosexuality! And I don't think he learned any of that from his Catholic religion. Homosexual acts were considered to be a crime against his Third Reich, and they called for imprisonment in a concentration camp. But for such as the SS lieutenant and his lover captain … oh ho ho ho ho! If their situation ever got upstairs to SS headquarters, then we're talking about *Lieutenant Lynched* and *Captain Corpse*. It could have meant execution by a firing squad. Because for them, as SS officers, it was more than a civil crime, it was treason! And they should have known that; in fact they did know that!"

"Imagine," said George, "that simple words of love could get a person shot."

"In this case, yes! But oh, it was so much more than that," Victor replied. "The statements he made in his letter became as though imprinted on my mind. Wonderful words they were, everyone of which spelled 'out'— Dani's release; for me anyway. Because those statements went on to describe how the captain's departure would, in the lieutenant's words, '*leave a gaping hole in my heart,*' that could only be '*filled by the warmth of your caress and the tenderness of your lips against mine.*'

"Oh, on he went, reminiscing about the ecstasy of their nights of passion, when they had realized that they were '*meant for each other.*' And he wrote that he yearned for the day when he would be able to gaze into the captain's eyes again, and '*feel complete*'; things like that. How he would '*hold him tight and never let him go again.*' Oh, I virtually memorized that letter for what it meant for Dani. It delighted me and made me sick at the same time. Then he ended by writing, '*Gedenke mein, mich nicht vergessen,*' meaning, 'Think of me, do not forget me.' and adding a long string of '*kuss, kuss, kuss,* and *ewig treu,*' that is, 'kiss kiss kiss, and eternal love.' Now statements like those could have gotten both of them shot!

"Now then, based on this *steamy* finding, and others, I concocted a devious plan; one involving that homosexual lieutenant and three of his subordinate ghetto guards. All three had wives, you see, and children back home in Germany; and all three of them shared Polish mistresses from the same brothel, there in Lwów. How about that? Now I won't go into the details, no need to. And maybe it was a cruel thing to do; but they deserved it, the scoundrels. And their wives were also entitled to know. I'll just say that everyone was about to find out everything about everybody.

"Besides, it was a far less cruel thing than what was happening to Dani, and certainly less than what had happened to her parents. And those were the things that caused the anger in me to boil up, enough to make me want to spill out to the Gestapo, everybody's dirty little secrets of homosexuality, fornication and adultery, regardless of the consequences; even if it meant death by a firing squad. And I was in a position to do this if they wouldn't do what I was ready to demand."

Valerie said, "Dad, you were vicious."

"You think so? Maybe I was. Anyway, I had it planned how to leverage their cooperation. So now I mailed them invitations, invitations to the holiday parties at the Winiarnia. And I also invited a few token peers from their units. I even gave them personalized and discounted entry coupons. Because remember, this was an *Italian* club; this was not for Germans.

"Now the invitations for those adulterous guards included an offer for them to get tickets for free drinks if … if they were escorting a female companion. And let me tell you, they loved that idea!"

Valerie's eyes sparkled with mischief. "Did any of them decide to bring their Polish mistress?"

"Oh, how I had hoped that they would. They didn't, but they fell right into my trap! On the night of the twenty-fifth, they arrived with other mistresses just as I'd planned. And they were required to show their military ID cards at the door in order to validate their discount entrance passes and their free drink coupons.

"So now I'm *really* learning things, connecting faces with names. And when the SS lieutenant showed up I greeted him with a bottle of Lacryma Christi. It's a fruity wine that the Germans seemed to especially appreciate. So in comes the lieutenant, and I have a drink with him before personally escorting him across the courtyard to the Officer's Club. No guns were allowed inside, so he agrees to leave his sidearm in a locker with the coatroom attendant. Then I introduced him to my dear friends, a pair of Sicilian lieutenants who were secretly expecting him, and I left.

"And the party was a great success. I had made personal contact with my target, the three ghetto guards, while my two Sicilian friends had been making the lieutenant feel right at home.

"So, by around eleven o'clock the three lieutenants were involved in a heated card game, gambling for rare stamps; stamps which I'd provided for my friends earlier; stamps that were probably better than money in that place and at that time. And according to our covert plan, the SS lieutenant was *winning*. In fact, he'd *won* several hands, raking in some very old Italian and German stamps. So he's feeling pretty good about himself; he's feeling lucky.

"Then in I walked … again, and asked if I could sit in. They all agreed and I sat down. Now this German, gloating over his winnings and having become pretty cocky from the wine, blurts out, 'I hope you brought some good stamps with you.' So I said, 'What have you got to play with?' And as if he had just won the battle for Leningrad single-handed, and with triumphal delight, he shows me his winnings.

"So now I said, 'I have with me one single stamp worth a hundred times what you've got there.' And he says, 'Show it.' And I laid it on the table.

"Now at this point all eyes were on him as he examined my stamp. I could almost see the question marks in his mind. Then he looked up at me—like he could kill. 'You must be joking,' he says. 'You must think I'm a fool, that I don't know stamps! This is nothing! Nothing more than a recently used, and I might add *worthless*, nineteen forty-one German Racehorse stamp.' I said, 'You're right.' And he said, 'You couldn't even mail a letter with it!' And I said, 'Oooh, but you're wrong, because a letter *was* mailed with it! You see, it's not the catalog value that makes this stamp priceless, it's the letter the stamp came from that matters.'

"So now he swears at me, barks at me in German, '*Was in der Hölle redest du?*' And in case you missed the meaning, and pardon my literal translation, he said, 'What in the hell are you talking about?'

"By now my two Sicilian friends had moved their chairs to his side of the table; one to his right and one to his left, and he was beginning to feel uncomfortable. But he had no idea how much worse it was going to get. And now my friend on his left said to him, 'We know *certain* things.' And my friend to his right added, 'About *certain* people.'

"Now this lieutenant, this … *Dutchman*, didn't like at all what was going on, and he bellowed something nasty in German as he stood up. So now my two Sicilian friends reached up, grabbed him, and slammed him back into his chair. And now it was my turn.

"I reached into my coat pocket; I pulled out his letter; and I began reading. '*I never loved any man more than the Führer … but then I met you … your departure left a gaping hole in my heart that can only be filled by your warm caresses and the tenderness of your lips against mine … I long for the ecstasy of our nights of passion when we realized that we were meant for each other.*' And I won't sicken you with the remainder of it as I went on.

"So what do you think, George? Have any idea of what an SS officer's face looks like when he knows his goose is cooked?"

George only smiled.

"Well, nobody else did either; not until the Nuremberg trials after the war. But my two Sicilian friends and I got our first glimpse of it at that Christmas party in nineteen forty-one.

"So now this lieutenant stood up again, and moved back from the table faster than my friends could grab him. And there he stood while he bawled brazenly, '*Ich mache mir keine Sorgen,*' that is, 'I'm not worried.'

"Now that did it! My anger returned and I stood up. I said to him, 'Fine! It doesn't worry you now. But I'll tell you this: if any harm comes to my girlfriend who's in your custody in your lousy ghetto, then I promise that I will personally see that the man you love is shot before a firing squad, and his blood will be on your hands.'"

"And then …?" said George.

"He sat down like he'd been poleaxed! And as I sat down, he said, 'What can I do? There's nothing I can do.' I said, 'Good! That's all I want you to do. Do nothing! I will personally escort my girlfriend out of your stinkin' ghetto, and you will do nothing to stop us from walking out.' Then while explaining that I had devised a plan for Dani's escape, I put his letter back into my coat pocket and took out the three letters belonging to his ghetto guards. I explained to him their situation, that they had also been invited, and that they were presently being entertained by their mistresses in one of the back rooms of the Winiarnia Italia soldier's club across the courtyard. I said he was to leave my rare stamps on the table, that he was to go over there and threaten them regarding their adultery, and to mention their incriminating letters.

"I told him to enter the Winiarnia through the back door, to walk in on them and to catch them in the act. He was to send their mistresses home, and then to have a stern *I-outrank-you* talk with the three about *German morality*. If there was any static he was to explain that he was in possession of their self- damning letters, and that if they repeated their immoral conduct he would forward those letters to their wives. Then he was to send the three back to their stations, and return to the officer's club where I would explain to him how the escape would take place."

Even in George Perantoni's living room, separated from the event by miles and decades, there was the feeling of imminent success.

"And what happened?" said George.

Victor was beaming uncontrollably. "Dani escaped! Lari, Stasi and I helped Dani escape!"

Valerie was virtually consumed with happy curiosity. "But how, Dad? she bubbled. "How?"

A wicked grin now and a gleam in his eye as Victor said smugly, "Well, it took some engineering. First of all—and let me say that it galled us to do this— but with Dani in mind, Lari and Stasi got themselves all floozied up on New Year's eve, looking like street walkers. And me? I dressed like a typical Italian pimp. Then off we went to find ourselves a real lady of the night. And that wasn't hard to do. Actually we found a pack of them, standing across the street from the Hotel George in Lwów's center square."

Then suddenly aware, he said, "Sorry my boy, but that was the name of the place." And they all laughed as he added, "It was a favorite *recreation* spot for German and Italian troops alike.

"So we stepped up to them, and I announced that I needed a third *companion* for a special and profitable New Year's party at the German guard station. Not surprisingly they all volunteered, but we were most interested in the one who smelled like a bottle of sour vodka. Because she was about Dani's size, and her hair was similar in color and style to Dani's, and also because she was already well lit, more than half blitzed.

"Well, the others were disappointed, of course, but off we strolled. That is to say, the girls and I strolled; the prostitute could only stagger. So we're heading for the ghetto, and Lari pulls a bottle of vermouth from her purse. Stasi took out a little bottle of apricot schnapps, and we started drinking and shouting, 'Happy New Year!' seein' to it that the drunken lush had the lion's share of the booze.

"Then after she was pretty well sloshed, we began feeding her Lacryma Christi wine, explaining to her about this SS officer who would like to join us in his upper chamber of the ghetto's guard compound. You should've seen her eyes light up! Let me tell you, the dirty mind is a continual feast. Some people can think of nothing else.

"So now we arrive at the ghetto's entrance, and I'm ecstatically happy to see that the SS lieutenant has done his part. The two guards were ones I recognized from last week's Christmas party, and they waved us right in, indicating that the lieutenant was expecting us. And if he'd completely followed my directions, the third guard had already delivered Dani to the lieutenant's personal quarters.

"By now the prostitute could hardly walk. So with her head hanging down and with us holding her up, and by delivering a couple of bottles to the guards, we schmoozed our way to the lieutenant's quarters where Dani was being held. The conditions were perfect for her escape.

"When we walked in on her, she couldn't believe her eyes. And from the way we were dressed she knew immediately what was happening. A couple more glasses for our street-walking companion, and she was out for the evening. Then it was just a matter of changing places. Dani put on the prostitute's dress, we put Dani's clothes on her, and left the poor girl on the lieutenant's bed, unconscious. Only minutes later, with Dani acting drunk, staggering between us, with her head hanging down, we walked out of that ghetto. Oh! And we took a moment to wish the guards a happy new year.

"And let me tell you; used correctly the corruption of a human can be a *wonderful* thing! And on that New Year's eve in nineteen forty-one, Lari and Stasi—and Dani too, bless her heart—along with yours truly, enjoyed, and I mean we enjoyed a happy private party in your grandfather Carlo's office at the Winiarnia Italia Soldier's Club!"

George threw his father a disparaging look; a look that spoke volumes, and that was not lost on Victor.

With a shake of his head Victor said, "Now don't look at me like that, George. Apart from fascism and international wars, the world had *some* morals back then, unlike today!" And amid a snicker of agreement from across the room Victor continued. "Nothing improper happened! But … we danced; we ate Pandoro Melegatti; we had Panettone Motta; we drank Asti Spumonte and we munched on Torrone Croccante. Without a doubt, despite the fact that conditions there in Lwów were more than terrible, that was the happiest New Year's party of our lives. And after that, just so that nobody could change their mind, you see, the three girls went into hiding in the surrounding countryside, Galicia's farm region."

Valerie rose now, and smiling brightly she walked to her father's chair. "Oh, Dad. I'm so glad all of that ended happily for you. And thank you for sharing the story. Let me take your cup to the kitchen."

Holding up a hand he said, "I can take care of it."

"I know, but let me take it. You and Gina sit here and talk with George. Would you maybe like to watch something on TV?"

He thought for a moment. "Umm, yeah, maybe." Then, "Yes, yes I think I would. I noticed that you've got the *All in the Family* series on tape. I'd like to watch that. Archie Bunker is such an opinionated butthead—like some of those German guards were. I like seeing him get his comeuppance."

Valerie was chuckling to herself as she left the room.

CHAPTER VI

Aging Victor was a respected man. To the several friends gathered for a barbeque the following week, he was like a neighborhood patriarch. Autumn's bite was in the air; the fire's coals were dying; glasses of various beverages were in evidence; and the gathering's conversation had gravitated to that of the family's discussion of several days ago. After bringing up to date those who had not been present previously, Victor was continuing his reminiscence.

"Three months had passed since Dani's release," he was saying, "and I was keenly aware that changes were in the air. News had reached us in Lwów that on the first of March the Russians had mounted a counterattack in Crimea. Rumors also had it that German losses in the fields were now calculated to be one and a half million lives. At the time we all thought that was pretty great. I can even remember some people cheering about it. But now I look back and I think, what was accomplished? Nothing."

Now he shook his head, as though to erase the memory. "And what was there to cheer about? Again, nothing. Why cheer about one and a half million people having died? And who were they: fathers, brothers, husbands? Were they uncles, cousins, nephews ... whatever? They weren't monsters. They had been people; and to someone they had been precious."

His eyes teared now and he paused. No one spoke.

Then composed he said, "It makes no sense to me now, but it seemed to at the time. We were also told that in France, the RAF was now raiding the industrial suburbs of German-controlled Paris.

"But I was occupied with matters of a more immediate concern, matters more personal. I'd been told by the commandante that I would no longer be allowed to remain in Poland." A smirk now, then bitterly, "Poland? Ha ha! It didn't exist. It was all kindly explained, of course, and I'd known formerly that it would eventually come to this; that I'd be relocated to a military training camp in Italy and be inducted into the Italian army. So it was no surprise. There were others to be relocated as well. And it seemed to me right then like the character of the war was changing."

And indeed it was. It would not be until later, after his relocation to Italy, when Victor would be angered to know that on the 17th of that very month the Germans had begun deporting Polish nationals to a labor camp in Belsen. Not until then would he also learn that late in the year the Germans were confronted with yet another problem. The Lwów ghetto was becoming overcrowded.

Thus, in the closing months of 1941, the matter of processing and deporting many hundreds of Jewish prisoners, shipping them to Auschwitz and Birkenau and to other death camps, became a pressing burden to an already understaffed and undermanned German garrison. And although a solution appeared to present itself in the form of additional help, such help failed to materialize.

All of this Victor related before saying, "You see the expected answer to the problem—the solution—had been the Italian Division, the Leopoli Division. The Nazi General Government had commissioned them, and they were expected to participate in this … (He made a rolling gesture with his hand.) … this effort to get rid of these unfortunate people."

Robert was refilling a glass for a guest as he remarked, quite matter-of-factly, "And the Italians didn't cooperate."

"You bet we didn't!" Victor snapped. "We had no issue with the Jewish people; that was Hitler's problem; at least he imagined it was. So now the Germans there in Lwów had something of a rebellion on their hands. Because the Italian soldiers had a pretty good idea of what was going on. They were not about to arrest Jews, and they wanted absolutely nothing to do with the deportations.

"You see, what had the Italians' interest, also, was that they foresaw an imminent invasion by the Allies. It didn't happen that way, not right away, but that's what they were expecting. Actually, to many Italians, like to me for example, it was not so much an invasion as it was a matter of being liberated from Germany. And I'll tell you this: when I finally learned about what had happened back in Lwów, I was furious! That liberation couldn't come soon enough." The group was quiet now as they waited for what would come next. "But I wasn't alone. The entire Italian military, throughout all of Europe, felt this same anger, this same discontented resentment of Germany.

"In Italy … (He shook an emphatic finger.) … "In Italy we could see everything going wrong. By the summer of 'forty-three the Russian campaign— Germany's invasion of Russia—was in some serious sauerbraten; and even the General Government was unable to supply the military with what they needed. O that poor wretched military!

"Can you believe it? Italian soldiers in Lwów were *selling* weapons and ammo to the underground—to Polish Partisans and to Jews. And why? you ask. Couple of reasons. Primarily because they needed living supplies; they needed food, which the partisans were able to provide. And secondly, they probably thought it might help to end the war."

Suddenly the old man stopped. Briefly he stared vacantly at nothing while his expression changed from one of contemptuous anger to one of deep regret. With eyes now glimmering with tears he surveyed the family and guests, each of them hanging on his every word as he said, "*Basta*! That's enough. No more talk of the war. No more." A great sigh now, and then: "Let's talk about something nice; let's talk about … how about racing—Formula 1 racing? The boys and I were talking about Nuvolari just a few days ago. Now there was a driver! Probably the world's greatest ever! Their grandfather knew him, you know." And the conversation went on for another hour.

Had Victor continued regarding the war, he would have said that July 25th, 1943, saw the end of fascism in Italy. The 20 years of enchantment with IL Duce Mussolini's fascist government had reached its end. He would have told of Mussolini's arrest by order of King Victor Emmanuel the third; of his imprisonment, and of Hitler having ordered his subsequent rescue by Nazi special forces. The Führer was still loyal to IL Duce.

What he most wanted not to talk about was the aftermath of fascism's fall in Lwów. As was true throughout Europe, Italian soldiers there were gradually relieved of their duties by the Germans. Then following Italy's surrender to the Allies on the eighth of September, 1943, the announcement being made five days later on the thirteenth, Italian soldiers in Lwów were preparing to go home. Discouraged and emptied after four long years of pointless warfare, they longed for the warmth of their families. It was anticipation never to be realized.

Two days later, on September 15th, with overtly calloused indifference to the sanctity of human life and with typical Nazi barbarism, German soldiers covertly massacred the entire Italian Division.

The event is said to have occurred in the forest of Lisentisky, west of Lwów. But there are questions. Soviet authorities, two years belatedly, released the news that they had discovered in Lwów—by then renamed Lviv in Ukrainian—the mass graves of some two thousand Italian soldiers. Included were generals, colonels and junior officers, allegedly murdered by the Nazis in 1943. The Italian Ministry of Defense, for whatever reason, denyingly replied that it was not so; that in those places and in that period, massacres of that size had often taken place. Who then were these poor victims? When were they really killed and by whom? Had these soldiers also been patrons of the Winiarnia Italia soldier's club?

The tragically macabre discovery is said to have resulted from the work of a student research group in Lviv, dealing with historical facts of World War II. Their leader, a Vladimir Demchak, had said that, "the names have already been identified; more than fifty officers killed." And he added that there were also witnesses to the massacre. A painter, a certain Semyon Gruzberg, remembered seeing the Nazis, "*accompany the column of gray-uniformed Italians.*" A certain Mrs. Yulia Moska Bukovskaya, age 60, confirmed the date of the massacre by saying that in September of 1943, she had seen Italians exterminated in groups, in the forest of Lisentisky. "*They were machine-gunned down in a sand quarry,*" she reported. "*The bodies were then burned in their sandy grave, and then the Germans planted trees over the grave pits, to hide the traces of their crime.*"

What was the official position taken by the new Italian government in the immediate aftermath of the war, in 1945 and 1946? And how did the new Italian Republic deal with the ever more pressing evidence of the facts? At first the news was rebuffed on the grounds that it was simply communist propaganda at a very sensitive period when new governments were being formed in European countries; and that this news—this propaganda—was intended to fortify the communist factions which, as Partisans, had fought long and hard against Fascism and Nazism, and who subsequently found themselves struggling against Republicanism.

So it was suggested that the only plausible theory was that the massacre had taken place after the 1943 Italian surrender, and not against the Leopoli Division, but against various Italian troops left on their own; abandoned in various European countries; and eventually arrested and rounded up by the Nazis, and then sent to Poland. Unfortunately, after that 1943 surrender date, the historical archive of the Italian Ministry of Defense was no longer able to collect official data on their troops abroad. And the Germans had also, predictably and perhaps conveniently, "lost all records."

Now there are many who remember the deportation of Italian soldiers— those rounded up by the Germans in the Balkans and elsewhere after the Italian surrender on September 8th, 1943. They remember sealed wagons, traveling for weeks in Europe, traveling to a point which was then in Poland—to Lwów, at the edge of the Russian front. And there, such men were put into prison camps.

Multiply now those memories of Italian veterans; add then the growing feeling among the Italian people, especially those Italian families with missing loved ones, that something had really happened out there—out there where the Russians say a massacre took place—and it certainly appears to amount to something.

Conversely there are those who exclude the possibility of a massacre by the Germans. There are even those who interpret everything as an attempt by the Soviets to invent another Nazi war crime, intended to justify the deaths of too many Italian soldiers who died in the captivity of the Red Army, and of whom nothing had been heard; not even citing the place of their burial. That the Division disappeared however—that the story of thousands of Italians vanishing without a trace even exists—is dividing public opinion among Italian citizens, wartime witnesses, and their heirs.

Another problem that the Commission of Inquiry had, was the task of solving why—regarding the alleged Leopoli massacre—why there was no trace in the archives of the Red Cross. However, among the documents of the Red Cross in Geneva, there was a report that provided some interesting details concerning Italian wartime internees.

In their report, submitted in August of 1948 to the Seventeenth International Conference of the Humanitarian Organization in Stockholm, it was stated that the number of Italian military and civilians interned in German camps after the September 1943 surrender of Italy, was as high as 550,000! But in Geneva, that list was never communicated. Why? Perhaps because during the final years of the war, Berlin had continuously denied open information on the status of prisoners of war. Berlin's position at that time was to deal with the problem only through the provisional government of the Republic of Salò, their own Nazi-Fascist outfit, La Repubblica Sociale Italiana—the RSI of Northern Italy. Thereby they excluded any international authority. The Red Cross claimed never to have been authorized for field visits, nor for the distribution of relief.

The Great Reich, in fact, considered itself above any law. And those of the RSI, headquartered on lake Garda with a fallen Duce, were only timid servants bowing before the Great Reich.

Whatever be the truth, over 2,000 of Germany's former allies, true sons of Italy, were thus destroyed in a mass execution—a mass murder. And thereafter the bodies, as reported, were burned and buried, trees then being planted atop the mass graves. Whatever really happened, the Italian Leopoli Division would become known as "The division which disappeared in 1943."

There are without doubt, somewhere in the world several persons, octogenarians who may have witnessed what transpired in early March of 1940; who may have even heard the crack of the rifles or the chatter of automatic weapons as thousands of lives were extinguished. Though the date of the event's occurrence cannot be targeted with precision, the date of its being ordered and its grisly product are beyond denial.

As reported in the press on April 13th of 1943, a mass grave was discovered in a forest near Katyn, Russia, some 12 miles west of the city of Smolensk. When the grave was opened, the stench was said to have been intolerable. For buried in that grave, along with others, were the bodies of some 4,000 Polish army officers. As for those responsible for the deaths of these men, there had been but questions, accusations and denials.

Let it be said however, and before proceeding further, that 4,000 is but a fraction of the multitude murdered at that location and at the suggestion of Laverentiy Beria, then the head of Stalin's Secret Police, the NKVD. Generally cited in connection with this event is the number 21,768, a number that must of necessity be viewed as a mockery of score keeping.

The victims of this sanguinary harvest included: an admiral; 2 generals; 24 colonels; 79 lieutenant colonels; 258 majors; 654 captains; 17 naval captains; 342 non-commissioned officers; 85 privates; 7 chaplains; 3 landowners; a prince; 43 assorted officials; 131 refugees; 20 university professors and 300 physicians. Along with them were hundreds of lawyers, engineers, teachers and writers. And in addition there were some 200 pilots.

It is reported that when the grave was discovered, the Soviets accused the Germans of having committed the massacre, and subsequently they refused to participate in an international investigation, their claim being that the matter was closed; the men had been killed by Germans. And it was thought that perhaps the claim was true, for it was determined that the shooters—whoever they were—had used German ammunition.

On the other hand, a German inquiry witnessed by Polish officials had concluded that the atrocity was the work of the Russians, and cleverly disguised by their having used German ammunition, which of course was alleged to have been stolen.

It may be said in retrospect that even then the Germans may have had the better argument. Because the exiled Polish government in London, of which General Wladyslaw Sikorski was the Prime Minister, had been wondering since 1939 about the disappearance of an entire Polish army.

Thus in December of 1941, when Sikorski had undertaken a visit to Moscow where he met with Premier Joseph Stalin, he had asked Stalin directly why these men, and others like them, had not been released according to an existing amnesty agreement. Stalin had responded by saying they had all escaped. Upon Sikorski asking to where had they escaped, and presenting a list of some 4,000 missing officers' names, he was then told by Stalin—the story now becoming patently plastic—that they had been released and had probably not yet returned home. According to the said agreement, however, Russia actually did release some of their Polish prisoners in 1941, but these were transferred to Iran, in order to prevent their subsequent fighting against Soviet forces in Poland. Upon their arrival in Iran, British officials were staggered to find no officers among these Polish soldiers. British and American authorities of the time, therefore, had little doubt that the Katyn affair was the work of Moscow.

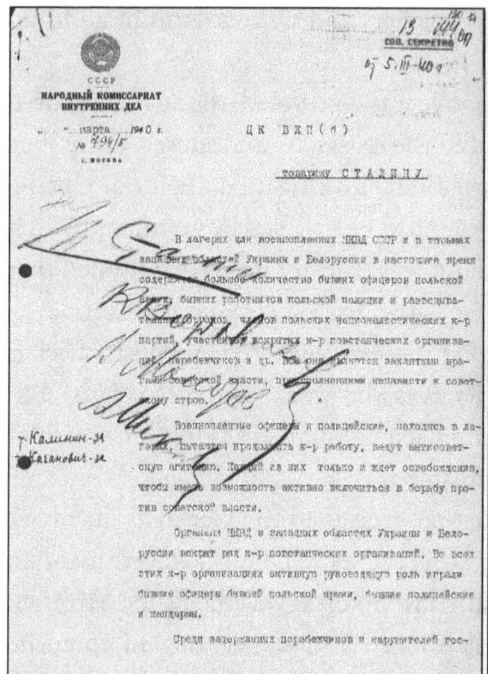

At left is an authentic copy of page one of the Soviet's execution order issued on March 5, 1940. It authorizes a massacre of some 4,000 Polish officers and other intellectuals. It is signed by Joseph Stalin, Vyacheslav Molotov, Kliment Voroshilov, and Anastas Mikoyan. It was published on April 28, 2010 to show Russia's *absolute openness* in telling the whole world what really happened. Evidently Russia felt it was politically useful after sixty-five years.

Ergo, it may be seen that the Nazis were not alone in their ability to commit such consummate and unthinkable atrocities; and that history would record objective analysts as attributing to Russian authorities the unconscionable slaughter of those thousands of Polish officers, soldiers, and civilian citizens some three years earlier.

Nevertheless, and with what many of sensitive conscience would contemptuously call a hypocritical looking away, there was to be no incrimination of their Soviet partner by the Allied forces. Indeed, one British official is quoted as having said, "There's nothing to be done." And no less a personage than Sir Winston Churchill is reported to have remarked unfeelingly, "There's no use prowling morbidly round the three year-old graves of Smolensk."

And thereby yet again is the ancient observation by Aeschylus reaffirmed: "In war, truth is the first casualty."

So, while the guilt for the massacre of the Polish citizenry remained officially unassigned, that is until Russia's involuntary and compassionless confession in 1990, there were other similar atrocities for which the responsibility was in no way a mystery. And Victor could remember such with painfully undiminished clarity.

He could recall, for example, that in the local dialect of Italy they were called *foibe*, the word being an Italian corruption of the Latin *fovea*, meaning a pit or chasm. The particular foibe at issue were rugged, yawning crevasses in the Carso Mountain range of the Eastern Italian Alps. But *foibe* was to become a dark word, a sinister word. It would become a word which, to those living at the time, would pulsate with terror. Later the word would come to signify the countless thousands of Italians who, after being forcibly wrested from their homes by Yugoslavian Communists, were thereafter bound into helplessness, brutally tortured and—were they to be so fortunate—shot before being dumped into any one of such rocky chasms. As inhumane as it sounds and was, as often as not such victims were still alive when dropped to the bottom of such a cavern. And there, wounded broken and bleeding, they died an agonizing death by starvation.

There are as usual, variances as to the number of such victims. But if an historian from the University of Trieste is to be believed, and there is little if any reason to doubt, the most conservative number of such victims is said to be rounded off at 3,500. According to the surviving citizenry, however, and according to the more than 350,000 expatriated refugees and their descendants, the murdered victims are claimed to be over 15,000.

It was then with uncomfortable ease that Victor could remember such horrors; such unspeakable mistreatment of his fellow countrymen during the years of 1943 through 1946, and some as late as 1949. He remembered also that as the war staggered on into its closing months, Yugoslavs had entered Trieste and the Istrian peninsula, an area that Italy had previously annexed following World War I, and which had thereafter been harshly Italianized under Mussolini's fascist rule.

Resultingly, thousands of ordinary citizens were tortured and killed for being hostile to an attempted annexation by Yugoslavia, or simply because they were Italian. Hundreds had been killed after the fall of fascism in 1943, and an additional tsunami of murdering came with the war's end, and continued some years afterward. Untold tens of thousands had also died after being deported to Slovenian detention camps. Perhaps due to a feeling of national shame and over a period of many decades, Italian Communists had tried to cover over the matter. And, as it would later prove so with the Nazi war criminals, there were some few minor personages who were tried and convicted after the war. But that was to be little if any consolation for those whose family members or friends had become victims of the foibe.

Added to that, Victor realized, was the fact that the pro-western parties that governed Italy, NATO's member nation during the Cold War, were at least reluctant if not totally disinterested in aggravating a Yugoslavia that was independent of the Soviet Union. Consequently, and despite all their justifiable and undeniable right to notoriety, for those same many decades the foibe killings continued to be overshadowed by the Nazi Holocaust. Few indeed are the histories that mention the foibe massacres.

But the Cold War ended and Yugoslavia disintegrated. And back around 1998, Victor had seen the debate intensify over the Italian Fascist collaboration with the Nazis, and the attacks by Italian resistance fighters that had resulted in Nazi retaliation. Thus, while it may have appeared good for some to shed light on this unconscionably brutal part of history, Victor knew in his heart that these old European animosities, these *vendette*, would never be settled.

Doubtlessly then, Carlo Perantoni had also been correct when he viewed Hitler and Stalin as two dogs arguing over a bone, the "bone" itself being Poland.

It is now approaching mid-summer in 1943. Victor's friend, André Frodel, now one of some 41,000 combatants and some 74,000 civilians comprising "Anders' Army," is joined with the Allied forces in Egypt. This Polish contingent sent by Russia's army, due to its current geographic location, has now come under British command. And as the Polish 2nd Corps, it is now part of what have been designated as the Polish Armed Forces of the West. And war's peculiar fortunes are about to manifest themselves.

Also a member of this unit is Franki Mrowicki. He has been such since its formation some 18 months earlier, and at which time he was also separated from his friend, André Frodel. For when André had been sent off to a gulag labor camp in Siberia, all communication between them was terminated. Franki, therefore, plagued now with the depressing possibility that André may even be dead, is without any idea as to what might have happened to his companion.

André, meanwhile, due to his broad linguistic skills, has been assigned to serve as an interrogator of war prisoners for the Allied armies in North Africa, most of such prisoners being Germans and Italians. As a serendipitous outworking of this assignment, a day was to come when André would be virtually electrified, a day when he was to be more than delighted—a day when he was to be as good as beside himself.

As with most any other day, André Frodel is busy. Apart from any precise details, and unaware of the High Command's plan for an amphibious landing at Anzio in January of the coming year, he and his fellow interrogators have been impressed with the need to acquire accurate information as to the disposition of German and Italian forces on the Italian mainland. Particularly was this so regarding positions held by them to the south of Rome.

There had, therefore, been a number of interviewees that day, many of whom had proven to be informationally fruitless, and no small number of whom had been equally and frustratingly stubborn. Such was the Italian colonel who now sat facing André, where he had been for the last 40 or so minutes. Compounding André's exasperation were the intermittent and all-too-frequent interruptions of his interviews; people coming and going, people asking questions. At the moment, and following one such interruption, he has resumed to addressing the colonel.

"Now then, sir, may we get back to the matter of ..."

Irritatingly, the office door opened once again.

A voice. "I was told to bring this prisoner ..."

Interrupting but never looking up, André barked, "Will you please get out of here and shut the door!" Then whirling on his chair he snapped, "I am seriously trying to …" The sentence was not to be finished.

Standing in the open doorway, prisoner in hand, was Franki Mrowicki!

"Franki?" André exclaimed. "I … Guard!" he shouted. And as an MP erupted through another door, braced for whatever anticipated emergency was suddenly at hand, André urged, "Take the aah … take the colonel and this … and this other prisoner away. I'll deal with them later."

As the two Italians were then hurriedly and summarily escorted from the room, Franki, as dumfounded as was André, stood speechless, wide eyed and slack jawed.

Then André virtually bolted across the intervening space. Grasping Franki by the shoulders he exclaimed, "Where in th … Lord, it's good to see you, Franki! Where *have* you been?"

Grinning, Franki said, "Well, there's a lot to tell, my friend, about the last year and more. But I've been with Anders' outfit since its formation. And since our arrival here in Africa I've been a guard at the Italian POW compound."

"This is unbelievable!" André cried. "Unbelievable but *wonderful!*" Then collapsing into a chair he said, "Sit down, sit down; take that chair there." And grinning with uncontrolled joy he said, "I feel like a … like a father who's just … just discovered a lost son!" And tears of emotion glistened in the eyes of both men.

For it was truly a grand reunion for these two. And that night they slept little as they exchanged experiences. Thus, after so long a time, after having been separated for seemingly endless months, these two philatelists—this pair of stamp-collecting friends from Lwów—were finally reunited. But more than that: André would now arrange for them to share the same living quarters.

Things are moving rapidly in the Mediterranean. It is mid-July; and even now the island of Sicily has already been invaded. In Italy, the city of Rome has been bombed and millions of leaflets have been dropped, warning Italy of its pending defeat, barring its immediate surrender. An invasion of the mainland is afoot.

His language skills having expanded his responsibilities beyond mere prisoner interrogations, André is now also involved in the coordinating of operations and logistics, this as an interpreter for the various multinational Allied forces now being assembled in North Africa. When he learns through channels that the bulk of the Allied forces there are now poised to invade the continent, to invade Italy, his excitement can hardly be contained.

It is late afternoon. The mess hall at the base is nearly empty. Sitting apart from the few scattered others who remained, André looked intently at his friend across the table. This was his first opportunity to share the news.

After looking about cautiously and then leaning forward as though conspiring, André said, "Franki," his voice intensely hushed and his eyes aglow with excitement, "We're going to invade Italy!"

"We're going to … are you sure?"

"Yes, I'm sure, and keep your voice down."

"Then all of this …"

"Yes! All of this *preparation*, as you were about to say, is to that end."

"But when?" It was a delirious response. "Does it mean that we're …"

"I don't have the date, Franki, but yes! Yes, it means that we are going to Italy. Finally we're heading back to the European mainland, our road back to Poland! Just imagine, Franki; we may very soon be able to see the Perantonis again: Carlo and Luigi, and the family!"

Franki was almost trembling. "Do you suppose they're still in Volargne?" His eyes were bright, sparkling with the hope he was feeling.

"I don't know, Franki, but wherever they are, we'll find them. And the girls … wherever they are—hopefully back home in Poland—we'll find them too."

And they finished their meal in silence.

It was later now and with greater privacy that they walked alone through the camp. As they did, they reasoned on the logic of the pending operation.

It was André who said, "It makes perfect sense, Franki. It's logical that the border between Italy and Germany would not be quite so heavily defended. What a perfect place to mount an attack."

"Well, yes," Franki agreed. "But the terrain there; it's is so much more difficult."

"True," André said with a nod. "So I don't think this is all there will be to reaching Germany."

Franki turned to look at him quizzically. "Oh? What then?"

"I think—and this is only my opinion—I think that the really big push will come from the north; from across the English Channel. I think the Allies, while trying to keep the German's attention drawn to Italy, will very likely make a landing somewhere in France."

"Really?"

"Yes, really. I'm no military strategist, but I believe that's what will happen, and there would certainly be less ground to cover en route to Berlin. And I feel, therefore, that this invasion of Italy is only a feint."

"Well, whatever," said Franki, grinning. "At least it's a move in the right direction for us; it'll get us back to our friends; and back to the pastasciutta and the wine!"

"Oh, yes!" André smiled reflectively, his enthusiasm likewise warming as he repeated the words. "The pastasciutta and the wine. O how I remember that! So … now we wait, Franki." And his face widened in a grin that threatened to reach both ears.

Meanwhile in Italy, with Victor's military service drawing to a close, he is more than ever intent on returning to Lwów. Repeatedly he has requested a transfer, and repeatedly it has been denied. And though he chafes at the reasons given, he concedes to their logic.

Firstly there is the heightened state of the war, and that of itself may have been all that was necessary. But added to that was the incongruous convenience of his dual citizenship. He was, after all, Austrian by birth and later Polish; and in Poland, therefore, his birth papers would immediately mark him down as an enemy of the Axis coalition. Indeed, he could well find himself opposing the very army of which he is an unwilling member. His papers would also likely force him to join the Home Army; the Polish partisans in their ongoing underground resistance to the Nazis. Reflecting then on those overtly inconvenient probabilities, he is resolved to remain in Italy. And the months pass by.

He is now 31. And with his military service behind him, Victor is in love; he may always have been in love of a sort, but now, near Volargne, he has met the light of his life: Luigina Zaninelli. From her hometown of Caprino di Verona, she is a beautiful girl; the daughter of an anti-fascist cheese maker. And although Victor still carries with him the photo of himself with Lari and Stasi—the one he had used in trying to locate the girls when he was last in Lwów—he is now truly smitten. He is struck virtually senseless, as it were, with a romance that is every bit as intense and as enduring as that of his storied countrymen of Verona: Romeo and Juliet. And thus enchanted, and before the summer ends, he marries his captivating Ginetta, as he calls her. It is a union that will last throughout their lifetime.

But for now they involve themselves together in the family's enterprise. Carlo is now 62, and to an ever increasing degree he defers the responsibility of running the business to Victor. They are still exporting wine to the Italian Division in Lwów; and despite the war's escalating nature they find themselves able to expand Carlo's business to the city of Mantua, some 33 miles south of Volargne. With plans to operate a wine-bottling shop, and with memories and visions of the Winiarnia in mind, they decide to also open a café bar inside the bottling shop, naming it "Caffè al Ponte Rosso," due to its proximity to a medieval red-brick bridge, a bridge that is constantly guarded by

German army platoons on both sides. Sadly, due to the wartime economy, and due also to the predominant Wehrmacht clientele who

rarely paid their drinking tabs, the shop and bar are only marginally successful.

Thus, their new caffé bar proves to be but a pauper's dream. For these few years have become a period of international trial and chaos. Entire families are being ripped apart; whole populations are being shredded.

So much is changing, and with such stunning rapidity. Indeed it is wholly unexpected when, later in July, a major change occurs when Benito Mussolini, their own leader, is abruptly overthrown by his own Fascist Grand Council. Immediately subsequent to that, King Victor Emmanuel orders him to be arrested and imprisoned. Such volcanic political upheavals, along with recent military actions in the Mediterranean, are causes for the Perantoni's wine business to wane. It is, then, but a matter of time before their connections with the Italian army's Leopoli Division in Lwów also evaporate completely.

CHAPTER VII

"Many of us thought it was almost over," Victor was saying.

It is an early October afternoon, a Sunday, and the waters of Lake Weston behind the two Perantoni homes glitter like azure lamé under a warming sun. The family has returned home from what many would call "going to church." But for them it had been a study of the Bible, current events being discussed in the context of Bible prophecies. For Victor it had been particularly cogent.

"Certainly everyone had *hoped* it was almost over," he went on. "Lord knows there'd been far more than enough suffering. I remember it being early in the month—like it is now, only in September; and with Mussolini now in prison Italy had finally surrendered to the Allies."

From behind Victor, George remarked, "Well, at least it was over for Italy." He had overheard the conversation as he had come from the house, glasses of iced lemonade clinking together on the tray he carried.

At the sound of the voice, Victor looked back over his shoulder. He smiled and nodded. "Yes, one would have thought so."

"You mean that it wasn't?"

"Oh! Would that it had been!" Victor took a lemonade. "No, apparently Hitler still felt a need for a line of defense in the south; and of course he was right. So in the same month—and surprising everyone—Hitler's fellow stamp collector, Mussolini, was rescued by the Nazis. I remember also Hitler restoring IL Duce to power, making him the head of a new Nazi-Fascist outfit that was called *La Repubblica Sociale Italiana;* the RSI for short. But this time he, Mussolini, would be only a puppet of the Reich, nothing more, and it wasn't going to work."

"I remember that the Allies were in Southern Italy by then, weren't they," Gina remarked.

"Oh, indeed they were! And for that reason the Germans had sent some of the best of their Wehrmacht to Italy. But there was also another reason for them doing that, one not so obvious. Because of General Badoglio's surrender to the Allies, on September eighth of nineteen forty-three, Hitler no longer trusted the Italian people, you see. So, like we talked about this morning at the meeting, like with Daniel, the handwriting was on the wall."

"And …?" said Robert, echoed by Mary.

"Well, the very next month, on the thirteenth, and as though to confirm Hitler's distrust, Italy joined the Allies. And not only did Italy declare war on Germany; they also declared war with Japan."

"So now," and George laughed, "everybody controls Italy except the Italians."

"*Esattamente!*' Victor exclaimed, and he laughed sarcastically. "The North of Italy was cut off from the Italian peninsula, and the whole Valpolicella region now came to be dominated by the Nazis. Unfortunately, Mantua and Volargne were in the center of it all."

"But what about all the Italian troops stationed with the Nazis all over the Mediterranean and Europe?"asked Mary.

Victor replied with a long sad stare. "Italian soldiers, who were deployed to war zones, were betrayed by their own government. Except for those fortunate ones who found their way back home, back to Italy, the rest were left to be arrested, imprisoned, and even murdered by their former Wehrmacht partners."

"Whew,"said Robert. "Just imagine being in a combat zone, in a frontline position, and suddenly you find that your allied flank, even the man in the same foxhole with you, has suddenly become your enemy! Yikes! To me, it's beyond conception."

"But it happened,"said Victor with a sigh. Then, "Aah! But no more about the war now." Rising with an effort and stretching, he said, "Sometimes I tire of remembering it. What about lunch, Val?"

"I can do it right now. Sandwiches okay? Or that is to say: *panini imbottiti?*"

"Buono!" said Victor, smiling. "Grazie, mio amore!"

'I tire of remembering.'

How often the aging Victor had said that. Yet tired though he would be, the memories came flowing back, persistent and inescapable; vivid in both their joys and their sorrows. Sitting in his home later that same evening, his Bible open in his lap, he looked over at Gina, sleeping so quietly in a favorite recliner. He was nearly ninety now, and the last several months had found him reflecting on the thought that perhaps it might be nice to fall asleep quietly in this war-weary world, and then, after a dreamless, timeless sleep, to awaken to a new and different world; a world at peace, where there were never any bad memories. And then his reverie was interrupted as he recalled being reunited with André and Franki after those many years. It had been back in June of 1944.

It was then he had learned that André and Franki had been at Cassino; that they and their comrades of the 2nd Polish Corps had struggled bitterly to capture the gutted ruins of a mountaintop monastery. Just why, neither of them could recall. Looking back it all seemed so unadulteratedly purposeless.

The aging 1,400 year-old monastery, incorrectly appraised by Allied intelligence to be a strategic German outpost, had undergone repeated bombings in February 1944. The place had thus been reduced to a pile of unrecognizable rubble. Both men had remarked that such bombings, contrary to Allied expectations, had rendered the old abbey even more inaccessible. The huge piles of debris, which fell all around the mountaintop's crest, provided instant obstacles to penetration by the Allies. It also provided excellent cover from which the enemy held out, and delivered a withering fire for well over four months, until withdrawing in the middle of May. Franki had said they counted themselves fortunate to have survived; losses among their companions had been severe.

Sitting there in his chair, staring pensively into space, he remembered also how thrilling it had been to hear from his old friend "Padre" Kolbuch. It had been at the same time of year, and the man had been in Vatican City. Although circumstances in Italy have not improved, Padre had finally been able to communicate with him through a network of fellow clergymen. He recalled as well, that thereafter he and Gina had extended Padre an open invitation; an invitation for—as they had phrased it—"pastasciutta and red wine, at our new café and bottle shop here in Mantua." Before that would occur, however, early that month the Allied forces had entered Rome.

Today was June 12th, a pleasant Monday afternoon; and they had been here since last Sunday. The city of Rome basked today in the warm summer sunshine, and some elements of normalcy had returned after weeks of chaos, during which German forces had tried to prevent the city's fall to advancing Allies from the south.

"Where do you suppose we'll find him?"

André took his eyes from the street briefly. "I have no idea, Franki, but the Vatican seems like a good place to start."

He had used his position with Operations; and having negotiated a Jeep from the motor pool, he and Franki were finally capitalizing on an opportunity to look for their friend, Padre. As they wended their way through the streets, not altogether sure of just how to reach the Basilica, they were impressed with the lack of the war's devastation in the city. How unlike Cassino and Salerno it was. They had noted that even the bridges over the Tiber were still intact, as were the city's historic sites. In fact, it was only the rail yards that evidenced the effects of the bombings. And now his fluent command of Italian afforded André the opportunity to ask the necessary questions. That being done, they had finally queried their way to Vatican City.

And now they were walking; they had been for some time. As they threaded their way through the people, eyes scanning the crowd in search of a priest, they were in awe of the grandeur of the city's ancient architecture.

But then they saw him; he was across the street. And André looked at Franki with a nod and a shrug of his shoulders. "It's a start," he said with a smile, and he crossed over to approach the man.

"Scusa, Padre." His Italian was that of a native. "But my friend and I are looking for a Padre Michele. Do you know him perhaps; Padre Michele Kolbuch?"

The man's responsive expression was one of caution and distrust. His eyes narrowed as he said, "Perché?"

"He's a friend of ours,"André explained. "From years back," Franki added. "We knew him in Lwów, but we've not seen him since …"

"Ah ha!" And the man's face lit up. "Cosi siete voi quelli!" And then he spoke English and smiled. "So you're the ones!"

"Th … the ones?" stuttered Franki.

"Yes, yes! He speaks of both of you often. Which of you is André?"

"Aah … that would be me."

And now the man virtually effervesced. "Please, let me shake your hand, André!" And as his clasp tightened on both of André's hands, he studied them intensely. "So … these are the hands that crafted that remarkable Vatican Travel Pass."

And now he grinned even more broadly. "I've seen it, André. It is incredible!"

Even under his deep tan, the blush was evident as André replied, "Well, I thank you; I thank you very much. But I'm afraid our time is very limited. Do you happen to know where we might find Padre Michele at the moment?"

The man did. "Yes, I believe I know right where he may be. There is a little restaurant …"

It was indeed a small restaurant, a coffee house. As the three looked in through the quaint, latticed window, they could see Padre sitting alone. Their guide gestured toward the window.

"I'll leave you with your friend," he said. "I've no doubt that you have much to discuss. I would only be in the way. *Godete*!"

Inside now, and despite the war's austerity, the atmosphere reeked of cheeses and garlic, of freshly baked bread and the heady aroma of dark Italian coffee. Padre chanced to look up and saw them, across the room and coming toward him.

"Ei, Paesani!" he shouted, the words ringing out above the murmur of the general conversation, his countenance suddenly brightening as he virtually leaped from his chair. Disregarding custom and customers alike, standing now with his hand in the air, he called for the waiter. "Ei, Cameriere! Portaci vino qui! Per favore, tre bicchieri!"

Handshakes were virtually useless; grossly inadequate to the occasion; immeasurably insufficient expressions they were of the flood of emotions that now surged through the three of them. Endless months of wondering and fearing for each other were now over. And they fell to hugging each other with uncontrolled and unabashed enthusiasm. And there were tears.

Those at other tables could only look on with curiosity; watching two Polish soldiers of the Allied Forces, clad in dusty battle fatigues, as they embraced a frocked priest with such overt affection.

Seated finally, and with glasses of bold Chianti lubricating tongues; with virtually indelible smiles on their faces and with nearly infinite information to share, they rattled away at each other for over an hour, endeavoring to erase with words the years that had separated them. The separation itself—over 4 years now—was mentioned but briefly, and thereafter seemingly endless questions flowed one upon another: How were the orphans? How was the trip to Rome?

Where were Carlo and Luigi? where was Victor? Where were Lari, Stasi, and Dani? So much had happened; so much needed to be known!

"Well, I certainly don't have all the answers," said the priest, "nor do I have enough. But as far as I know, Carlo and Luigi—and their families—are still in Volargne, and I've had some communication with Victor. Actually, he's married now; I'm sure you didn't know about that, and living in Mantua. He and his new young wife are operating a bar and wine-bottling shop there."

"Really!" Franki remarked, grinning. "It's hard to imagine Victor being married. He's now reduced to only one woman; seems like he always had at least two."

Curbing his amusement, Padre said, "Yes, I seem to remember him that way too. By the way, they sent me an open invita … wait a minute!"

"What?" André was surprised at the breach in the conversation.

"They aah … they sent me an invitation to visit, but it makes no mention of how many may respond." An impish smirk now. "Why don't the three of …"

"YES!" Franki blurted. And people around them turned to look. "They have no idea that we're here, do they. Let's surprise them!"

His head nodding vigorously, André said, "Great idea, and I agree! But we're going to have to wait. The Nazis still hold a line at the Po River. It's their last line of defense in Italy, and the Alpine foothills beyond the plain constitute their escape route into Germany. They'll not yield that easily."

His face darkened now as he added: "And I can but wonder what the situation is like there—the Germans still in control."

The month had turned. In Poland, the Russians had begun a July offensive that would gradually push the Germans out of Lwów. The Russians would then overrun the city, and the entire region would again come under Soviet authority. But even with the routing of the Nazis, there would be no sense of liberation.

Because, like once before, Lwówians and their partisans had regained their previous foe, the Red Army.

In Northern Italy, in the district of Victor's and Carlo's little town of Volargne di Dolcé, where German troops had once been viewed as polite guests and where they had so conducted themselves, they now grew surly. Angered perhaps at realizing their cause to now having been purposeless, they became brutal. They became as a pack of paranoid animals; looting and drunkenness was the order of the day.

Much aware of the Allied advances in the south and central parts of the country, the German morale, and that of the RSI of Northern Italy, had sunken to unimagined levels. Virtually to a man they were hopelessly disheartened. Miserable and fearful, despair could be seen in every countenance.

For it was patently clear by late 1944, that Germany was losing the war on all fronts. As for Hitler's hope of the possibility of a "final victory"—as for his dream of a 1000-Year Reich—they had devolved to nothing more than empty promises. Fear of the Allies and anger towards the Italians was now evident in all their faces. As the Allies continued their northward advance, the Nazis gradually retreated toward the road leading to the Alpine Brenner Pass, historically the proverbial Gateway into Germany.

For well over 3,000 years it had been an avenue of passage used by those whom ancient Rome had considered to be barbarians. And now facing certain defeat, the hordes of retreating Nazi barbarians are forming a bottleneck there in the Western Valpolicella region, adjacent to Lake Garda.

On the lake's opposite bank and in the town of Salò, lie the headquarters of the RSI, the Nazi-Fascist government of Italy's ousted IL Duce, Benito Mussolini. It is then in the midst of all this, that Victor, Carlo and Luigi find themselves, along with their families. They are isolated from the Italian peninsula; they are isolated from Lwów in Poland; and they are as if trapped in the snarl of a military bottleneck— in the retreat of a drunken and emotionally drained Nazi army. But it is also an army driven by desperation. And as they yield ground, they leave their mark.

"Just look, Carlo, at what they're doing to our country!"

Carlo nodded. He and his friend, Count Valentini, are standing on the porch of Valentini's spacious villa in Volargne.

"They are pleased to call them *engineers*," Valentini fumed sarcastically. "The *Einsatzgruppe Italien*. And their German officers have chosen to set up their headquarters on my property! Why, the poor devils are nothing but slaves, and they're *our people*, Carlo; the people of Volargne!"

Carlo nodded his agreement. "Yes, I know, Signore Valentini, and I share your anger. Indeed, I've personally spoken with some of them.

But they say the Germans are doing this everywhere: in France against the recent Allied invasion, and even in Germany against the advancing Russians. The war has brought their manpower down to its very dregs. Some time ago, Fritz Todt, the Reich's chief engineer, died in a plane crash, and his organization needed a new boss. So along comes this … this *Dutchman* architect, a personal friend of Hitler, whose name is … Aaah … Speer; that's his name, Albert Speer. So he's the new man in charge, and he's authorized this einsatzgruppe to organize any number of civilians into forced labor, this in order to construct barriers at every entrance to Germany. So now our friends—*i nostri Volargnesi*—are being forced to destroy their own countryside, building defensive positions and military obstacles."

The Count cocked his head quizzically and looked at Carlo in a wise way. "The Germans don't really believe that this is going to stop the Allies, do they?"

Carlo thought for a moment and then said, "Madmen think differently than we do, Signore Valentini. But then again, maybe it's what they're drinking."

"Oh? And that would be …?"

"Wine that I supply. Victor and I have been ordered to supply wine to the German quartermaster. So, we don't like it but we're supplying the wine. It's not that they get the good wine, you understand; it's been cheap local stuff, and it's often delivered in bottles that are chipped and scarred. When they complain, I say to them: What can I do? It's the bad roads, the craters. Up until now, they're contented."

The Count smiled and threw an arm over Carlo's shoulder. With a wink he said, "Well, my friend, you keep up the good work—or the bad work. Meanwhile I salute you; all Italy would salute you."

"Papá, we have a problem." Victor's face wears a worried frown.

Carlo looked up from his work in the bottle shop. "Oh? And what is that?

"Yesterday, Signore Dieter, the quartermaster, threatened me." "Really! He threatened you? Why?"

"He told me that unless we began delivering good wine in good bottles, that there would be—as he put it—reprimands. Now I don't know exactly what he means by that, but you know the Germans."

Carlo nodded. "Umm, yes I do; I know the Germans. Well, we've obviously got to do what he says, but is there some way we can use this to our advantage?"

In Orlando, Victor had been relating the experience over dinner. "And that was the problem that we suddenly faced." And now Gina had tactfully interrupted. "Pass the lasagna, please."

As the aroma-laden dish traveled up the Perantoni's table, Victor's riveting tale paused briefly. Then came Robert's question.

"So how did you and grandpa deal with the German's order?"

Allowing himself a conspiratorial grin, and using that familiar Italian gesture, Victor said, "By now, of course, we'd been delivering the wine for some time, but since they were now getting testy we decided on something different. I'll tell you what we did." And he paused meaningfully.

Mary's mock impatience prompted a chuckle from everyone when she said, "So get on with it, Dad! What did you do?"

Victor took a leisurely sip of his wine. "It was a curious thing," he said. "We got to thinking about the fact that German soldiers were less brutal when they were drunk from our Italian wine, than when they were drunk on their Nazi ideology. So we decided to give them wine that was *WINE*!" An almost demonic smile as he added, "We decided to give them freshly fermented wine, wine laced with uncooked mosto from recently stomped grapes, and deceitfully covered over with extra-strong *g-r-r-r-r-rappa*!"

George said, "Explain that to everybody, Dad. Tell them what grappa is."

Victor grinned like a mischievous elf. "Literally, grappa means 'grape stalk.' It was a brandy we used to make by distilling the residue—the grape skins along with the stems and seeds—that was left over after the pressing. Originally we made it to cut down on waste, using the leftovers at the end of the season.

"But now this was potent stuff. Like I said, it's distilled—it's about a hundred and twenty proof; that's sixty percent pure alcohol. So now your grandfather and I begin delivering some very fine wine, as requested, and it's all hopped up with our grappa. Well! These German soldiers have been used to the usual wine, alcohol about twelve percent. And they had probably never tasted anything as good as our mixed grappa wine; at least not since they left home. To them, this was like their schnapps back in Germany—like a grape schnapps."

"Mmmm, sounds good," remarked Mary. "I think I'd like that."

"It does sound good; I agree," said Victor, "But let me give you a little chemistry lesson. Uncooked *mosto* is the first strain from pressed or stomped grapes. Very rich in bacteria it is, especially if they were stomped by children with dirty feet! That's why a person should always cook the mosto if they're not going to ferment it into wine. And, of course, it blended perfectly with the wine and the grappa."

"Tell everybody what this mixture does, Dad." George was snickering now; he knew what was coming and he could hardly wait.

"Ah, yes. Well, used moderately—and what did the Nazis know about moderate—this uncooked under-fermented wine-grappa mixture is what we might call *a digestive drink*. What I mean is, Ex-Lax should be so good."

"I've changed my mind," said Mary. And everyone at the table began sniggering.

"Talk about healthy bowels!" Victor went on. "Realizing that the average German soldier had virtually no concept of enough, not when it came to wine. The Whermachjt's Wehrmacht's super troopers were suddenly *souper poopers*. And that's spelled s-o-u-p-e-r. Oh, and you'll love this!" He was himself laughing now. "Now guess what they thought was the problem. They blamed the problem on some change in the local water! Aah ha ha ha! And that, of course, just increased their use of the wine! Aah ha ha ha haaaa! "

And now the entire table was in hysterics. Victor, still grinning with childlike satisfaction, went on to explain that the Italian partisans then stepped up their harassment, taking advantage of the drunken disorder, the logistical mayhem and the ongoing confusion that he and Carlo had caused.

And on that note, with stomachs satiated, with laughter still in the air, and with Valerie, Mary and Gina beginning to clear the table, dinner came to an end.

For all of its humor, however, both at the Perantoni's table and at the time of its occurrence, such a situation as had been generated by Carlo and Victor was but an all-too-brief emotional reprieve from the grisly reality of war.

For those who have never tasted its bitter dregs, the pageantry of flags and of uniforms, the stirring, brassy music of bands and the glitter of medals, exercises a mesmerizing power. *Tunes of Glory*, a writer had once said of it. Perhaps *Tunes of Gory* may have been a more appropriate phrase.

For there is the probability, it would appear, that there exists a level of inhumanity so abysmally debased, so purely demonic, as to cause an otherwise sane person to shelter himself in sheer, self-imposed madness. Indeed, for those who have never experienced it—even as fortune has granted to most pesons—the bloodshed, the dismemberment, the chaos and the irreplaceable loss of precious friends cannot be altogether fathomed.

But Victor had seen it; he had looked into the grim visage of war. And later that evening, as he lay in the quiet of his own bedroom, he reflected on the emotions that can be generated by that which is called patriotism. In his mind, it was as a cancer, a cancer that destroys humanism. And he viewed it as one of the most insidiously demoralizing things ever to beset the human family. As he thought on it, he recalled the words of Bertrand Russell; Russell who had once said, "Patriotism is the willingness to kill and be killed for trivial reasons." And he felt that pretty much summed it up.

Lying there in the comfort of his bed, he allowed his mind to dwell on those words, and on those poor young Germans whom he had known; young men who had served in Hitler's armies; men on whose belt buckles had been the words "Gott Mit Uns." That is, "God With Us." Had they been patriotic? Indeed they had. And for what had patriotism inspired them to fight? For the Fatherland, they had been told. Not for fathers or for fatherhood, but for the Father*land*—for the *land*; nor did they think they were fighting for a trivial thing.

He thought too of this country's Revolutionary War, a war fought over the issue of freedom from British sovereignty and from what had been considered as unjust taxation. He reflected on the tens of thousands of young men who had died in that war, and did anyone remember them. And what really was different now? Nothing, he concluded. Nothing at all. In England, as well as here, people still got up in the morning; they went to work; they earned money; they built houses; they raised families—unjust taxation is still with us, and with them— and they die. Nothing had changed.

Indeed, he thought, both countries are still linked politically. True that they are individual nations, but they are still linked—inseparably it would appear —in international interests, in trade and in mutual defense. They had even fought together, side-by-side in both world wars, as if they had been brothers. So the only thing that patriotism really produced back in seventeen seventy-six, or thereabouts, was a lot of dead people. And neither nation is really free.

This country's own Civil War then rushed unavoidably to his mind. And again the issue had been freedom—freedom for power-hungry people to do what they wanted; to have what they wanted; and this at the cost of other people's freedoms. Yet it had been no trivial thing in their minds. And for what had they fought? Some had fought for *The South*, whatever that had been; and those on the other side had fought for *The Union*, another insentient abstraction. And all of this killing had been prompted by the spirit of patriotism.

But then a conflicting thought as he turned onto his other side. Was there no place in one's life for loyalty? And then it struck him: loyalty has a much different connotation than patriotism. True that they are similar, and there are some shared nuances; yet there is a kind of nobility attached to loyalty. And he thought of the loyalty he felt toward Gina, lying there beside him. Never would he violate that relationship. But he felt no patriotism toward her. And there was the loyalty he felt for la familia. And it occurred to him that loyalty is the child of reason; of deliberate, rational thought. Whereas patriotism is often nothing more than misdirected enthusiasm.

And then came the realization that patriotic fervor can obliterate moral distinctions altogether. And if moral distinctions are erased, that which is actually trivial may be made to appear as inordinately important. Yes, he thought, moral distinction was the issue, and patriotism seems to involve little morality. Assuredly there had been nothing moral about the indiscriminate butchery that had gone on in the wars he had just recalled. But he had to admit: there had been a great deal of patriotism.

Sleep had nearly overtaken consciousness now, and a drowsy mind wandered back to a time in 1942. He had been standing in a military formation, and had chosen to express his opinion out loud; that it made little sense to him that he had been drafted to shoot at men who had been drafted to shoot back at him. It proved to be neither the brightest nor the most opportune thing he had ever done. And not surprisingly his commanding officer had reprimanded him on the spot.

And now it was November. It was growing cold; temperatures were dropping into the low thirties and it rained much of the time. While Carlo spent the larger part of each day in their Mantua bottling shop, formulating their wine-grappa combination—their "caca cocktail"— Victor and Luigi kept themselves busy delivering the spiked wine to the still unsuspecting Wehrmacht.

As for the Germans, they had now concentrated the major part of their remaining forces in the vicinity of Volargne, La Chiusa di Ceraino, and Dolcé. Thus, the last of the German lines of defense in Italy had withdrawn to the Alpine foothills of the Adige River valley. They are, therefore, close to their escape route via the Brenner Pass, where temperatures are now reaching sub- zero levels.

Plaguing the Germans still further, beyond the inexplicably communal diarrhea, other local citizens are courageously carrying out additional acts of sabotage. And these are increasing significantly. Nevertheless, and although retreating in defeat, in the Nazi mind there remains to be completed the executing of their Füeher's murderous orders. Like an insane clockwork, therefore, the deportation of Jews and other political prisoners is accelerated; it is still a priority. No opportunity is to be missed of capturing Hitler's victims before the Wehrmacht are forced from Italy altogether.

Hence the trains, the seemingly numberless trains transporting Jewish prisoners, are given precedence. Because deportations of Italian Jews were not conducted during Mussolini's regime, and now that IL Duce has been reduced to nothing more than Hitler's marionette, the Nazis are accelerating the deportations; they are endeavoring to make up for lost time.

Arrests are intensified, and from all regions of Northern Italy's RSI, the dispatching of deportation trains filled with prisoners is expedited. Clattering out of Volargne, their very sound as if a death rattle, the trains are headed north, through the Brenner Pass and into Germany.

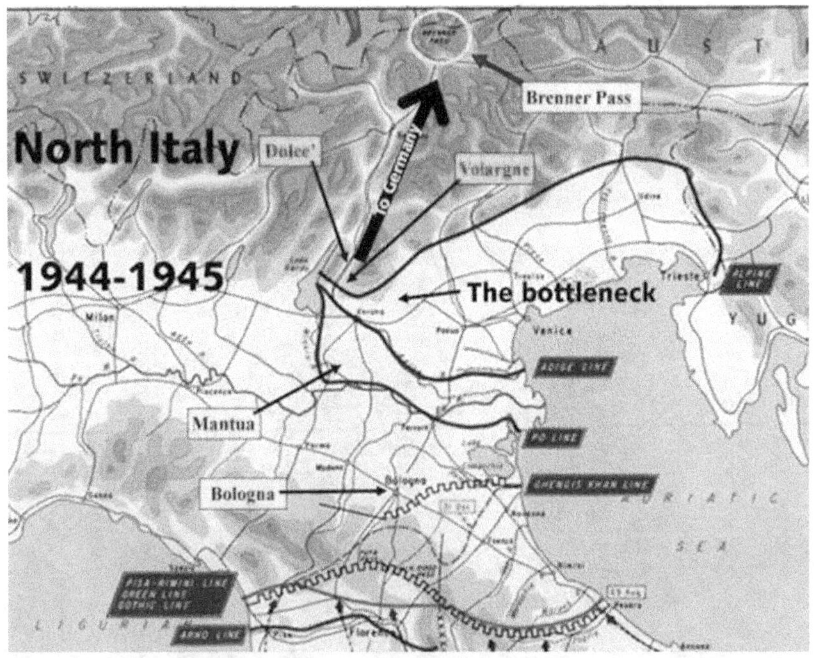

However, this unreasoning insanity of Hitler's is causing a near impossible snarl of traffic, aggravating the problem caused by an already excessive volume of German military rail movements. And all of this was converging at Volargne's railhead. The result is delay upon delay, officially inexcusable delays; long periods of time wherein local train station workers search for and find opportunities to assist numbers of prisoners to escape.

More to be concerned with, however, is the inexorable advance of Allied forces from the south. For while the Brenner Pass is a route of escape for the Germans, it is simultaneously an open doorway to Germany for their enemies.

With that unacceptable reality thus in mind, the unthinkable was conceived by the German High Command.

Perhaps it was Hitler's architect, Albert Speer, or Herr Todt's engineers who suggested that they implode the beautiful La Chiusa foothills. Those great masses of rock, hovering high above the Adige River, would cascade down to block that river, flooding the valley and closing, perhaps forever, that ancient gateway into Germany. It would be the culminating defense of the German retreat: a cataclysmic, flamboyant—yes, a pyrrhic exit—worthy of being extolled in symphony by Richard Wagner himself. But it would require an explosion of Vesuvian proportions; something that would virtually parallel the extinction of Herculaneum and Pompeii.

It would then be mid-November when the infamous train of 15 cars would roll into Volargne.

CHAPTER VIII

In Orlando, Florida, Victor is home alone on this decidedly chilly October afternoon, and he could recall the day as easily as he could remember breakfast that morning. Outside, an autumn rain was hurling itself against the windows as he watched *National Geographic's* televised recounting of Hiroshima's destruction.

"Yes," he said quietly, remembering Volargne. "It was very much like that." And the memory came flooding back with all of its mind-searing reality.

He remembered that the train, from the very time of its arrival, had been shrouded in mystery. Because this was not a train for prisoner deportation as was so often the case. What was not known, save by only a few, was that the 15 rail cars were the property of the German Army's Ordnance Division.

For several days the train had sat there, little more than 100 yards from the town of Volargne, Victor's town. Guarded closely day and night by German soldiers, it was parked on a siding only a few miles south of the bend in the river, a bend that was called *La Chiusa*.

Literally the name meant "The Lock," or "River-Closing." And doubtless it was the very secrecy surrounding the train that imbued it with such an ominously sinister and somber quality.

To the townspeople of Volargne it represented something darkly menacing, something evil. Indeed, had they but known its contents, they would not have slept easily.

For these railway cars comprised part of a munitions train. Packed to their capacity with multiple tons of TNT, they were to be detonated inside the railway tunnel located on the southeast side of the river, in the La Chiusa foothills. It goes without saying that the secret was tightly guarded.

However, as though in compliance with Aeschylus' axiom, that truth is war's first casualty, there was a young man from Switzerland employed as an interpreter with the Todt organization of engineers. And this young fellow was altogether aware of the train's contents. But more than that. Being of Swiss nationality and therefore a neutral—in his self-perceived allegiance at any rate— he was agreeable to selling that information. And this he did. To the Allied forces.

Victor remembers now that it had been a bright Tuesday afternoon, November 21, 1944. He had been in the process of making routine deliveries of the Perantoni's *Liquor de Latrine*—the spiked grappa-wine—to the mess tents and canteens of the German quartermaster. He had parked his delivery van near that bend in the river, and had continued his delivery rounds by pedal cart— civilian motor vehicles not being allowed inside German compounds. After delivering the wine in Volargne, he had restocked his cart from the van and had begun pedaling towards the mess tents near Dolcé.

Faintly at first; and then as with a crescendo in music, growing in volume as he made his way past the marble foothills of Ceraino, he heard the sound of warplanes. And then suddenly, as if rising from the very earth behind the massive foothills and flying very low, they came roaring directly over his head. Then just as suddenly they disappeared over the next foothill.

He could not see what happened next. For with their target then in sight, the aircraft had opened fire.

The town would literally stagger under the blow.

In Orlando, Victor now sat staring into space, the television scenes of Hiroshima forgotten. In their stead he saw himself, looking off in the direction of the planes' flight. Then abruptly, in his mind's eye, the sky over Volargne turned red, and then it was white and then black; it all occurring as though in an instant.

Back then, as he had stood watching on that infamous day, there had come the sound. It was a sound he would never forget—could never forget; a deep, thudding sound, followed by the reverberations of an inconceivably thunderous explosion. It was as if the very air had been blasted apart. He had felt a piercing pain in his ears; had felt the ground shudder uncontrollably. And it was as though the world had suddenly ended. Before his very eyes he saw every bottle of wine in the pedal cart shatter. Less than one second later, the events being virtually simultaneous, he had been thrown to the ground. And there he had felt his entire body, as though by some unearthly demonic force, being compressed. Immediately thereafter the pressure dissipated, and it became as if there was no air at all; no air to breathe, while his hair and his clothing were pulled in the direction of the explosion.

He had watched with wonder then as the wine, pouring from the cart and as though in slow motion, became airborne, flying horizontal to the ground, southward towards Volargne. Even as he had watched then, the air came rushing back. Suddenly he could breathe again. And as his breath returned, so did his hearing, allowing him an awareness of the re-echoing reverberations; of the spasms of the cosmically devastating convulsion of the very elements themselves. Caroming from foothill to foothill, the shuddering pulsations had been as a circle, threatening to return and finish him off—to destroy him!

Doubtless, the Allied aircraft had executed their mission with near perfection, the only flaw being to their own injury. The strike on the munitions train had resulted in a cataclysm of truly volcanic dimensions. Of such awesomely immeasurable power had been the detonation, that a generated vacuum had literally sucked one of the planes into its lethal vortex, hurling it to the ground. A second aircraft, though surviving, had carried away in its fuselage a wheel from the demolished train. And yet another had found itself riddled with fragments of the train, as though with shrapnel. Not even imagining what enormous havoc they would wreak, they had flown too low.

As for those buildings adjacent to the railway and facing the tracks, the initial impact of the blast had resulted in their being literally pulverized. The remaining buildings in the town had been seen to either crumble or to be knocked down by the explosion's colossal force, or to implode, due to the rapid and radical change of the barometric pressure. Others, when suddenly surrounded by a vacuum had exploded from the inside. Likewise, and for the same reasons, the dead and wounded of the populace had been afflicted by similar internal injuries; the eruptions of arterial and venous blood vessels.

Throughout the entirety of the river valley, throughout the entire Valpolicella and Lake Garda region, it had been as an apocalyptic trumpet blast, a gazette as it were, that the very Devil himself had taken Volargne as his own. By reasonable estimate, 96 percent of Volargne's buildings had been destroyed absolutely. In retrospect, the damage was at least equal to that sustained by the town of Cassino. There, however, over four months of battle, bombings and shellings had produced the wreckage. But here, in Volargne, it had occurred in an instant of time. The town was no more.

Some few moments had been required before Victor was able to regain even a semblance of composure. With his mind a-whirl, filled with near panic and dread, he had remounted his pedal cart. Ignoring the wine that still streamed out of the carrier, squinting against a "snowfall" of white dust that made it difficult for him to keep his eyes open, he had traveled hurriedly back towards what had once been Volargne.

Down along the river bend he went, there to stop and gaze down the hill. But he had seen no town. He had seen only a cloud of dust where once the town had been. At first he had imagined himself to be still disorientated, or perhaps he had traveled in the wrong direction.

But discerning that the river was to his right, and that it was flowing southward, that wishful thinking had been short lived.

The rain outside his window in Orlando had stopped now; and as water continued to drip from the eves, he remembered how he had watched the dust cloud slowly beginning to settle, how he had begun to see the jagged, surrealistic heaps and piles of unrecognizable rubble; the gaunt, disjointed skeletal remnants of walls still standing. And across what had been the city, fires burned out of control, dense columns of acrid smoke ascending.

Down the hill then to the town he had gone—down to where the road had ended, to where the rubble had begun. Then leaving his cart he had started walking. As he did, he had recalled his visit to Lwów after returning from Switzerland; had remembered the chaos that had confronted him there. But there was no comparison to be made. For here the devastation was greater by magnitudes; here the destruction was absolute.

> "A sunny afternoon became night in one instant, and an apocalyptic end-of-the-world came into view after the dust settled and daylight came again, and survivors covered in dust and blood emerged from the rubble, like ghosts."
>
> *Quote by survivor Luigi Ferrari, Cavaliere di Vittorio Veneto. From 1985 interview on 41st anniversary of Volargne's destruction.*

It had seemed impossible. Less than an hour before, on that sunny, bucolic afternoon, he had been loading and unloading wine in that charmingly beautiful town. Then as by the war's witchery, he had found himself standing in the midst of a scene of apocalyptic proportions. And then the survivors, many of them wounded and bleeding—like apparitions in their coverings of dust, they had begun to emerge from among the shambles.

And he remembered now that he had been as a madman.

For the conscience-shattering scene that had lain before him was sufficient to prompt the very essence of unmitigated despair. It had been as though grief and anguish themselves had been distilled—as was his grappa—and then poured with malevolent intent over the little town; that the place should become irrecoverably intoxicated with misery. Feeling thus, he had been able to do no more than stand amidst the ruins and hurl his limitless hatred at the sky.

With loud screams and cries he had released the consuming anger that had been fermenting within him since the day when the Nazis had invaded his homeland of Poland. With vitriolic rage unadulterated, and with confused political loyalties, he had given voice to obscene curses against his former hero, IL Duce Benito Mussolini, cursing him for having betrayed Italy. At the same time and at the top of his voice—with near-endless tears making flesh-colored tracks through the town's dust that covered his face in mime-like fashion—he had cursed Adolf Hitler for having taken away IL Duce from the Italian people.

As he had stood there ranting away, appearing as a man bereft of all sanity, a platoon of German soldiers had arrived. They had stopped to observe his mad soliloquy, and had remained silent. For they too had been horrified, staggered by the enormity of what had happened to Volargne. While they had stood watching him, he had turned and began throwing pieces of dusty rubble at them, screaming aloud obscene curses against Germany and against the German people; against National Socialism; against Adolf Hitler and his idiot puppet, Benito Mussolini.

But the soldiers had chosen to ignore him; and walking away in bewilderment they had left him sobbing out his vulgar accusations of treason against Mussolini and Fascism. Abandoned to his pitiable psychopathy, he had fallen to his knees in an agony of inconsolable grief. And there, watched by curious survivors, he had ripped from the lapel of his coat the PNF party badge that IL Duce had given him at the Winiarnia fifteen years earlier. Then using a piece of brick from his shattered town, he had beaten and flattened the badge beyond recognition; and with a ferociously angry shout, vilifying IL Duce's name, he threw it far into the Adige river.

Although past his believing at that moment, the truth was that consolation would come, that others would come; that Carlo and Luigi and Gina would come from Mantua to join him. And here they would stay, throughout the night and the following day. There would be recovery of a sort. Italian soldiers and others would begin searching for victims in the rubble; perhaps even some Germans would help. An Italian Army hospital tent would be hastily set up near the riverbank, beyond the parameters of the obliterated town. And there the wounded would be helped to heal.

He remembers Wednesday passing, the 22nd. And that evening he returned with the family to Mantua, there to enjoy some much needed food and rest. But dinner had been an unhappy affair, very somber and quiet. There had been little conversation. Thereafter, Carlo had poured large brass mugs of Lacryma Christi for everyone, along with smaller glasses of aged red Vermouth.

Luigi had thanked his father and immediately fell to drinking. "Tonight is the right night to get drunk," he had said angrily.

But Victor remembers being at disagreement with his brother. "No," he had countered. "That would be of no use at all. Besides, all the wine in the cellar could never wash the taste of Volargne's dust of death from my palate." And then he remembers that he too proceeded to get blessedly drunk.

In Orlando, twilight was darkening an already overcast sky. Triggering the remote control, he turned off the television. Then rising, he went to the kitchen, poured a large glass of Cabernet, and looked at the clock: almost five. The family would be home soon. It was Thursday morning in Mantua. The wine still sat on the table. On the label: Lacryma Christi, the "Tears of Christ." Painfully fresh in the minds of all were the events of the last two days.

How ill named. The thought had come briefly to Victor's mind as he read the bottle's label through the spread fingers of both hands. As he held his bowed and aching head he reflected: *Maestro Jesus would never have done this to us.* And he was right, of course.

With Gina still sleeping, the three men had gathered themselves at the breakfast table, there to share, as it were, a debilitating communal hangover. Their stomachs too were still in a state of riot, and again conversation had been minimal. Even sotto voice, the sounds of words seemed to batter the air like the ringing blows of a blacksmith's hammer. Rather, they quietly and cautiously nibbled at some home-cured Valpolicella raisins, and some of Carlo's special sun-dried peaches and figs.

From demitasse cups they sipped dark Italian coffee—rich, potent and mildly sweet. Across the room and sitting on the counter, the espresso machine hissed and bubbled away. One after another they consumed cups of the placating brew. For obvious reason, the wine was left untouched.

Finally breaking a silence that had prevailed for several minutes and pointing, Victor said softly, "Dad, why did you ... why did you serve us from that bottle last night?"

Though not seen, his head being bowed, there was a quiet smile that warmed Carlo's face. For Luigi, such a question would have been fully in character; he having always been more spiritually inclined. But Victor was one who virtually never spoke of religion, and this kind of question from him was unexpected. Even so, Carlo knew exactly, that about which his son was hinting.

Lifting his aching head now and looking across the table, Carlo avoided a conversational response. "Why, you ask me ... why? Because it's vino delizioso, that's why. And you always said so yourself."

Victor shook his head and immediately wished he had not; the pain ratcheted up. But he was nowhere near satisfied with his father's response. So he now picked up the bottle and tapped the label.

"Isn't there a story," he said, "about this wine; about Christ crying over Lucifer's fall from heaven; and that when he saw the Devil plunge into Vesuvius, his tears fell on the land, fertilizing the lava flows and inspiring the vines that grow there?"

It was a clumsy way to introduce what he wanted to talk about, but it was Victor's way. And Carlo understood what his son was driving at. Moreover, he was pleased to hear Victor make an effort to discuss a subject not among his favorites.

Carlo stood now, rubbing his forehead. Walking to the coffee maker and pouring a fourth cup he said, "Yes, that's the story. At least it's one of two or three; but all of them are obviously myths. So how about the truth?"

And now Victor pressed the point. Obviously confused he said, "Well isn't it the same thing you tried to explain to us at the Winiarnia, back when Mussolini had visited us fifteen years ago?"

Addressing his sons with a look, Carlo said, "No, it's not at all the same thing. Myths are legends, and if they're written, they're not worth the paper they're written on. Just think about it for a minute.

"First of all, spirit creatures in Heaven don't cry; they have no need for tears. Furthermore, why would Christ have cried if he was the one who threw Satan out of Heaven in the first place, and for what purpose? Go, please; go get those Bibles I gave you fifteen years ago, and let's read the truth about the Devil's fall from Heaven."

It was the beginning of a lengthy discussion, several hours in fact. With chapter 12 of the Bible's Revelation as their focus, in particular verses 7 through 9, Carlo began by explaining that Michael was Christ's angelic name; that it meant—in the nature of a challenge—"Who is like God?" and that the war in Heaven, therein described, was the direct outworking of the first regal action taken by Christ following his enthronement as king in 1914.

"Note to where Satan was cast," Carlo said. "To the earth; and note too that this would mean woe for earth's people, as it's foretold here in verse twelve. Now this was precisely what brother Russell was talking about way back in nineteen ten, when I met him in Warsaw. And now you tell me, please: was there woe for the earth in nineteen fourteen?"

He paused now, letting the question linger unanswered. Then he said, "You know the answer. And there are many people—many intelligent people, insightful people—who feel it beyond doubt that the global events—unspeakable events in some cases—which have taken place since that time can only be the result of malicious demon influence."

Angrily now, he went on. "Because never before has mankind carried out, or seen, such insanely concentrated and coordinated evil. And you've seen it!" Again he paused. Then pressing the point he added quietly, "Like never before, my sons; like never before!"

The sun was setting now, the passing hours having constituted an unusual day. For as those hours had passed, and with their headaches gradually subsiding, the men had spent the entirety of the day in periodic discussions together. Gina had been there, of course, and listening. But it had been the men, recuperating from the mind-reeling events surrounding Volargne's destruction, who had spent those several hours reflecting on the far too numerous tragedies they had witnessed or been part of over the last four years—ever since the Nazi's invasion of Poland.

And from the vantage of his years of experience, Carlo had used the opportunity to expand his sons' limited understanding of world affairs. With additional facts and with supporting figures when necessary, he undertook to explain the deeper meaning of the things which had happened since that infamous day—the day when a young Serb, 19 year-old Gavrilo Princip, had assassinated Austria's Archduke and his wife on the 28th of June in 1914. And there was much to explain as to how and why one event had segued to another.

"It was like … well, it was like a bad lasagna," Carlo said, illustrating his point. "It was as if each of the ingredients were okay, but when they were put together it was … it was a disaster; it was not done well. Not everybody can make really good lasagna."

He told them, for example, how Austria-Hungary, dissatisfied with Serbia's response to their inevitable ultimatum—one which rightly called for the assassins to be brought to justice, but which in so doing nullified for all practical purposes Serbia's sovereignty—had declared war on Serbia on that very day. That Russia, bound by a treaty to Serbia, had then announced that she was mobilizing her vast army in defense; a sluggish process that would take them well over a month to complete.

"And then Germany," he went on, "allied with Austria-Hungary by a treaty, was swift to assume that Russia's mobilization was a belligerent act against Austria-Hungary. So, after giving no more than a scant warning, it too declared war on Russia. That was on August the first.

"Then there was France. Now, I guess a body might even pity France in a way. 'Cause there she was, bound by treaty to Russia, and she suddenly found herself—and not by choice—in a war with Germany; and by extension in a war also against Austria-Hungary. Well, the result of that was that Germany hotfooted it to invade Belgium, which at this point was still neutral. But believe me when I say that Kaiser Wilhelm didn't care a rat's patooti about that. Because going through Belgium would be his quickest way to Paris.

"So now what? Enter Great Britain, allied to France by what was called the *Entente Cordiale*. It was not really a treaty; what it basically said was that they'd be nice to each other, whatever that meant. So while they may have felt a moral obligation to defend France, Britain's real reason for joining the pending fray lay in another direction. Because, by the terms of yet another treaty, a real treaty, some seventy-five years old, she was obliged to defend Belgium as well. So then, on August fourth, with Germany having invaded, the Belgian King appealed to Britain for help. And later that same day, and like it was with France, Britain too found herself at war with Austria-Hungary.

"And you know what? So cocksure these British were; so elated with their imagined Anglo superiority … Off they went; off with the bands a-playin'; the flags a-wavin'; and people singin': 'When Johnnie comes marchin' home again' blah, blah, blah. And everyone was saying it would all be over by Christmas. *HAH*! In a pig's eye!

Postcards of 1915 titled: *"Auf Wiederschen!"* German Occupation of Lemberg (Lwów)

"But … the United States was different. They wanted no part of any war in Europe. So they declared themselves absolutely neutral, an official position that would last until nineteen seventeen. That's when Germany allowed herself the liberty of unrestricted submarine warfare. Then came the sinking of the *Lusitania*, and it turns out—that besides the ammo they were illicitly carrying— there were a lot of Americans aboard. Well! The U.S. didn't take kindly to that! And besides, since America's commercial shipping was now being threatened, and since that was almost entirely related to the Allies led by Britain and France, America finally felt itself sucked into the war. That was in nineteen seventeen, on April sixth.

"But before that came what you could call the domino effect. Because Britain's colonies and dominions, feeling a kind of companionship with England—places like Australia and Canada; like New Zealand, the Union of South Africa and India, all responded rather naturally by offering military and financial assistance.

"And over in the Pacific at the same time, and recognizing the need to honor their military agreement with Britain, Japan now got into the brouhaha. That was also in August of nineteen fourteen, on the twenty-third. And two days later this was followed—it could almost have been predicted—by Austria- Hungary declaring war on Japan."

And now Carlo brought the matter close to home. "And what about us Italians, you're asking? Well, by making use of a clause in an alliance Italy had with both Germany and Austria-Hungary, a clause that committed us to defend both countries in the event of a defensive war; we insisted that their actions had actually been *offensive*. So Italy also declared herself a neutral. And we stayed that way until May of the next year, when we finally sided with the Allies against our two former partners.

"So you can easily see how all of this … this political *spaghetti*, brought virtually the whole world of mankind into the war that everyone believed could never happen. Matter of fact, I once read about a Danish fellow, name was Peter Munch. Seemed like an unusual name; maybe that's why I remember him. Anyway, back before the war, around the late eighteen hundreds, he'd said that all the evidence was against the probability of a European war. He even went so far as to say that the danger of war would disappear in the future; said it had happened time after time."

Quietly Luigi said, "But he was wrong, wasn't he, Dad."

"Oh, yes he was, Luigi! Like so many others of the time, he was wrong, dead wrong. He realized it later on, but he was wrong. Actually, he even wrote in his memoirs, and retracting his previous prophecy, that the war of nineteen fourteen was the great turning point in the history of humanity. He said that we had gone from what he called a bright period of progress to an age of disaster, horror, and hatred, with insecurity everywhere. He even speculated that the darkness, as he called it, which came upon us at that time, might even mean the permanent destruction of mankind's entire cultural structure."

And now it was Victor who said, "It seems to me, Dad, that all the agreements—all of these treaties between the nations—were actually the problem. Suppose they had all disregarded the treaties and everybody had stayed home?"

"Well now," and Carlo grinned, "what an interesting speculation; it would have been different, I suppose. Personally, as I look back at it, I too feel that all of these alliances were themselves the cause, at least the human cause, a contributing cause in escalating the enormity of that conflict. But ... the interesting thing is that the Bible had said that it would be the way it was; and so it was."

All of this he was able to explain to Victor and Luigi; and how that war, resulting from that assassination, the Great War, had never really ended in 1918; that it was continuing at that very moment in what had been Volargne, and elsewhere around the world. Together they had looked closely at the major societal and political events occurring from 1914 to the present day. As a result, Victor and Luigi began to see clearly the subtle yet obvious connections between the Archduke's assassination and the destruction of Volargne.

Of particular interest had been certain other related prophecies from the Bible. And Victor was finally beginning to understand what his father had been trying to tell him 15 years ago.

Then Carlo said, "Victor, go get your stamp collection; the part you brought with you from Lwów."

"My collection? Why?"

"I want to show you something. Just get it, please … and bring your Bible."

With the collection then on the table, Carlo turned his Bible to the 146th Psalm, suggesting that Victor do the same.

Then he said, "Now look here." And they read verse three. "*Put not your trust in princes nor in the son of man in whom there is no help.*"

"Now then, Victor. Choose a volume from your collection, any one of them, and open it to any page." That done, he said, "What do you see?

And there they were: the *"princes;"* the *"sons of men,"* the uniformed and medal-bedecked nobles of nations around the world. Carlo then spoke softly.

"Now then Victor, and you, Luigi, if you think about these so-called noblemen, I believe you will agree that not a single one of them may be credited with having given their people anything genuinely useful; nothing beyond what God himself had already given them. No. What these men and others like them have given the world, is a plutocratic struggle for superiority. And blinded by nationalistic rhetoric, by patriotism, the people are even inclined to call them benefactors." He shook his head now. "Such a *delusion!*"

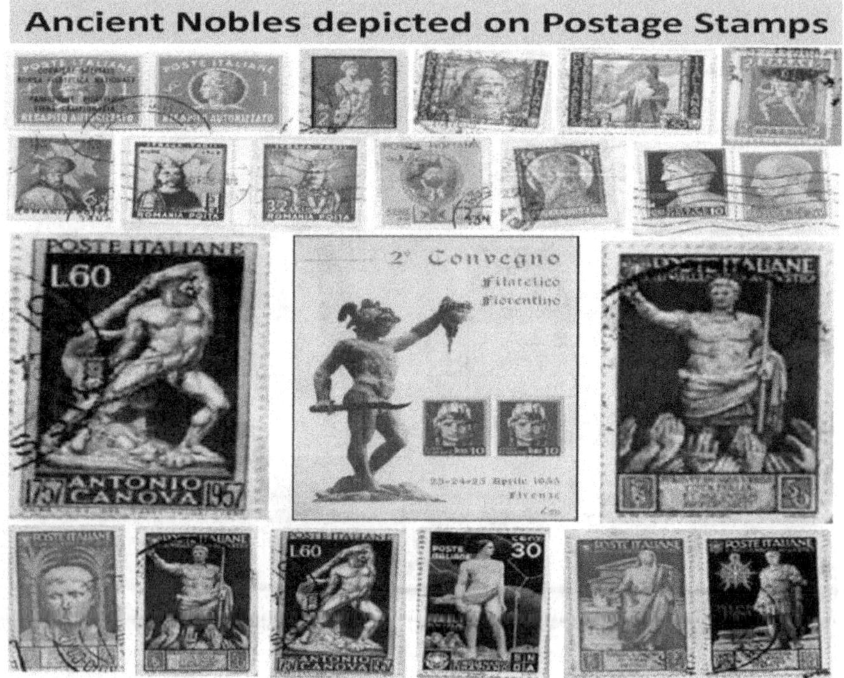

While Victor and his brother nodded in agreement, Carlo turned a few more pages in his Bible. "And now read this," he said, as though crowning his argument.

And there, in verse 9 of Ecclesiastes chapter 8, inspired by God and written by Solomon, they read: *"All this I have seen, and applied my heart to every work that is done under the sun: there is a time wherein one man ruleth over another to his own hurt."*

With the haunting vision of Volargne's recent destruction emblazoned vividly in their minds, and giving consideration to Lwów's disastrous plight over the past five years, the men each looked from one to the other.

The unspoken consensus could be seen in their faces; it was inescapable. Without exception, each of those nobles there portrayed had indeed been guilty of *'ruling over another to his own hurt.'*

CHAPTER IX

The year had turned; it was now 1945, February. In Yalta, Crimea, on the 4th of the month, Prime Minister Churchill and President Roosevelt had conferred together with Joseph Stalin. It would become known as the "Big Three Conference." There, in the same infamous manner of Hitler and Stalin previously, they had determined upon how to divide and reorganize Europe; the unconditional surrender of Nazi Germany now being for them a reasonable preclusion.

Thus did the Yalta Conference refine and confirm Poland's new borders, borders which had already been established more than a year earlier in November of 1943, in Tehran. At both meetings, decisions concerning Poland's future had been made and agreed upon; decisions, not one of which was known of or approved by the Polish people. Nor was any approval expressed by their exiled government in London. And the chief player in this game of political intrigue—that person most instrumental in causing Poland to lose the eastern half of its land to the Soviet Union, was Marshal Joseph Stalin himself.

On that same day, February 4th, 1945, amid what had been many days and nights of bombings and shelling during an escalated offensive in Northern Italy; and delivering prematurely due to those very bombings, Luigina Perantoni had given birth to Victor's first son, Roberto. Yet on the day he was born he was robbed; both his family's

Polish heritage and his birthright being stolen by political highwaymen; by Stalin, Roosevelt and Churchill.

During the following week, and while still at Yalta, Churchill and Roosevelt had agreed to give Lwów, East Galicia and all of Eastern Poland—territories that neither of the men had ever owned or could ever own—to Joseph Stalin. Galicia, for those unfamiliar with the name, is an historical region in Eastern Europe, currently divided between Poland and Ukraine. This gift was to be in exchange for Russia's participation in the war's Pacific Theater. And Stalin had accepted their offer. It was not until after the war, however, that most of the Polish soldiers stationed in Italy, and elsewhere, would learn of this nefarious, underhanded agreement; would become aware of the impact and the consequences this transaction would have on their lives. As a result of the subsequent Cold War, Lwów would never be the same.

When this news would later reach Victor in Mantua, he would come to realize that he had lost forever his beloved Lwów; that the Perantonis would never return to their wine import business; and that the Winiarnia Italia would never again be anything but a memory. Along with their 8-unit apartment building and all their other assets in Poland, these things would become as if they had never been. Though it had not been spoken, Victor had unknowingly said, "Arrivederci Lwów"— "Arrivederci Leopolis."

One day had followed another, and February had become March. The war had plodded along, appearing to be eternal in the minds of some, and nearly a year had passed since André Frodel and Franki Mrowicki had met with their friend Padre in Rome—a year since they had planned their visit with the Perantonis in Mantua, an event that had never been given an opportunity to occur.

But now in Northern Italy, Allied forces—André and Franki being among them—have crossed the Po River; *Operation Grapeshot* having initiated their penetration into the Lombardy plain. Ahead lies the town of Bologna, geographically the next of the Allies' premium targets, the battle for which would begin on the 9th of April. And not far south from there, the two reluctant warriors find themselves but about 65 miles from Mantua.

It was then close by San Lazzaro di Savena, a small town a few miles southeast of Bologna and at a little farm, where they proved to be among Fortune's favorites; where chance alone had put them in company with a fellow postal worker. For upon his learning that Franki had also worked briefly for the postal service, and that he was, as well as André, a fellow philatelist, a warm friendship was struck. And when they had explained to him their desire to contact a friend in Rome, he had made clever use of avenues with which he was familiar, and had thereby reestablished their communication with Padre Michele at the Vatican. That having been done, the three Lwówians planned again for a visit, the long awaited visit, to the Perantonis in Mantua; this for stamps, songs, pastasciutta and red wine.

Only hours later in Rome, Padre had been nearly beside himself; it had been so many months. Effervescing with excitement and not allowing for a moment's delay, he could have been seen packing his bags. Having also learned from his friends that an Allied offensive was imminent, he reasoned that traveling to Mantua during such heightened military activity would likely be difficult, perhaps even dangerous. And there would need to be a valid reason as well. Therefore he packed extra priestly garments, because strategy too had been uppermost in his mind. He remembered also André's incomparable skills as a printer and forger. So packing an assortment of blank Vatican forms and climbing into a car sporting Vatican plates, one which few could afford—a 1936 royal blue Lancia Astura, with a convertible top, skirted rear heels and a rakishly inclined grill—he put down the top and headed north. It was a joyous reunion.

"Carissimi amici!" Padre shouted, leaping from the car upon arriving.

Then throwing his arms around his friends' shoulders, he rattled on in Italian: "Despite all you've been through, the two of you look wonderful, absolutely magnifico!" Then turning to the postal worker and extending a hand, "And who is this?"

"This is Guido," Franki explained. "He's the reason you're here; he made it possible to get in touch with you."

"Guido, I am in your debt," Padre said emphatically, clapping his hands together, his eyes sparkling with appreciation.

Then shaking a finger at the man he said, "And for you I have brought something."

Turning quickly back to the car and reaching into the back seat, he took out two packages. Handing them to Guido he said, "These, mio amico, are for you."

The man was speechless. When he hesitated, Padre said, "Please! Open them. As I've said, they are for you."

When the wrappings had finally been torn away, Guido was seen to be holding a giant Italian salami; a Roman salami. While on the car's hood lay an autographed photo of the pope.

"Oh, Padre mio," he said, his tears brimming. Humbly he muttered, "But I cannot accept these. These are ..."

"These are just what they should be," Padre interrupted softly. "You've risked your life, Guido, in your caring for my friends and in helping to get us together. So these are but nothing." And for almost a full minute there were no words.

"Now then," Padre remarked sharply. "We have much work to do, much work. When is it that the Allies are pushing for Bologna?"

"It'll begin tomorrow; on the ninth," Franki responded.

"Tomorrow!" Padre exclaimed, startled. "Well, the two of you can't go driving about the country like a pair of tourists. Good Lord! I'm glad I brought what I did." And the work began.

The next few hours were little short of panic. As a halfway believable story was concocted, André busily falsified Vatican documents. From his skilled hands came special travel orders for three clergymen. And as though by some manner of wizardry, along with those papers there appeared also a purchasing order, an order allowing for the acquisition of a special purified wine—a sacramental wine—from a certain Carlo Perantoni of Mantua.

As to the quality of the forged documents there was no question, and language would likewise pose no problem: André and Padre being fluent in both Italian and German. Franki, however, was another matter; he was potentially the weak link. He spoke only his native Polish and a smattering of Russian, words he had picked up over the years. But neither would be of any value. It was decided, therefore, that Franki would become a mute, a monk sworn to silence; his role would be that of a special Vatican wine taster and purification inspector.

As for the plausible story, it would be said that the recent bombings of Rome had damaged the Vatican's wine purification facilities. The priests' instructions, therefore, were to transport Perantoni's wine back to the Vatican, there to be consecrated by the pope. At its very best perhaps, the plan was a house of cards.

Even so, thus equipped and rehearsed, late on the following afternoon André and Franki donned their priestly garb. And with Padre in the driver's seat, they said their good byes to Guido. After all of these many months, they were finally on their way to Mantua.

What an evening it was when they arrived!

The ancient Bacchanal itself could not have been more festive. Added to the natural joy of seeing each other after so long a time, was the delight of the surprise. Carlo, Victor and Luigi, busy in the shop when their visitors had arrived, had dropped their work on the instant. Indeed, hardly had the men gotten out from the car before the hugs and kisses began. And there were tears— tears of immeasurable joy. For not since the beginning of the war, almost six years previously, had all of them been together.

And now the very spirit of the Winiarnia was seen to be revived. In the kitchen, Gina cooked pasta al dente. In a large pot, a mouth-watering meat sauce, *a la bolognese*, absolutely reeking of the flavor of Northern Italy, was brought to the level of gourmet perfection. Cheese was set on the table and bottles of wine were uncorked. And with such a lavish board, a cheer-filled evening of—as they were so accustomed to phrasing it—stamps, songs, pastasciutta and red wine began.

As the evening progressed, as the wine worked its Aesculapian alchemy, hearts were made lighter and the war became as if it were not, momentarily fading from their consciousness. Proportional to the wine consumed, the volume of the singing rose, the night air trembling with the sound of their happy voices. And it was then that Victor remembered.

Separating himself from the bubbling merriment, he went into the shop's small office. Finding there the object of his purpose, he returned to the group. It took some time; but as the clamor of the singing subsided only briefly, and standing with one hand behind his back, he interjected his announcement.

"Silenzio, cari amici! Per favore! I have something to say." And he waited, it taking a moment before the room was sufficiently quiet.

"You will remember, André, and you also, Franki, that both of you left something behind in Lwów, at the Winiarnia." And now the room was as silent as a tomb. "You left it with the hope that it be found and safeguarded." Victor was now beginning to have difficulty in speaking, his throat thickening as he felt the emotion of the moment.

"I was fortunate enough to find what you had left. I have it with me and I would like you to have it back." And with that he handed them the stamp collections he had found under the floor of the shattered Winiarnia.

The men were dumbstruck. Their hands trembled as they held the treasures. Tears of deep-seated joy and appreciation welled in their eyes, streamed down their cheeks.

"O, mio fratello!" André murmured, and they both crushed Victor in a brotherly masculine hug.

With halting words Franki said, "I could not … I could not have asked for a better gift at a … at a better time. On this evening, Victor, you have made our joy complete. Grazie, grazie!"

And there was applause before André resumed. "But now I would ask—that is, we would beg—yet another favor. Will you continue to safeguard these for us—until the war's end? I think it will not be too long."

"Of course, my friends. "Non c'é problema."

As Victor walked back to the office, carrying the treasured stamps, the party and the singing resumed. Nor did it end soon, for it continued throughout the following day and evening. It was a reunion that exceeded by far all of their expectations.

Thursday morning however, April 12th, was almost demoralizingly different. Stepping out of the command car that had parked in front of the Perantoni's shop, a polished battle helmet in place of his officer's cap, the Nazi colonel swaggered arrogantly through the front door. At the back of the shop and having seen him arrive, Franki and André scrambled for the wine cellar.

Addressing himself to Carlo, off to one side of the room as the man had entered, the officer announced, "We are going to need your shop as a field hospital. And as I drove up, I noticed that you have a Catholic priest here."

"Well, yes," was Carlo's hesitant reply, "but he is only visiting."

"No matter," snapped the officer. "He will do. Equipment will be brought in and casualties are right behind me; within the hour they will arrive. The fighting has grown very heavy, and we need additional space to care for our wounded." Then with a sweeping gesture and in a tone that brooked no contradiction, he added: "You will make whatever adjustment are necessary." And he stalked out.

It was then, less than an hour before Padre, anxious now at being suddenly in the midst of the German army and surrounded with a growing number of casualties, found himself working alongside a German Chaplain, a Lutheran with whom he was at odds nationally, and with whom he felt no spiritual companionship whatever. Apart from the sham in which he was involved, however, his concern for the wounded was genuine, as was his administering of last rites to the dead and dying.

As the hectic hours wore on, and in the ongoing confusion, he worried about the virtually predictable discovery of his friends; that someone would eventually find their way to the cellar and that André and Franki would be found. And it happened.

Arriving at the bottom of the stairs and surveying the two priestly-clad men with suspicion, the patrolling soldier asked why they were there. "*Was machen Sie hir?*" he barked.

Franki started to turn. Then remembering that he was allegedly mute, he stopped short. Tapping André's arm and looking back over his shoulder, he displayed savoir faire beyond his ability as André, casually and matter-of-factly explained.

"Why, we're sampling wine for the Vatican; we're testing for wines suitably pure for sanctification by the Holy Father." Sounding the least officious as he possibly could under the circumstances, and after reaching into his cassock, he held out the authorization for purchasing.

"Here. See for yourself."

Turning their backs then, leaving the document in the soldier's hand and showing as much disinterest as was possible, André muttered to himself as they resumed their pretentious wine testing procedures. But suspicions were in the air now; and following his being informed about the two men in the cellar, and having been shown the forged purchase order, those of the German army chaplain became of particular concern. All of the pretenders felt a great deal of apprehension. Indeed, the air became thick with it.

Sensing this, and in an effort to alleviate matters, Padre Michele acted quickly. Telling the German chaplain that he was going to the basement, he swiveled his way authoritatively among the cots toward the stairs.

In the cellar now, and having been followed by the soldier, he personally began to sample the contents of the casks. After several such tries, he handed a sample to the soldier.

Lapsing into German and with a disarming smile he said, "*Versuchen Sie hier dies.*" Surprised, the man jerked back.

"*Bitte,*" Padre pleaded. "*Dies ist gut.*"

Finally accepting the sample and tasting it, the man grinned. "*Oh, ya!*" he said. "*Das ist Gut! Das ist gross gut! Danke schön!*"

Padre smiled. "*Bitte schön.*" Then turning back to André he said, "Yes, this one will do nicely, and that one over there as well." And after having approved the two barrels for Vatican use, he made a great show of ceremoniously attaching an official looking label to each one. Then using red chalk, he marked each barrel with a date and his initials.

Upstairs now, he approached the German chaplain. With an air of restrained superiority, and citing a church of some inconvenient distance away, he said very boldly, "I carry no money with me, of course; not in these days." A knowing smile as he added, "And I'm sure you understand why. It's much too risky. So it will now be necessary for Signore Perantoni to accompany me to the church for a transfer of the funds. But we will not be long."

And with that officious summary of matters, he and Carlo climb into Padre's car.

But an air of anxiety had now settled down upon all who were involved in the impromptu charade. As Luigi and Victor watched the Lancia pull away, and as the German chaplain began expressing his suspicions to the commander of the field hospital, Luigi turned to his brother.

"I think we'd better get these barrels into the van as quickly as we can. Because without doubt, if André and Franki are taken as prisoners—if they're seen as spies—they'll be shot ... and we'll probably be shot right along with them."

It was now patently clear; their long-planned holiday—their anticipated respite from the war—had itself become part of the war, potentially a matter of life and death. Victor, therefore, with André and Franki crammed into the back of his van, had driven to Luigi's house with as much abandon as seemed allowable. And it was not unlikely, being as he was in the man's hometown, that the name Nuvolari may well have come to his mind.

At Luigi's now, where Padre and Carlo had agreed to park the Vatican's car, they found the two of them in the garage and in the process of removing the Vatican's official plates. Padre looked up as the brothers came in with their friends.

With one plate in hand he said, "We'll be needing these later, when we head back toward Bologna. But right now we need to get out of here and leave this car."

"And what's the situation in Bologna?" Franki asked. "Has the city been captured?"

"I'd have to say that my guess is as good as yours," Padre replied with a shrug. "But with German casualties still coming in the way they are, I'd venture that they still control the city. However, that's really beside the point. Regardless of the situation, you and André really need to get back to your unit."

"Perhaps we should leave the car on the street somewhere," André suggested. "That way there'll be no connection to Luigi."

"Oh, no, not a good idea," Victor countered soberly. "Any strange car, especially a car like that Lancia Astura, and here in Mantua! Why, it'll draw the German's attention like … well, like Da Vinci's *Mona Lisa* at a rummage sale."

"Yes, or the Star of David on the front of the Reichstag," suggested Padre.

"Yeah, like that." And Victor grinned. "But I believe I know where we may be able hide it with no suspicion attached; no questions asked. Let me talk to my father. Meanwhile, we'll take the van over to my house. You Franki, and Padre, can hide up in the attic's colombaia for a few days. It was used as a granary for messenger pigeons about fifty years ago, but it's very clean now. Actually, Luigi and dad use it to season the summer's almonds, and the Castagna chestnuts of late autumn. I'll bring some mattresses up there; Gina can cook; we can have some wine …" Then a cavalier chuckle as he added, "And who knows? Maybe we can even gamble for some stamps." And becoming nostalgic he said, "Like we used to do at the Winiarnia."

By now it had grown dark. With the Lancia parked in front of the home of Carlo's friend, he and Victor climb out. There are no lights in the house, but on the porch now they knock. The man who answers the door is lean, his face angular in the pale shadows.

"We're sorry to disturb you at this time of night, Tazio, but we need your help."

Tazio Nuvolari looked beyond their shoulders, his eyes drinking in the Lancia parked at the curb. A smirking grin played with his face as he said, "I can't believe it, Carlo! You've stolen a car." And then he smiled; a crooked- toothed smile.

"No, it's not stolen," Victor offered, "but the Nazis are looking for it."

And Carlo added quickly, "Actually, Tazio, it belongs to the Vatican."

"Oh ho ho ho! Now that's really clever!"

"Yes, well maybe. But we do need to hide it, Tazio, hide it where it'll not attract undue attention. As you know, I'm more than aware of your fancy automobiles, and I thought that ... well, that maybe you could include this one in your collection, for a while anyway." Then pleadingly, "Can you help us?"

The smile broadened, the eyes sparkled. "Come in, gentlemen, come in. We'll have some wine and we'll talk."

As it turned out at Victor's home, and in an effort to lessen their fear of discovery and capture, they relaxed somewhat by gambling for stamps up in the colombaia, but in dim candlelight and with less fanfare than before. And three days passed during which they did as Victor had said: they ate Gina's cooking and drank Carlo's wine. But there was no loud boisterous singing as there would have been at the Winiarnia. There was no spirit of the Winiarnia as there had been upon their arrival in Mantua.

Much rather was there a growing feeling of tension, with everyone's focus on the routine street patrols by German soldiers, and the arrangements being made for André and Franki's escape. For while none of them were being sought as a saboteur—as being guilty of espionage—and while the Germans authorities were still uncertain concerning the sudden presence of three priests in the town, along with a missing luxurious car with Vatican plates, the situation was both unusual and dangerous at the very least. So while German patrols were searching for them from house to house, Carlo and Luigi were planning on how to alter the wine barrels.

It was then early on the morning of the 14th when Carlo, in the garage with Luigi, rolled one of the two barrels between them; barrels from which they had emptied the wine and from which they had removed one end.

"I've given this a lot of thought, Luigi, as I know you have; and here's my idea." Then smoothing his hand around the barrel's opening Carlo said, "I believe we can install a little lip around this inside edge, with an opening on opposite sides." He pointed as he said, "Here and here. Then if we alter the top, giving it two little ears that will fit into those openings and under the lip, the top can be put in place and turned from the inside to lock it."

Luigi saw it easily in his mind, and nodded thoughtfully. "Yes, that should work fine, Dad. It can be opened and closed from the inside, but with no outside handles."

"Exactly. And if we also allow for the bung to be opened and closed from within, there will be no lack of air."

Again the nod. "Right. I think it should work perfectly."

"We agree then. Let's tell the others."

It was shortly after seven o'clock, and the morning sun shone brightly in the kitchen windows of old Victor's Orlando home. His hand trembled a little as he lifted his coffee cup. Robert sat next to Mary, listening to his father's telling of the story.

"And that, Beto, is the way your grandfather and your uncle Luigi figured it out. So the next morning, April fifteenth it was, everyone was ready to chance the escape. Your grandfather had already put the Vatican's license plates on my delivery van, and Luigi and I were now wearing the frocks and cassocks. I also remember that we felt pretty silly. Now it had been decided that I should be the driver; Luigi would sit next to me up front, and Padre would sit in the back with the barrels. So then it was just a matter of getting André and Franki—both of them armed and back in uniform now—into the barrels."

"I'd like to have watched that," Robert said, chuckling at the thought.

"Oh, you did, Robert, but you wouldn't remember. You were only two months old at the time. But I remember your mother standing there in the garage with us that morning, holding you in her arms and laughing with the rest of us as André and Franki squeezed themselves into the barrels. It was tight and almost comfortable. And since it would be a trip of over fifty miles, it was decided that the barrels should travel on their sides. That way the men could be lying down, rather than in a continuous squat.

"Of course they reeked of wine—the barrels I mean; those staves were soaked with good claret—and it was André who joked that they might well be drunk by the time they reached their destination."

Visualizing it all in his mind, Robert chuckled softly and Victor continued.

"Anyway, we loaded the barrels; we said our sad goodbyes to Carlo and Gina, and to you of course, and then dressed as clerics we piled ourselves into the van. We were on our way.

"Oh! I just remembered something I haven't mentioned. Padre had sealed the barrels. I mean he'd put flashy red wax seals, with a papal embossing, on each one. So as we left, he was sitting in the back, next to the barrels, and holding an attaché case that contained various documents, including his counterfeit Vatican travel pass and purchasing orders. Now those orders—orders he had drafted—required that he personally maintain visual supervision of the transport of the pope's purified wine. This would preclude any contamination, as required by Vatican rules.

"Now other than the fact that our adrenaline was running pretty high, it was an uneventful trip until we were stopped by a Wehrmacht platoon manning a checkpoint, a German military outpost about thirty miles south of Mantua. You see, what we didn't know was that the German troops throughout Lombardy had been alerted. So now they're on the lookout for three suspicious Vatican emissaries—two priests and a mute monk. But … they're looking for them to be in a Lancia convertible.

"Anyway, they stopped us, and right away they wanted to know where we were going. So one of them said—probably the one in charge—'*Dove state andando?*' And we thought wow! At least one of them speaks Italian. When we said we were going to the Vatican, they wanted to know about the mute monk. '*Dové il monaco muto?*' says the one speaking Italian. 'Where's the monk who can't talk?' Well, Franki the monk, now back in uniform, is in the barrel of course.

"So Luigi and I start complaining; I mean we complained loud and long, explaining that the deaf-mute was part of another group, and that their wine cargo had been stolen by—as I recall phrasing it, and in German so they all could understand—by the *barbar Verbindet*, the barbarian Allies, somewhere in the vicinity of Florence.

"So now these soldiers order Padre to open the barrels, to lift the lids. Well now! We couldn't very well do *that*! So now it's Padre who starts to complain; I mean he's making a show of it! "

"Really! The Padre, eh!" Robert had crossed the room and was refreshing his coffee.

"Oh yes! Now I'd have to say that it's generally understood that priests don't lie; but Padre Michele stood there and lied like a veteran. I mean that if his religion really had a hell, he was guaranteeing himself an uncontested seat. He claimed that we were the fourth group to make this wine procurement trip for the Vatican, and that the pope was highly upset because he'd had to postpone the Holy Easter Sacraments due to the lack of purified wine; and all of this caused by bungled military interference by—and these were his exact words— '*Narren wie Sie;* ' by 'fools like you.'

"Then he really pressed the point! He told them that if they broke the seals on the barrels they might just as well steal the wine. Because, as he put it, its purity would have been compromised by men of war. Then he went even further. O Beto! He was inventive; he was *magnificent*! Padre should have been a fiction writer; he should have been an actor! He said they should know that a plane from the Luftwaffe, with neutral Swiss Guard markings, was standing by in Rome, waiting to deliver the sacrament's holy bread and wine to the Füehrer himself in Berlin, and that it was already two weeks late!"

Robert sat down with his coffee as Victor said, "And you'd never guess what happened next." Another few sips of his coffee while he allowed the matter to hang for several long seconds.

Finally Robert, consumed with curiosity said, "So …?"

"So you could hear the thumps of mortars and the thunder of the Allied artillery in the distance—to southeast. And these German soldiers—probably all Catholics, or maybe Lutheran; Hitler was a Catholic—were almost terrified. Just kids they were. And having no way to check on any of what we said, they bowed down, hugging and kissing the supposedly sacred wine barrels. Can you imagine it, Beto? They even asked us for a special blessing."

And now a great sigh. "Actually, as I think back on it, it was really a … really a very sad time. Amusing now, but back then those were frightened men— frightened kids. There they were, isolated, ordered to wait for the combat that would soon reach them as the Allies advanced. They were just awaiting their doom.

"I tell you, son: although it was a sham on our part, it was really quite moving. Because each of those soldiers at that outpost—perhaps about thirty in all—removed their helmet, they put down their weapon, and they got on their knees—on their knees, Beto—while Padre, Luigi and I, hypocrites that we were, acted out a ritualistic blessings for those poor frightened young Nazis."

A long pause now, Victor's mind dwelling on the memory while he stared thoughtfully into his cup. Then shaking his head and looking up at Robert he said "I'll never forget it, Beto. Never."

Another pause and he continued. "Anyway, an hour later we were stopped by a British infantry patrol. They asked some questions; we asked some questions; and finally—it was only a matter of time—they asked what was in the barrels. Well, when they saw André and Franki crawl out, reeking of wine but totally sober, the Brits started laughing. And the more they laughed the funnier it became, until it was almost hysterical. When we'd all finally regained our wits, and as we'd requested, they very kindly directed us to the Polish Second Corps. And there André and Franki were reunited with their unit.

"And just think. This all happened because Franki and André, and Padre, wanted to visit us at our shop in Mantua. Such a vacation! So now it was just a matter of Padre, Luigi and me driving back to Mantua. But you can bet that we used a different route. Oh, yeah; and we all wore civilian clothes this time, even Padre."

A wistful sigh then. "And Beto, if you don't mind, I think I'd like to sit in the patio for a while; and if you'd be so kind, would you refill my coffee?"

It was now mid-afternoon. The patio was bathed in autumn's warm sunshine. At Victor's elbow, a glass of Robert Mondavi's burgundy. Throughout the passing hours his mind had often dwelt on what had been discussed that morning. Particularly had he reflected on the return trip to Mantua; a part of the story he would perhaps share with everyone later.

He recalled that as the three of them had bounced along over the road, having left the area near Bologna the following morning—the empty barrels clumping away in the back of the truck—it had been a time of reflection. So clever they felt they had been, and indeed they had; outwitting the Germans at every turn: at the bottle shop; hiding the Lancia at Nuvolari's house, and spiriting André and Franki past the Nazi checkpoints. But as the euphoria of their exploits subsided, along with their braggadocio, their conversation took a decidedly surprising turn. It had been largely due to Luigi.

They had stopped for lunch, it being near noon, and after breaking out some bread, some onion, salami and cheese, along with some of Carlo's fine Valpolicella vintage, Padre had sat munching in the passenger-side door opening. Victor had elected to sit unceremoniously cross-legged on the ground, and Luigi had stood lounging against a nearby tree; one leg crossed in front of the other. Just why Luigi chose that moment to initiate the dialog that ensued will never be known.

Abruptly he said, "Tell me something, Padre, that is if you don't mind, why do we call you Padre; why do we call you Father? After all these years, why don't we just—why don't we just call you Michele?"

Padre swallowed a piece of cheese he was chewing on. "I suppose it's tradition, Luigi, just tradition."

"Yes, I know, Padre, but why? Where does the tradition come from?"

Victor was now looking at his brother with something like surprise, or maybe it was embarrassment, or shock. And Padre scratched his head thoughtfully.

Finally he said, "I think it was Paul, you know, the apostle—who said, somewhere, that he was a Father to the ones he had taught. It's in the Bible; book of Corinthians … I think."

Despite his erudite training, Padre had a reputation for seldom being able to actually put his finger on much of anything in the Bible.

"Okay," Luigi agreed, a condescending smile giving his face an impish look. "But what did he mean by that? Was he saying that was his *title*, or was he just saying that he was *like* a father to these people, that he cared for them, that he loved them, *like* their own fathers would?"

Padre was obviously embarrassed. He blushed. "Well, I …"

"Now don't get me wrong, Padre." Luigi was chuckling. "Lord knows we're friends, and this isn't meant to become an issue between us; I'm just curious. Because the other day … well, have you got a Bible with you?"

"Yes, I have one in my bag."

"Would you get it, please? I … I'd like to share something."

Padre slid from the seat, sat his wine on the running board, and went to the back of the truck where he opened a leather satchel. Taking out his copy of a Douay translation of the Bible, he handed it to Luigi and picked up his wine.

"It's here in Matthew," Luigi said, thumbing the pages. And after a moment: "Yes, here it is. It's in chapter … in chapter twenty-three; it's in verses eight to eleven. And this is what it says: 'But be not ye called Rabbi: for one is your Master, even Christ; and all ye are brethren.'" He paused now, and then said, "And here's the point: 'And call no man your father upon the earth: for one is your Father, which is in heaven. Neither be ye called masters: for one is your Master, even Christ. But he that is greatest among you shall be your servant.'

"So now. It looks to me—according to Jesus, that is—that God is the only one we should call Father, that is to say, in a spiritual sense."

For several long seconds, the buzzing of some flies was the only sound to disturb the silence.

"So then," Luigi continued, "this got me to thinkin' about some other things. We're told that God and Jesus are the same person, for example. So when Jesus died I wondered, 'Was God dead?'; and who resurrected him? And what about Limbo … and hell! Is hell really a place where Satan is the aah … is the *capo*—the boss? Or does he maybe work for God? Does God really torture people?"

Padre, his brow furrowed, had returned to his seat and was savoring a bit of provolone. For a while he nodded wordlessly. Then: "I must admit, my friend, that I've never been challenged in just this way; that you have some valid points there. And quite honestly—and I've never told this to anybody—I too have questioned some of those same things. And I concede that in some cases I don't believe they're really true. I know other priests who feel the same way, but that's what the Church teaches."

"More tradition?" Luigi suggested quietly. "But if you don't believe some of these things, why are you a priest?"

Padre allowed a dismissive shrug. "It's the way I was raised, Luigi, and … and it's a living."

Luigi nodded his understanding. "Hey! Everybody needs one of those. But let's carry this a step further; that is, if you don't mind. Other than that they don't believe in Jesus, why are Jewish clergy called Rabbi? Jesus specifically said not to do that. But then, why are the clergy of so-called Christianity called Reverend? Where do they get the authority for that? More tradition? The word means worshipful, deserving of awe. I looked it up. And with all due respect to you, Padre, and admiring you as a friend, I've never met a man deserving of awe, of worship.

"Did you know, Padre, that the word 'reverend' only occurs once in the entirety of the Bible that my father gave me? It's a protestant Bible, of course, a King James translation, and the word is in Psalm one-eleven, verse nine. It says there that God's name is to be reverend. So how are humans now reverend; are they putting themselves on the same level as God? Because it looks that way to me."

Padre allowed himself a cynical chuckle. "I see what you mean, Luigi; and very honestly," he shook his head, "I have no argument. Indeed there is no argument."

"So, my very dear friend," said Luigi softly, "in view of all we've said, why are you a priest; why do you have people call you Father?"

For a time, Padre looked wordlessly at the ground, his lips pursed, his head nodding slightly. Then looking up, adjusting his wire-framed glasses on his nose and looking at Luigi, his eyes filled with humility. Softly he said, "I've never been confronted with such questions before, nor with such kindness. People were probably afraid to ask. But they're valid questions, Luigi; and I think the answer is that ..." And there was a long pause. ". . . that otherwise I'd have to get a job and go to work."

And laughter suddenly erupted refreshingly into the air. It was such a brutally honest evaluation from such a genuinely honest man. For this man, Padre Michele, so widely traveled; a man who had seen not only all of Europe, but all of the United States, Australia, Canada, South America and more; a man who had met and knew important people everywhere; had dined on the finest cuisine and had tasted the most exquisite of vintages, had now poured out his soul, as it were; had humbled himself to these two friends of his.

The laughter subsided, but Padre's smile remained, brightening his face as though he had just been released from a prison. "I share your sentiments, Luigi, and I agree. Very honestly, I've always felt rather uneasy whenever someone would call me Don Michele. Because Don is an abbreviation of Dominus … that is to say, Lord. And if I recognize one thing, Luigi, it's that I'm no lord. And when I think of all of those times when …" Now he shook his head. "So from this moment on, to you my good friends, I am Michele. I'm no longer Padre Michele, nor Don Michele. And you know what?" Laughing he said, "I feel wonderful!"

With André and Franki soon to be included, the Bologna offensive, a major assault against the German forces there, had begun as scheduled on April 9th. Opening with a devastating air and artillery bombardment of the German's positions, it was followed that same evening by American and British units engaging the German flanks, while Polish units broke through into the city. By the following day, those same Polish forces had pushed the Germans away from the Senio River.

And now on the 17th, the two men had become a part of the battle. It was not to be a long engagement however. Because on the 21st, the 3rd Carpathian Rifle Brigade of the Polish 3rd Carpathian Infantry Division entered the city, a city where only isolated pockets of German resistance were still to be found. And by 0615 that morning, the Polish units, inclusive of the 6th Lwów Infantry Brigade, along with the 16th, 17th and 18th Lwówski Rifle Battalions, had secured the city.

In retrospect, it may appear fitting for that task to have fallen to the Polish 2nd Corp, and particularly to those Lwówian units involved. For the seemingly interminable months from September of 1939 through May of 1945 were indeed the years of The Lion's War. After all, Lwów and Eastern Poland were the bones over which the war between two rabid dogs was started—Adolf Hitler and Joseph Stalin. And its people, especially the citizens of Lwów, suffered immeasurably due to the resultant social and political butchering of Europe's cultural geography. It was that city which suffered the most, during the war and thereafter. Lwów, a city whose Latin name is Leopolis, *City of the Lion*."

Of that Polish 2nd Corp it has been reported that during the last two years of the conflict—1944 and 1945—its military units fought with particular distinction in the Italian Campaign. Outstandingly was it so during the final Battle of Monte Cassino, the Battle of Ancona during *Operation Olive*, and the culminating Battle of Bologna.

For as history would later come to see it, the battle for Bologna was to be the last battle of the Polish 2nd Corps, an engagement that liberated most of the Lombardy plain. It was also to be André's and Franki's last military involvement. For on the 22nd of the month their unit was taken out of the front line.

As they could now begin to see the war in Italy reaching its end—as the German Army evacuated Mantua and as it retreated toward the rubble of Volargne en route to the Brenner Pass—these two men, along with all the Italian citizenry in the Lombardy region, experienced a feeling of freedom, however small, a freedom that had not been theirs in too many years.

Indeed it was only days later, circumstances permitting and again in Mantua, when these two friends from Lwów were once again enjoying the companionship of Carlo and his wife, of Luigi and Michele, Victor and Gina; and were again savoring the cheeses, the pasta and the wine. And being as they were, philatelists to a man, they saw the many opportunities—opportunities of which they could and would take advantage.

For while this was a joyful time for them, it was a critical period for Italy, even as for the rest of the world. Things of landmark historical import were occurring, things of a truly unique nature. And for these men that meant new stamps—stamps having a similar historical import and of a correspondingly unique nature. Each of them, therefore, made a point of placing advance orders with Victor's philatelic connections in Mantova, Verona, and Milano; orders for complete sets of new stamp issues in full size sheets—stamps commemorating the defeat of Northern Italy's former Nazi-Fascist organization, the outfit that had been called La Repubblica Sociale Italiana—stamps to be acquired at special discounted prices.

Enjoying their relative freedom even further, they have occasion on the 28th to be in Milan, to be the guests of Gogliardo Grassi, a close friend of Victor and a fellow stamp collector.

And here again was the opportunity to collect and trade stamps unique in their character; to avail themselves of singular, never to recur postmark opportunities, those associated with the imminent fall of Hitler's Nazi-Fascist RSI; and this occurring even while the puppet Duce was attempting to escape to Germany, disguised in the uniform of a German soldier.

But for Hitler and for Germany the proverbial handwriting was on the wall—had been for many months. In Lombardy, American and British troops had completed their encirclement of the Germans forces north of the Reno River, and the 8th Division of the Indian units had crossed the Po River. The complete surrender of the remaining German forces in Italy was imminent.

Such news having reached them in Milan, and being now in high anticipation of the rumored issuance of a new Italian Republic stamp, Gogliardo's guests leave requests with him; that he would acquire for them mint-condition sheets of the new stamps. They also order future sets to be mailed on letters, thus to be postmarked on the day of issue as well as on the day of the Italian reunification. Either of such postmarks will assure the stamps' distinctive nature and their subsequent rarity and value.

But now other news reaches them as well, electrifying news—news that comes the following day as the five of them are preparing to drive to Milan's main post office. And it comes with all the force of the Euroaquilo, a fierce and fearsome Mediterranean storm with which Italian seamen are all too familiar. IL Duce has been arrested and executed!

While accounts of the event are generally in agreement as to the location of the capture, the character of the several reports is mixed, as is so often the case with news surrounding high-profile personages.

One report had it that a partisan commander, known by his *nom de guerre*, Eduardo, had dispatched ten men and an officer to arrest IL Duce. According to that report, they had found him and his mistress in a hillside cottage outside the village near Lake Como. It was reported also that when IL Duce saw his fellow countrymen approaching, he had joyfully embraced his mistress, thinking that they had come to liberate him. Upon learning, however, that he was under arrest, it was said that his face had turned yellow with fear and fury; and that he had cried, "Let me save my life, and I'll give you an empire!"

A less flamboyant telling had the man and his mistress being captured while trying to escape in a German convoy. After being summarily identified, and sans any legal process, they were thereafter shot.

Whatever the truth of the matter, *il popolo Italiano*—the Italian populace— were no longer to be had for mere promises. They are done with Mussolini's *Empire*. For while he may have caused the trains to run on time, such industrial efficiency does not, and would not ever, adequately compensate for the loss of sons and families, of homes and of businesses.

CHAPTER X

Milan is in a state of absolute anarchy.

On this sun-drenched Sunday morning, April 29th, the populace of the city, the very city wherein Mussolini launched his concept of fascism, is reacting with the kind of speed that breeds terror. As Victor and his friends arrive downtown, their attention is immediately riveted on the riotous commotion of a large mass of people in Piazzale Loreto; a place since renamed as the Piazza Quindici Martiri, in honor of the 15 anti-fascists having been executed there.

Out of their car now, having parked some distance away, they are swept along with the crowd, curious as is everyone regarding this uproarious bedlam of civil chaos. But the scene that finally confronts them is beyond anyone's believing.

From the overhead framework of a gas station, surrounded by a crowd of shouting, cursing men and women, hanging upside down as if so much meat in an unsanitary barbarian slaughterhouse, are the dead and bloodied bodies of Benito Mussolini and his mistress, Claretta Petacci. Strewn carelessly about on the ground, ropes attached to their feet in preparation for hoisting them up in a similar fashion, are the blood-smeared bodies of an additional 16 high-ranking fascist leaders.

But the crowd is not yet satisfied. Smarting from years of war and privation, having forgotten perhaps what measure of good Mussolini may have brought about for Italy, the crowd is growing ever more vicious. As Victor and his friends look on, the enraged mob surging and swaying about them like an angry sea, the absolute savagery of the moment holds them in a state of unwilling fascination, Suddenly shots ring out; a woman not far away emptying her pistol into IL Duce's body.

"Five shots!" she screams. "Five shots for my five murdered sons!"

Others were shouting also. "He died too quickly!" said one. "He should have suffered!" But the hatred of many was far beyond the words of contempt or animosity to be found in any lexicon. And now the people begin spitting on the corpses. Then stones and other objects are thrown at them.

And finally, as though not altogether capable of fully venting an anger that knew no depth, as though the hanging bodies were little more than grisly piñatas, they begin beating on Mussolini's unfeeling head with sticks and clubs.

Were it not so before, it now devolved to an indescribably gruesome scenario, a veritable feast of fury. The face of Mussolini ceases to be recognizable. Indeed, it ceases to be a face, having become but a bloody, gelatinous mass of battered flesh and shattered bone. It is a scene of unfathomable depravity, of unconscionable horror. A veritable carnival of carnage.

It is demonic!

And now Victor's nausea has risen beyond his control. Looking away, he vomits. And hardly had that occurred before Padre Michele

— having done nothing but look on in grief and revulsion — is threatened by an enraged communist partisan.

Brandishing a handgun the man shouts, "Don't even think it; don't even think of giving IL Duce his last rites, or even a blessing!"

Quietly and wisely ignoring the man, André says, "Come. It's time for us to go. We've been here far too long."

With emotion tortured faces, sober faces, they make their way back through the heaving, jostling crowd. Behind them they can hear the wordless roar of the angry mass crescendo. Without a backward glance, they know that the other bodies are being raised up to hang in ignominious disgrace; perhaps, indeed likely, to undergo a similar beating.

While in Berlin, shortly after midnight of the very same day — in the Reich's Führerbunker and with hypocritical solemnity, Adolf Hitler marries his mistress, Eva Braun.

Adolf Hitler: the man who in 1941 told his General, Gerhard Engel, "I am now as before a Catholic and will always remain so." Adolf Hitler: the friend of the pope, and who by him was never called to answer for his crimes; who according to his cousin, Anton Schmidt of Spital, Austria, was the man who at age seven wanted to be a bishop; Adolph Hitler the child, who built an alter with benches and pretended to officiate a mass; Adolph Hitler the little boy, who demanded that all his playmates kiss his hands.

Hitler the man: aware now that Germany's defeat is a foregone conclusion, is also aware of the public's growing disenchantment, as well as that of many of his officers. If it is not yet so, within hours he will learn of the fate of Benito and Claretta. Realizing in that knowledge that a similar fate may well await him and Eva, they have planned their marriage to be a mutual suicide.

Loyal SS officers will oversee their secret cremation and burial.

The Hitlers' marriage will last but a matter of hours. As a baptized Roman Catholic, his last act in life will be to make a mockery of marriage. The Beast of Berchtesgarten is to be no more.

Sic transit gloria mundi – thus passes the glory of the world.

The house in Orlando is quiet on this Sunday afternoon in mid-October. The family has gone on a picnic, and a cool breeze gently ruffles the water of the lake behind the house. Sitting in the patio, a glass of Carlo Rossi Burgundy on a table at his side, Victor watches the sun appear to ignite the water's little wavelets, causing them to sparkle like myriads of little fires. Bright avian melodies are in the air as he allows his mind to drift back over the events of the past few weeks. He recalls his conversation with George, here on this very patio. Less than a month ago it was; a conversation that had taken him all the way back to 1929.

Other talks there had been since then, conversations with the family wherein he had, on more than one occasion, stressed to them the significance of 1914. And it was not because of their being unaware; it was, rather, because he wanted them to never forget. For him, as well as for a multitude of insightful historians around the world, the events of the past 88 years were as but the fruitage of a single vineyard in a single season:

World War I; the second World War of his own experience; the various hotspots of the Cold War; the war in Korea; the war in Viet Nam; the never ending contentions between Israel and the Arab nations; the ongoing slaughter in the Middle East — yes, the destruction of New York's World Trade Center — all were of the same harvest.

True it was, he thought, that for Italy and for its people, 1945 had seen the end of the war. The insanity that had begun six years previously in Poland had finally ended. Yet, while the country had started on a program of recovery and healing; while the shattered Italian government had begun proceedings to become a reunited democratic republic; these had been matters of which he had wanted no part. For Victor had by then been firmly of a mind that only a government by God himself would solve humanity's problems; would provide everlasting peace and a genuine security.

Even so, at the time he was still an avid philatelist at heart, maybe even a bit fanatic about his passion for stamps. And having previously had many contacts with the Mantova post office, being then keenly aware of the postal systems' lack of needed organization, he realized that therein lay an enormous opportunity; one to be seized on the moment and in the manner of the irrepressible lieutenant Covasech.

For he vividly recalled the understanding had by that man — the Lwów Stamp Club's president — of the critical postal situation in the Austria-Hungarian army in 1917; how he had created his own set of commemorative stamps following the Battle of Caporetto. And now, in 1945, Victor had wanted to do a similar thing. Having then subsequently obtained the help and cooperation of the friends of Mantova's post office, he promoted the idea and then initiated the production of stamps — stamps which have become rare and renowned as the PSI MANTOVA overprints.

Circulated only by the Mantova post office and appearing nowhere else in Italy; existing but for the moment — only one issue ever being printed — Victor's PSI-MANTOVA stamp was to have commemorated the political and military reunification of Northern and Southern Italy, the South having separated itself when they surrendered to the Allies soon after the 1943 invasion. Northern Italy then became Hitler's and Mussolini's infamous Repubblica Sociale Italiana, continuing its resistance until 1945. However, although Victor's PSI Mantova overprints were meant to be non-political and well intended, they were to become an effort gone awry.

For among Communists and other anti-fascists of the time, the thought was promoted that the initials PSI stood for "Partito Sociale Italiano," the original foundation of fascism. It being a time, therefore, when people were being shot in the streets for supporting or trying to revive defunct fascism, he recalls having personally come under immediate accusation and threat; of having been in serious danger. Victor therefore, and without delay, had gone into hiding at the home of his dear friend and fellow philatelist in Milan, Gogliardo Grassi, the man they had been visiting when Mussolini had been so atrociously murdered.

Indeed, not until his father Carlo, explaining in front of a mob of irate men at a town meeting — armed men demanding to know Victor's whereabouts — that PSI really stood for "Piena Sovrenitá Italiana," that is to say, Full Italian Sovereignty — was there a quelling of the Communists' hue and cry for Victor's life. And to further appease their lack of understanding, Carlo undertook to distribute 25 cases of gift bottles labeled as PSI wine – fine, local Valpolicella wine.

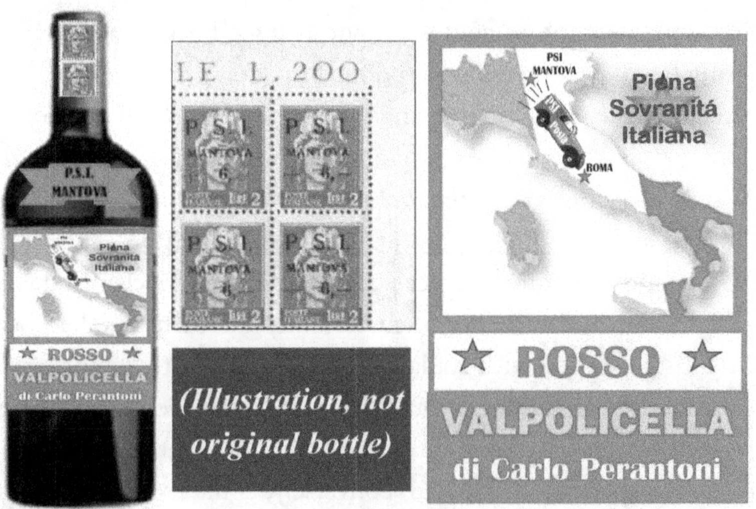

Bottled in frantic haste the night before by Carlo and Luigi, and bearing labels hurriedly drawn by André and printed at an Allied military press in Monte San Giusto, Macerata, it was ready for delivery by the following morning. André himself, along with Franki, would make the urgent, overnight label delivery to Mantova. The PSI labels, displaying an illustration of a mail truck driving southward down the Italian "Boot," had clearly spelled out "Piena Sovrenitá Italiana." And each bottle was tax-sealed with a gummed PSI- MANTOVA stamp, the taxes having been paid by the Perantoni family.

As it turned out, the arrival of Carlo and Luigi at Mantova's town meeting that evening — this in an Allied Jeep and accompanied by two Polish soldiers in uniform — made an indelible impression on the angered partisan mob there assembled. It was clear and obvious evidence that there was no spirit of fascism within the Perantoni family. And it had a discernable mollifying effect on what had been a murder-bent mob in hot pursuit of Victor.

Indeed, the communist majority of that hostile assembly, so attracted by the fancy red labels and the red stars on the wine bottles, wasted no time before starting to sample the rich fullness of Carlo's ruby Valpolicella vintage. And it was not long after when their stomachs were filled with it. So having happily accepted Carlo's explanation, along with the wine of course — not a single bottle being left at the meeting hall — and having abandoned the doing in of Victor, off they marched. Unsteady to be sure and wavering, rifles slung on their backs and swinging a bottle in each hand; they were singing loudly: *"Avanti Popolo … Alla Riscossa … Bandiera Rossa trionfera'. . ."*

It all seemed so long ago now. Victor had been 33 years of age at the time, and after all these years he still remembers clearly the whole botched affair. If not before, then certainly thereafter, he had become utterly disenchanted with Italian affairs of state; with the unreliability and instability of Italy's various forms of government; with so many new administrations; with cultural separations and discords he had personally experienced. He had, conversely, come to firmly believe the factual evidence presented in the Bible.

In his mind it had now become a matter of Bible Truth versus the World's Philosophy. And now, nearing the age of 90, it was often when he would think back to the time when Mussolini had visited the Winiarnia in 1929; to when his father, Carlo, had tried so hard to help him understand the significance of that cardinal year: 1914.

Now he sipped his wine, remembering how in May of 1945, he and Gina, with their infant son Robert, had begun preparing for a new life's journey. Germany had surrendered on the 8th, and he had been anxious to make the long awaited return to his beloved Lwów. There, if possible, he would reclaim his family's belongings, restore the winery tavern, and resume the family's wine import business. It had seemed such a bright time. He was fondling that memory when he heard car doors closing. The family had returned.

It was nearing 9:00 o'clock now. Amid the pale amber light bathing the elder Perantonis' living room, amid its warm, bronze shadows, he and Gina sat with their eyes closed—the music soothing away the day's cares.

"I was just thinking," said Victor, his words interrupting the muted strains of an aria from Verdi's *Aida*.

"Oh? About what?" Gina's sotto voice response.

There had been no dinner as would have been the usual; the picnic having sated everyone's appetite save that of Victor. On his lap, therefore, as he enjoyed the music and the comfort of his favorite recliner, a small plate of savory Stilton cheese and crackers.

"About André and Franki," he replied, "and of all the splendid times we had together. They were such fine fellows."

Then shaking his head resignedly he said, "But as with all good things, they end, as has this day." Then allowing himself a plaintive sigh, "I'm ready to go to bed."

A week had passed; October was drawing to a close. Two days ago the chilly fingers of a cold front had reached deep into the state, and no longer did the weather invite the family out to the patio.

Staring vacantly out of the kitchen window this afternoon, George thought, *Winter's coming.* And in that context he thought immediately of his parents, Victor and Gina. Life's winter was already upon them, and Victor's mind would occasionally wander. Had he but known it, Victor would be lost to them in the coming year.

Then shaking his head in an effort to dismiss the somber thoughts, he finished preparing a tray of snacks. He would come back for the coffee.

"Well now, aren't we the domestic," Valerie said brightly as George came into the living room. And he grinned.

"Just some snacks. I've used some of the cheese from the picnic, but I couldn't find any of the ham."

"That was a week ago, George," Valerie reminded him. "The ham is long gone."

"Oh, of course," he said, "it would be." Then pausing briefly before turning to his father he said, "And by the way, Dad, speaking of things 'long gone,' and particularly of people having disappeared in a similar way, I got to wondering the other day about Franki and André, about Michele—that whole bunch. You've told us so much about them, but they've just drifted off into some sort of a historical fog. What ever happened to them? But don't answer that; not yet; not until I come back with the coffee."

It was but a minute later, with coffee all around and with George now seated, when Victor said plaintively, "Curious you should ask about them. Just last week Gina and I thought of them. But in all truthfulness, George, and to begin answering your question, it's hard for me to believe that André died back in 'sixty-three. He had always seemed to be so very alive. But it's anyone's guess as to whatever happened to Franki. Even André lamented, up until the year he died, that he'd lost all contact with Franki."

"Why?" said George. "How did that come about?"

"Well," Victor began, "by nineteen forty-six the remains of what had been the Polish Second Corps, and that, of course, included both of those men, were housed in England, waiting to return home. But the months went by and they gradually understood that they'd been betrayed by virtually the entire world. Brave soldiers they had been too, that Polish Second Corps. But they finally came to the sad and rather ugly realization that they'd been used by the two chief players, the Russians and the Anglo-Americans, and then discarded when no longer useful. It was a terribly unhappy truth, George; especially painful when they would remember those many who had died in the process."

He paused now, mouth pursing as he mused over what he was about say. And Valerie asked, "What made them think that?"

"Oh, Valerie; and that's the really sad thing. Nobody ever explained this to them. But this conclusion of theirs was reached upon learning the demoralizing fact that Polish soldiers in England would not be invited to march in London's Victory Parade. That too was in nineteen forty-six. What a sad way to learn of your betrayal."

"Well, were there any others excluded?" George queried. "Perhaps there were …"

Victor became angry now. Interrupting he said sarcastically, "I can't imagine who they would've been, George, because most all the rest of the Allies were represented. There was Australia and New Zealand; the United States.

"There was France, and Belgium; Holland and Luxembourg were there, along with Norway, Brazil; Denmark and Czechoslovakia. And … let's see. Oh, you can also add Egypt and Ethiopia; add Greece, Iran, Iraq and Mexico. Many others too. Did I mention China and Nepal? There was even … there were even representatives from Transjordan, mind you. But Poland? Oh, no! No, not the Polish troops!"

"But why not, Dad?" said Valerie softly. "It makes no sense that …"

"Aah, not to us it doesn't; but to those who organized the parade it did. It mattered a lot. And to answer your question … because Russia wasn't invited; that's why!

"You see, by nineteen forty-six the British government had recognized and accepted the new Polish government, the one in Soviet Warsaw. And what an outrageous humiliation that was for those ill-fated Polish soldiers who fought the same common enemy; now more than one hundred sixty thousand of them housed in England!

"*Every one of them* should have been in that parade; they should have *led* that parade!"

Now he stood. Pacing the living room he snapped, "But how disgraceful, how very *shocking* it was for these brave men! And for their families too, assuming of course their having survived at home in their beleaguered Poland. Imagine these valiant soldiers gradually finding out the veiled truth of their betrayal, just getting bits and pieces of the facts. Over several months they waited, anxiously anticipating a happy and triumphant return to their homeland, a reuniting with their families. But even today the majority of those families continue as torn apart. And that includes even General Wladyslaw Anders and his family."

"Dad, that's terrible. That's every bit as bad as …"

"What? The Germans?" He spun and looked directly at Valerie. "Oh ho ho, yes! You're absolutely right. And it wasn't until forty-five years later, *forty- five years mind you*, in nineteen ninety-one and with the dissolution of the Soviet Union, that the tragic truth about those returning soldiers was released and reported by the world's media.

Victor shook his head in bowed respect. "O those poor soldiers! We found out, in nineteen ninety one, Valerie, that those who returned to Poland from the west were arrested and persecuted without exception. There was no G.I. Bill for them; there was no glory even from their own homeland, a homeland which was forced to become a deeply communist Soviet satellite. Some of those gallant soldiers were actually imprisoned, while most others were required to work at menial jobs. And they were also prevented from getting either a higher education or a respectful position. Very likely, Franki was not allowed to finish college." A pause now. "No, the Polish war veterans were destined to live the rest of their lives as marginal citizens in their own country. All this because the Soviets felt it necessary to crush any possible sources of Polish nationalism."

Now the old man sat down angrily and picked up his coffee.

Realizing now his father to have gone off on a tangent of history and emotions, George repeated the question that had triggered the whole conversation. "So then, Dad, what happened to André and Franki?"

Victor looked at his son out of the top of his eyes. "George, I'm an old man; give me time. I was coming to that. Let me calm down for a minute."

He drank the remains of his coffee now.

"Of those Polish soldiers there in Britain, while the vast majority decided to stay in the west, there were only some sixty or seventy thousand who returned to Poland. And Franki was one of those few. And among some forty thousand who were given aid to move to other countries, there was André."

"Aah," said George. "I can see where they began to lose track of each other. So where did André relocate?"

"Well, he wrote to me on his arrival; said he'd received a farming land grant in Alberta, Canada. Said he wasn't charmed; described it as … how did he put it? Oh, yes, 'A god forsaken frozen tundra.' Aah, ha, ha. ha," he laughed. "That's what he called it, frozen tundra. He wasn't a farmer, George; never would've been. So … he sold the land and moved to Vancouver.

"Of course he needed work when he got there, so he used his artistic ink- and-paper skills to make a modest but honest living as a philatelic artist. And yet again he found himself producing fantasy stamp art. None of it was to defraud anybody, you understand, but it was to be sold as high-quality stamp art.

"And because most of his friends and acquaintances were philatelists, and since he really was a great artist, there was a market for this sort of artsy thing, and with hardly any competition. Can you imagine this, George: that man could slice a stamp in half! What I mean is that he could separate the gummed side from the printed side! Don't ask me how. Then he could turn the halves around and rejoin them upside down or backwards, making the image appear reversed.

"So, using this and others of his secret methods, he was able to produce some amazingly beautiful philatelic stamp art. He even had a process of dissolving a stamp's paper and lifting the print! Oh, let me tell you, George! His art was often displayed in frames and hung on walls at hobby shops and stamp clubs. Even some doctors and lawyers have decorated their offices with his art.

"The sad thing however, is that several years after his death he would become renowned as one of the greatest stamp forgers in the history of philately."

"A forger?" said Valerie, taking another piece of cheddar from the plate. "Why a forger?"

"Well, that's what they called him: a forger. But forgery usually involves deceit, and like I've already explained, never would there be found a grain of dishonesty in my friend André Frodel. He was an upright and noble person. More than that, he was a man of great courage. What many don't know is that he was awarded nine decorations for valor in World War one and World War two. Does that sound like a forger?

"No, he never defrauded anybody, and nobody has ever accused him of fraud. He was an honest man, a talented artist who sold his products as art. Why, some of his stamp-art even bears his initials on the back. He never pretended that his stamp fantasies were anything other than just that, certainly never postal originals. And like I said, he died in 'sixty-three."

George said, "But didn't some of his work get sold as real philatelic postal rarities? Weren't there some …"

"Oh, yes. Yes, several years later, *after his death*, some of his art was fraudulently sold as genuine collectable postal oddities; as high-priced postal rarities. But this was done by unprincipled swindlers who had to convince their naïve buyers that the items were so very rare that even the stamp catalogs had missed them! Actually, in the late nineteen seventies it prompted the Canadian Postal Department to investigate some of André's stamp fantasies, which had been sold as rare postal originals. And it then became evident that if André had really intended to defraud any stamp collectors, it would have been much easier and less risky for him to produce cataloged stamp rarities. Those would have been high priced items, easier to produce, and their circulated existence would have been obvious in any catalog!

"Today, André Frodel's fantasy stamps are highly prized and valuable; they have become collectable, unique hand-made art. I know it would please him immensely if he were alive."

Valerie looked at her father-in-law with a smile. "Dad, you have known some of the most fascinating people, and André is certainly among them. But what about Franki? You said he'd returned to Poland, and that's where you left us."

"Uh huh. Well the last I knew," said Victor reminiscently, "was that in nineteen forty-seven Franki had relocated to Gdansk. And he chose Gdansk because he was not allowed to return to Lwów. Lwów, you see, was now part of Ukraine, and the Soviets had expatriated the Poles. So he too, although unknowingly, had said, 'arrivederci Leopolis.'

"Then too, he was also hoping to regain his old job at the Gdansk post office. As a matter of fact, all through the late nineteen forties he wrote often to André and to me. But it became obvious to both of us, as we read what he wrote, that Franki had mailed us far more letters than we had received. And we eventually realized that he could write only what the Soviet censor would allow. So while the calligraphy in Franki's letters was beautiful, it was not what his heart meant to tell us. And that's about all I know of the dear man. As I said, it's anybody's guess. So I'm like André in the matter.

Letter from Franki Mrowicki, July 1945. One may perceive the nostalgia in Franki's letter. Note also that while the Germans surrendered 2 months earlier, on May 8, the Polish troops had not yet been able to return back home.

July 8, 1945

Dear all

I send you a letter just a few days ago, so I can talk to you, and be with all of you despite the distances I miss you, my very good friends – You Vittorio and wife. You both were so good to me and helped me so much when I needed it. One more time thank you very much for what you have done for me. I am saying this from the bottom of my heart. I will never forget those happy days we spent together. I wish… But I am in the army now and I have to do my best so we can all go back to our homeland, and you Viktor can go back to Lwów you love much. I am in the same place but nobody knows how long we will stay here. I am O.K so far; just miss all of you and Giovanna very much. I do not know how she is doing and what she is thinking about me. Viktor, I hope that you did not forget me I and you will write a few words. You know me, I can keep a secret, and I will never put you into the trouble. I often think about all what happened back then I still remember fantastic taste of the salad your wife used to prepare for us. So again thank you very much for everything. I have to finish this letter now. I send my best wishes and a thousand kisses for the Family.

Franciszek

Especially I am sending greetings to Miss Giovanna Veronni and aunt.
Stay with God
Good night and Good Bye

"Then in the fifties — you were only a year old then, George, and we were living in Australia — communication to and from Poland, including that with Stasia, ceased entirely due to the escalation of the Cold War, and partly, I think, because André and I had addresses in Canada and Australia, countries considered to be enemies by the Soviets. But from Italy, however, Luigi and grandpa Carlo did manage to continue some censored correspondence with Stasia during that period."

A long and thoughtful pause now before Gina, having listened quietly all this time, said, "Yes. Yes, I remember André and Franki very well. And I think of them often, and of Padre." Another pause before she smiled, adding with a suppressed snicker, "Ha ha ha, and of their crazy ride in those wine barrels."

Victor grinned quietly. "It was crazy, wasn't it. *Assolutamente pazzesco*! But it worked!"

She said, "Yes, it worked. Do you still remember the difficulties we had in trying to return to Lwów?"

A cynical chuckle; an angry chuckle. "Oh, yes. As much as I'd like to, I'll never forget those days. People could hardly go anywhere; all that political folderol — passports and visas being held up; until after that pointless conference —that *circus*, in Potsdam, Germany."

"We'd been ready to leave Mantua back in May, hadn't we," she said quietly, "and there we were in the middle of July."

"Yes, July," he said, echoing her remembrance, "while Stalin, Churchill and Roosevelt spent two weeks — *two weeks* — deciding on what had already been decided at Yalta years before, and at Tehran even before that — that Russia would control Poland, and that the exiled Polish government in London was to be considered defunct."

And now his mind became troubled. Tehran, Yalta, Potsdam: names that were bitter to recall; names that smoldered in his memory. These were names which at times would leave him fuming. And had he but known all that had transpired behind the closed doors in London, Washington and Moscow, he would scarcely have contained himself. Inwardly he railed against them all, but toward Stalin was his anger most intense.

Though consistently portrayed in the press as the grandfatherly patriarch —the kindly benefactor of his people set upon by the vicious Nazi Beast — Stalin was in actual fact a murderous sociopath; an insidious liar who artfully cast "bones" to his Western Allies. While craftily promising imminent democratic elections in Poland, he failed to disclose the Soviet definition of what was democratic. In agreeing to the planned post-war demarcation zones — zones that would have allowed French occupation of Germany alongside the United States, Great Britain and Russia — he gave the impression of collaborating with President Roosevelt in support of the establishment of the forthcoming United Nations. Indeed, he even appeased the President by offering to reduce the number of Soviet votes in the U.N., and ultimately by agreeing to send troops to the Pacific Theater for the war against Japan.

These then were the "bones" with which he mollified his Western Allies, thus obtaining for himself almost half of Poland, limiting its land to George Curzon's disputed border of 1919. In effect, however, Stalin's promises were short lived at best — if ever they were intended to be fulfilled — proven by time to be nothing but frauds, brazenly committed in the face of the world, and with Lwów and Eastern Poland as the victims of those frauds. And now his thought returned to the present.

"As I think back on it now," he went on, "the conclusions reached at Yalta were a betrayal, an outright betrayal of Eastern and Central Europe. It was a *Benedict Arnold sellout*! Those leaders there at Yalta gave no consideration whatever to Poland's rightful future. They seemed to forget that Polish forces had fought the Germans longer than any country since the beginning of the war. Indeed, Poland *was* the beginning of the war. Thereafter they'd fought right alongside U.S. and British troops, alongside the Russians, and this in most of the major campaigns in Europe. They'd even fought in the final battle for Berlin."

"So many lives lost," Gina said, "and nothing gained."

"Yes, nothing gained. Altogether they'd committed almost one and a half million men, hundreds of thousands of whom had died. Why, in the final stage of war — after the Russians, the U.S. and the British

— the fourth largest military force in the world were the Polish. And its government, exiled there in London, was an official ally of the U.S. and Great Britain. And all this was ignored when Roosevelt accepted that this Allied government — this *amica* — was to be dismantled and replaced with a puppet communist government!

"And while all this was going on, even while Roosevelt was planning to hand Poland over to that butcher, Stalin; men of a Polish armored division in Europe were *still* battling the German Army and the Hitler Youth SS Panzer division, trying their best to link up with an American division, part of Patton's Third Army, and to close the trap on the German armies in Normandy."

Taking an angry bite of his cheese, he looked at all the family sitting there: Gina, his *Ginetta*, for whom he would literally give his life; George, the Orlando carpenter, and his wife Valerie; Robert his oldest, the Milwaukee aeronautical technician and his wife Mary, the cute Milwaukee blonde who loves to lie on sandy beaches and worship the Florida sun.

"I'm sorry," he said. "Didn't mean to be so historical. But I'm tired and it's late." Then turning to Gina he said, "Let's go home." And they headed to their home next door.

CHAPTER XI

Inside, Victor was exceedingly angry. Even now, in the late autumn of his life, he felt it impossible to accept the plight of the world, a world so very unlike that of his youth; a world inflicted on his family and on others. In earlier years he would have simply placed the blame somewhere, on someone, and then have looked hopefully for the relief which he hoped would come. But no longer could he do that; and there would be no relief, no human relief. He could only lament what had happened over the last few decades.

Sitting in his living room the following evening, Victor wondered quietly: *And where should I find fault tonight? With the Atlantic Charter perhaps? And why not?* It seemed to him as good a target as any.

Given its newsy but unofficial title by some writer at a London newspaper, the *Daily Herald,* and drafted by Roosevelt and Churchill in 1941 before their alliance with Joseph Stalin, whom some called "The Beast," the Atlantic Charter's signatories agreed not to seek post-war territorial advantages. Rather, the so-called Charter purposed to maintain the right of all peoples to choose that form of government under which they wished to live, and to assure a permanent system of general security.

But to Victor's way of thinking and to that of others, and in regard to honoring the spirit of the Charter as a whole, England's Prime Minister and the American President had failed. Pointedly he felt this to be so in the matter of the Charter's points No.1 and No.2: these regarding territorial gains and adjustments of territorial boundaries.

For these two presumably insightful statesmen had naively believed that the Soviet Union would also agree, that unity with their Russian ally would be easily achieved, especially after Russia had been so treacherously attacked by Germany, and only one year after *Time* magazine had named Stalin as the Man of the Year.

In what Victor felt may have been a spate of verbal diarrhea, Churchill had laid the groundwork for the Charter's major malfunction; that Charter point No.3, stating that all peoples had the right to self determination, would not apply to Stalin's Soviet Union. In a September speech in 1941, Churchill stated that the Charter was meant to apply only to those European states then under German occupation. Why, Victor reasoned, could the Charter's point No.3 not also extend to countries then under Soviet domination?

Then he answered his own question. The likely reason was that Britain had never intended for this principle to apply to them, to their colonies in India and Africa. Nor would this principle be brought to bear on other European countries which also held pre-war colonies, even after their anticipated liberation from Nazi Germany.

James Groppi then came to mind, his Italian friend and neighbor —Milwaukee, Wisconsin's civil rights priest of the 1960s; the renowned activist protester and the originator of Milwaukee's open housing marches, the most famous of which became known as "Selma of the North." When both had lived in Milwaukee, Victor had often discussed with him the frequently questionable politics of World War II, and the subsequent betrayal of Poland. Looking at the matter with hindsight, Groppi had remarked that the Atlantic Charter appeared to him — particularly in light of Churchill's Charter-emasculating statement — to have been written solely to benefit certain European imperialist nations during the Nazi oppression, and never for the people outside of Europe; not for those countries which, after the war, would be labeled as "third world."

Groppi's keen sense of racism had enabled him to detect its subtle machinations, no matter where and no matter how deep. A champion for oppressed peoples' struggles for equality, Groppi had once startled Victor by even stating that something good had come out of that 1939-1945 war. Although he roundly condemned both the Dictator's philosophy and his actions, he said that Adolf Hitler had, though inadvertently, shown certain elite Europeans what it feels like to be under the heel of an oppressor, to be colonized; what it feels like to have their lands occupied by a foreign power; their resources exploited; their people oppressed and even murdered.

Victor remembered that Groppi had taken great personal satisfaction in making that observation. "Imagine," he had said, tongue in cheek, "by accidental chance Adolf Hitler actually did something good for the world."

And perhaps Groppi had been right, Victor thought. Because Nazi aggression had shown colonialism and imperialism — generally accepted by the League of Nations prior to the war — to be what they really were: political slavery. And by the end of the war they had seen their day. The ancient glory of colonialism was forever tarnished, and the future of imperialism was at least in question, if not ruined.

Indeed, the resurrected League, now the United Nations, had established the Special Committee on Decolonization. And by the early 1960's such decolonization was in progress. How ironic, Victor thought, that such as Hitler had given European colonists a taste of their own medicine; that by default he had inadvertently taught the world a much needed lesson.

But Lwów, Poland would receive no such benefit. Decolonization was to be on the Western side of the "Iron Curtain." Due to the Charter's failure, more pointedly the failure of the Anglo-American leaders who drafted it, Stalin gained for himself and his Soviet Union many new territories, thus creating a second world: the Warsaw Pact nations of Communism. To the citizens of these countries he vehemently denied any benefits of the Charter's point No 6. Namely, freedom from want and fear.

Exasperated now with his own thoughts he surprised his wife. "Oh, Gina, Gina, Gina! *Basta*! Enough, mio amore. Thinking about it makes me angry." "About what?" she said, confused and looking up from her reading.

"I was just thinking, and it made me angry. I don't want to be angry." He smiled as he added: "Right now I'd just like to sit back and listen to some more of Verdi, to forget what the rest of the world is like. Makes me feel like I'm sitting on a two thousand year-old limestone step-seat in the Arena of Verona."

Had he continued his reflections that evening, Victor would have recalled that he and Gina were still waiting in August, waiting anxiously in Italy for passports and visas, for permission to relocate to Lwów. He would have recalled also that while they had waited, out of Potsdam had come a declaration.

The powers there assembled, having grown weary of war and having been joined by the Republic of China, had issued to Japan a demand for its surrender. It had been a caustic ultimatum, stating unequivocally that if that empire did not surrender it would face prompt and utter destruction. It had been but words, however; and Japan, not easily intimidated, had rejected the ultimatum outright.

But other news had also reached Victor and Gina, news heard by the rest of the world as well; news that during that two-week conference in Potsdam, the president of the United States, now a Mr. Truman, had spoken of what he had called "powerful new weapons." Weapons intended for use against Japan.

It was high rhetoric, of course, but rhetoric nevertheless. Japan, therefore, was no more impressed than had been Joseph Stalin when he had heard similar boasting from the Nazi propagandist, Joseph Göebbels. For that man too had spoken of his Germany having new miracle weapons. But time had demonstrated his words to have been impotent, nothing but empty threats intended to strike fear in the hearts of Russian troops as they had advanced toward Berlin. And it would again be time, and that only, that would or would not supply muscle to the words of Mr. Truman.

Stalin, conversely it may therefore be assumed, was no more impressed by Mr. Truman's revelation to him at Potsdam concerning an atomic bomb, than had been Emperor Hirohito. Nor would such have truly been news to the Soviet leader, as Soviet espionage had already brought to light Nazi Germany's nuclear research, as well as the Manhattan Project at Los Alamos, New Mexico and at Hanford, Washington. Indeed, Moscow had already taken steps to develop its own nuclear program. What was finally confirmed at the Potsdam Conference was Stalin's agreement, on August 15th, that he would join the Allies in their war against Japan. He had no need to do so, other than to collect what he himself had proposed and that had been agreed upon at the Big Three Conference about six months earlier in Yalta. Namely, Lwów and Eastern Poland up to the 1919 Curzon line.

In preparing to fulfill his promise, Stalin had already moved his Red Army into Manchuria, this on August 9th, 1945, the same day the United States bombed Nagasaki. Thereafter, and because Japan had accepted the allies' terms of surrender, Stalin's war with Japan ended before it ever began. Without delay, then, he turned his army around, having fulfilled his obligation without ever firing a shot in combat with Japan.

It has been reported, and is perhaps noteworthy of mention, that some of the conscripts assigned to fight in this final battle of the war were older, middle- aged Polish men — men who had previously been classified as Ukrainians; men whom Stalin had drafted from Lwów and the Soviet-occupied Eastern territories of Poland; older men who had been put into Soviet uniforms to fight the Japanese. Had they but fought and been victorious, their solitary reward would have been to lose their country to the Soviet Union!

In actuality, however they had already lost it to the Soviets in 1939. Thus, Lwów and Eastern Poland will always be seen — must always be seen — as the historical center of World War II — the very heartbeat of the "Lion's War."

CHAPTER XII

Monday morning in Orlando. Under skies of scudding gray clouds and in diametric contrast with yesterday's weather, rain is pelting down. Occasionally the murmuring of a soft rolling thunder can be heard. Walking in at breakfast, Victor finds himself suddenly immersed in a sparkling conversation about the world's political complexion. George, in fact, had initiated it by reviewing with the others what they had learned over a week before, about what had happened to André and Franki after the war.

And no sooner had Victor sat down, than George began with the questions. "I'm sure I speak for all of us, Dad, when I say that you satisfied much of our curiosity a few days ago, about André and Franki. But we've been talking this morning about Padre. He wasn't even mentioned at the time. Whatever became of Padre?"

Head down and cocked to one side, Victor looked at George as he so often did, almost through his eyebrows. And speaking aside he said, "Valerie, would you please pass the toast." And everyone waited.

And now his knife scraped over the crusty bread, spreading the butter. With mock sarcasm he said, "Would you mind terribly, George, if I'm allowed a bite or two before the interrogation begins?"

The murmur of amusement went round the table, and George said, "I'm sorry, Dad. I didn't mean to ..."

"I know," and Victor waved a excusing hand. Then after swallowing some scrambled eggs and a bite of the toast, he took a sip from his coffee. Nodding he said patiently, "I understand, George, I understand. It's the impetuosity of your youth, and you're an Italian."

As the laughter subsided, Victor said, "I can say this about Michele. Sometime in the nineteen fifty's, he was appointed as the General Consultant for the Holy See, and from here in America he relocated to Rome permanently."

"Is he still in Rome?" It was Robert's question.

"Couldn't really say, Beto, but I doubt it. Michele would be … well, he would be ninety-nine now."

A pause. "Huh! Hard to imagine him that age; he always seemed so young."

"Did he ever write?" said Valerie.

"Oh, yes. Padre wrote many times, and I've saved his letters. But in the nineteen sixties they gradually became fewer. I'd always supposed it was due to the very heavy workload and the responsibilities assigned to him during the Second Vatican Council. Anyway, his mail eventually ceased; but not before grumbling to me about having less free time at his new job, and how very much he missed the good old days of leisure in Poland, at the Winiarnia before the war."

1940 letter narrating the Lwów bombings, sent to Victor by "padre" Michele Kolbuch.

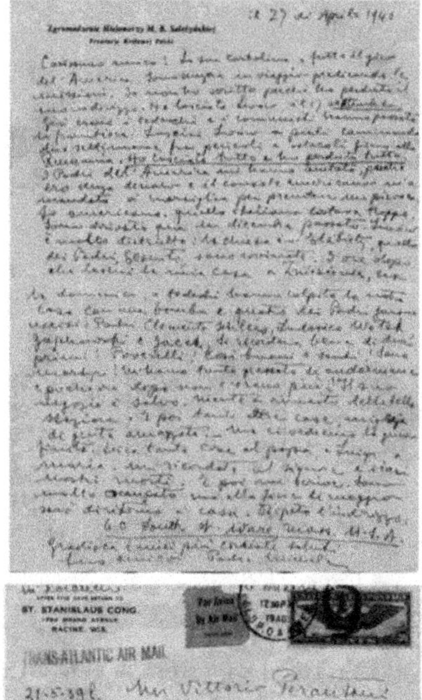

27 April 1940

Dearest friend,

Your postcard went all over America. I am continuously in travel preaching the missions. I did not write because I had lost your new address. I left Lwow on 17 September. There were Nazis, and the Communists too had entered our borders. I left Lwow with the children and we walked for two weeks through dangers and obstacles until we reached Romania. I left everything and I lost everything.

The American Consulate allowed me to board an American ship in Marseille France, because the Italian Ships were too expensive, and the missions in America helped with the cost. I arrived in the U.S.A. in December. Lwow have been destroyed. The church and the Jesuit building have been destroyed. It was Sunday when I left Lwow, and 3 hours after my departure a bomb fell centered on our parish home and 4 of the Fathers were killed : Fathers Clemente Schleis, Ludovico Wotes, Fathers Zujchowski and Jaced. You certainly know the first two. Poor souls ! How good and saintly they were ! They have become martyrs ! They had been urging me to depart on my journey, and only a few hours later they were no more !

Your winery is intact, but nothing remains of our beautiful train station. And so many other homes and buildings destroyed, thousands of people killed. But we will reunite at the end of the war. Tell all these things to your father, to Luigi and Maria. Remember me to the Lord and to all our dear dead ones. And then write to me. I am very busy, but by the end of May I will be back home. I repeat my address : 60 South St. Ware, Mass. U.S.A.

Receive my most cordial 'saluti'.

Your friend,   Padre Michele

"And the girls?" said Robert.

"I can tell you about Stasia," Victor said, a voice bright with increased enthusiasm. He nodded now. "Stasia Alexiniska; what a beautiful name; it's like music." And a broad smile lighted his face. "She kept in touch with your uncle Luigi and your grandpa Carlo while we were in Australia. Married a certain Polish fellow finally; name was Rozankowski. And I remember that in the late nineteen fifties she and her husband were expressing their desire to leave Poland."

"And did they?" Valerie's query.

"Yes, eventually; after receiving some encouragement from your grandfather. That was during a nineteen sixty-two ballet theater tour in Vienna. Matter of fact, Grandpa Carlo died that same year. So it turns out they were among the fortunate ones; the ones able to defect. Like most refugees, they would have preferred to stay in Poland, but not after it became part of the Soviet Union."

Gina suggested, "Tell them where they went, Papa'."

"I was coming to that, mio amore; you're almost as impatient as George." And he grinned as he laid a hand on that of his wife.

"In nineteen sixty-four, soon after our family arrived in Milwaukee, I was able to sponsor her and her husband as immigrants, and then as Polish refugees. And without too much difficulty, the Rozankowskis were granted asylum here in the U.S.

"Actually they followed the same procedures, the same *expedient* immigration steps, that I had used to bring our family here, coming as Polish refugees." Some eyebrows went up, and Victor took note. "Oh, you're surprised, are you? Ah ha! Yes, even our Italian family came to this country as Polish refugees."

"Oh? Why Polish?" said Valerie.

"Ah!" He said. "You see, the Polish immigration quotas were consistently low and seldom filled during the Cold War. So U.S. embassies everywhere in Europe gave Polish refugees priority over other immigrants. Consequently the Rozankowskis arrived here in 'sixty-five, settled in New York City, and there Stasia started a seamstress shop, making ballet outfits and costumes. Not surprising. It was exactly what her mother had done in Lwów."

"And Dani and Larisa?" Valerie persisted.

Victor's tone now became more solemn. Shaking his head he said, "I'm sorry. I don't have much if any information about them; I wish I did. Stasia did tell me that after that wonderful nineteen forty-one New Year's Eve party at the Winiarnia, Larisa's father, Mr. Doroshenko, arranged for Dani to live on his brother's farm in Southeastern Galicia, on the Ukrainian side of the border. He didn't, however, reveal the community's name, wanting probably to preempt any possibility of her being interrogated.

"She said that Larisa had gone with Dani to the farm, and had stayed there for a while, and that during that time her own father died.

So, soon after the second Russian occupation, Stasia and her mother were forced to evacuate to Western Poland.

"After that there was no contact with either Dani or Lari. They both may be dead by now. But I've often prayed that they may have survived the terrible war crimes of that region, and I still pray about them, that they be alive and well."

The room had become quiet and somber. And then Robert broke the silence. "Thanks, Dad. I know that wasn't pleasant. So if I may," and he picked up his coffee, "I'd like to change the subject."

"O please do!" Valerie urged quietly.

"Good! So … I was reading in *Time* magazine," he went on, "some interesting information about Bush. In this article by Ron Suskind, he said that a certain Bruce Bartlett—he was a treasury official for George Number One—had said he thought that a light had gone off for people who've spent time close to Bush: that the instinct Bush is always talking about is a weird sort of idea; a Messianic concept of what Bush thinks God has told him to do."

Valerie laughed, cynically surprised. "*God* has talked to George Bush?"

"Whatever," said Robert, chuckling. And he went on. "Anyway, Bartlett believes — according to Suskind — it's the reason why George W. is so clear-eyed about Al Qaeda and an Islamic fundamentalist enemy. Bush believes you have to kill 'em all, that they're extremists that can't be persuaded. Bartlett says that Bush understands them because he's just like them, and it's why Bush dispenses with people who confront him with inconvenient facts.

"Suskind actually quoted Bartlett as saying that Bush truly believes he's on a mission from God; that absolute faith like that overwhelms a need for analysis; and that the whole thing about faith is to believe things for which there is no empirical evidence. Then Suskind quoted Bartlett as saying, 'But you can't run the world on faith.'"

Victor looked knowingly at his son, sitting to his right. "Hitler thought he could—faith in himself. And so did Mussolini; so did Hirohito, Japan's emperor."

From the opposite end of the table George said, "And they were wrong."

"*Assolutamente!* Victor snapped. "Because just four days after that meeting we talked about yesterday — the one in Potsdam — on August sixth of 'forty-five, this country dropped the first atomic bomb on the city of Hiroshima."

"That was the one they nicknamed 'Little Boy'," Robert recalled.

"Right! And it killed … no, it vaporized — instantly — more than eighty thousand people. *Eighty thousand people!* And most of them were civilians." Looking down he shook his head. "Never knew what hit them."

"And when that happened," George interjected, "although we didn't know it at the time, it marked the beginning of tensions between the U.S. and Russia."

"Yes, and out of that came the Cold War," Robert added.

"Right," said Victor. "But first — and pointlessly I would add — two days later, on August the eighth, Stalin declared war on Japan.

"Now there was no logical reason for him to have done that, none whatever; the Pacific war was a done deal. His purpose — his only perceivable purpose was to honor — if that word may be properly used in connection with a politician … " And here everyone chuckled. ". . . was to honor his part of the Yalta agreement. And when he did, he sealed the fate of the citizens of Eastern Poland and Galicia, including Lwów."

Victor looked down then, staring into his cup of coffee. After a moment's silence and with a sigh he looked up. "And while Gina and I didn't know it then, our hope of a life in Lwów ended that day; we had said arrivederci to Leopolis — to Lwów."

Though it was a somber note on which to end their breakfast, it was perhaps in keeping with the weather. The rain continued until early in the afternoon.

It may have been a subliminal thing, possibly in compensation for the rather dreary morning. Whatever the reason, the family decided to have a barbeque. And though the air remained humid, reminiscent of the morning's rain, it was pleasantly and unusually mild for an October evening. And lacing the air like savory pheromones, was the smoky, appetite-whetting aroma of beef sizzling on a grill. Hearty glasses of Chianti Rosso would make for light hearts.

Perhaps it was predictable that later, with appetites sated and with the wine prompting memories of old Italy, the conversation would eventually reconnect itself with that of the morning. It was not, however, because they were unaware of how the war had ended. It was, rather, that they were much aware— far more often than was desired—that Victor would not be with them forever.

They found great pleasure in listening to the old man's stories, and to his arcane wisdom. He seemed at times to know things that no one else knew. It was then George who brought up the subject.

"You aah … you kind of left us hanging this morning, Dad."

An elf-like smirk on the old man's face. "Yeah, I do that now and then."

George smiled and the others chuckled. "So how was it that things worked out for you and mom?"

Victor sipped thoughtfully at his wine. "Well, George, as I said this morning, the news about Lwów was … well, it was dreadful; it was just unacceptable. And not fully understanding what it meant, your mother and I still remained hopeful of getting back to Lwów. What I mean is that it seemed to us that society — I mean the culture and the traditions of Lwów — were far too well established for a government like Russia to make too much difference. But …" and here he shook his head, ". . . it turned out to be nothing but wishful thinking. Boy! Were we ever wrong!

"What we didn't know was that Stalin considered himself *bigger* than culture, bigger than tradition; what we didn't know was that he was planning to expatriate all Polish nationals, along with their traditions, and then generate a total cultural transformation from Polish to Ukrainian … and do it in the Soviet style. Gina and I couldn't even imagine such an accomplishment. So now you're asking, how did he do it?"

Eager now, Robert said, "Well, yes, Dad! How *did* he do it?"

Victor bobbed his head and raised an emphasizing finger. "It was not until later that we discovered — that the world discovered — that

Stalin had already begun deporting Poles eastward, soon after the nineteen thirty-nine invasion. From the Soviet occupied regions of Eastern Poland, over one and a half million Poles went to labor camps in Siberia and Kazakhstan. And by nineteen forty-six, if you were Polish and still living in Lwów, you were arrested. Release came only after you'd signed an agreement to leave Lwów.

"After that, the rest was simple. Stalin made Ukrainian the official language; he changed the names of the streets; he changed everything else that needed changing. He even changed the alphabet! Most of the remaining Poles packed up and moved to Western Poland; and those arrested were given the option of doing the same or settling in Siberia. Obviously, most of them chose Western Poland. And still in nineteen forty-five, more than a hundred and twenty thousand of the city's remaining resident Poles left Lwów. But now it was no longer called Lwów; it was called Lviv. So there was no Lwów for us to go back to. Actually, the only thing left was the significance of the city's name: Lions. And if we'd known then what we know now — if we'd understood the reality of what was taking place — I suppose it might have been … well, it might have been much like the loss of Volargne, but without that awesome explosion.

"Anyway, the following year was difficult for us, very difficult. The Italian economy was *in the toilet* as we're now inclined to say; the new republic's bureaucracy made it even more difficult for merchants and other businesses to stay afloat; and now that fascism was gone forever, Italy was struggling with communist influence in their multiparty democratic government. They called the leading party *"Christian Democracy."* Phew! They didn't know the meaning of the word. For your mother and me it would have been a laugh if times hadn't been so tough.

"In the meantime, and half way around the world, the United States dropped its second atomic bomb. That was on August the ninth — a twenty-two kiloton monster nicknamed 'Fat Man.' And apart from obliterating Japan's industrial seaport of Nagasaki, it atomized more than thirty-five thousand people in a flash; I mean literally in a flash.

"And now listen to this if you will: it was determined, a year or two later —there are people who like to keep records of these things — that the two bombings had resulted in post-attack radiation casualties of more than double the original number of fatalities. So now, we take the original number — a hundred and fifteen thousand dead from the two bombings — we double it to get two hundred and thirty thousand; and we add them to the original one hundred fifteen. Total: some three hundred and forty-five thousand people."

Gina looked over at her husband with sad eyes. She knew exactly what Victor was feeling. And Valerie, her voice soft with melancholy said, "Oh, Dad! That's awful!"

"Yes, it was. But now let me tell you something else; something that you probably never read in your schoolbooks — probably something nobody ever will ever read. What I'm about to tell you is no secret; it's just something that's never talked about."

Allowing the family to wonder what he was about to say, Victor rose and walked to where he poured himself another glass of wine. He took his time, and the suspense grew. Finally it was Robert who simply said, "Well, Dad?"

"Patience, Beto, patience. I'm coming to it."

Seated again, Victor said, "Now then. Before the bombings, Japan was ready to surrender." And now everyone was on the edge of their seats.

"They were ready," he said, "if only one condition could be met. That is, if they could retain their emperor; that the surrender not involve any demand that would prejudice the prerogatives of the emperor as a sovereign ruler. The Allies, however, demanded — *demanded* … an *unconditional* surrender."

And now the silence was disturbed only by the lapping of the water along the shore. And everyone waited.

"Actually back in July, on the thirteenth, Japan's Foreign Minister, Togo, had sent a wire to Ambassador Sato in Moscow, purposely to find a negotiated way out of the war. In part the message had said that the unconditional surrender was the only obstacle to peace; that it was the emperor's heartfelt desire to see a swift termination of the war."

"Really? So why then did the United States …?"

"Exactly, Valerie! Why? Why indeed? Because if the Japanese were so fanatical as to have already lost millions of lives and still not have surrendered, why did they in fact surrender after losing only a few hundred thousand at Hiroshima and Nagasaki?"

There was a silence on the patio that could be felt; that was virtually solemn in its nature.

"And consider this," Victor went on. "It was concluded by no less than the United States' Strategic Bombing Survey, and following interviews of Japanese decision-makers immediately after the war, that Japan was indeed on the verge of surrender. It would have surrendered even *without* the bombing of Hiroshima and Nagasaki — and without that hideous loss of life and all of that prolonged suffering."

The silence remained unbroken.

"Oh, the bombings helped to speed things up all right, but so would the United States' acceptance of that one condition the Japanese had asked for: the sanctity of the emperor. Anyway, on August fourteenth, nineteen forty-five, Emperor Hirohito accepted the allies' terms of surrender. Publicly, *publicly* I say, it was an unconditional surrender, but in actual fact it did allow for that one condition to be met. So in the end, Hirohito's requested condition had been accepted.

"So, on the following day his surrender speech was broadcast by radio to all the Japanese people. Then MacArthur, General Douglas MacArthur, very tactfully convinced the emperor to make another radio speech to the Japanese people; one that aired on January first of nineteen forty-six. In it he would plainly reject the Shinto claim that he was a god. And with that speech, Hirohito himself *threw in the towel*, so to speak, as to his sanctity. Come to think of it, Hitler too, and Mussolini as well, had also been looked to as gods of a sort. Were they not? It might even be said that in nineteen forty, the three of them had been a trinity; in ancient Rome they would have been a triumvirate — an *Axis Trinity* of false gods."

A bitter laugh as he added, "Because without doubt, hadn't parades been held in their honor; had they not been saluted and bowed to?

Hadn't human sacrifices been offered to them? Because when one thinks about it, isn't that what those men who died in the war really were — sacrifices? I mean, what more do gods get?"

Heads were nodding thoughtfully as George rose. As he began cleaning the grill, and as the wives began gathering dishes, he said, "It really was a stupid war, wasn't it Dad?"

"Pshaw! Aren't they all? In nineteen fourteen it was 'the war to end all wars.' In nineteen thirty nine, it was the war to correct the wrongs of the nineteen fourteen war. In nineteen forty-one, it was the war to 'make the world safe for democracy.' Then came Korea and Vietnam and the rest of the conflicts. So here we are, in two thousand and one, and the fact is that the world's not safe for anything!"

He paused briefly and then said, "I can remember Will Rogers once making an interesting comment. Referring to so-called peace conferences, he said they were simply occasions for nations to get together to choose up sides for the next war."

Along with the others, George laughed. "It's about like that, isn't it Dad."

"Yes, it's just about like that. No, it's exactly like that! And I'm reminded of another observation I heard the other day; that war occurs when the demons are playing with their toys. I swear, George; only a government ruled by God himself is going to solve all of mankind's problems, is going to provide true peace and a lasting security." Then turning to Gina he said, "Hey! It's been a wonderful evening, but let's go home." And they walked across the lawn to their home's back door.

It was late now, nearly eleven. Gina was sleeping and Victor sat reflecting on what had been said, and what had not been said. He thought of how, on August 16th in 1945, Joseph Stalin had initiated the border agreement between Poland and Russia, a move that cemented the arrangement that had been made at the Yalta conference; that solidly finalized Russia's acquisition of Eastern Poland and Galicia, limiting it to the so-called Curzon line, a 1919 line of demarcation. It was an action that had robbed him — for the next 46 years — of the second town of his youth: the city of Lwów.

The events of which he and his family had spoken over the past several weeks had reminded him again that faith in human governments is poorly founded; that these current "ships of state" are, without exception, shabbily commanded by incompetent people and leaking badly. And as with all of their predecessors, they will inevitably sink. Human government, whatever it be, is founded on a lie; the lie being found at Genesis, chapter 3 and verse 5; that by usurping God's authority one may "be like God, knowing good and evil;" that one may wisely and successfully choose one's own course.

But such usurpation had not resulted in such wisdom, nor would it ever. Therefore, great Egypt of the past and mighty Babylon are no more; the empires of Rome, Medo-Persia and Greece — all are gone; each having passed away, as have the soaring towers of New York's World Trade Center.

Victor had not been there, of course. But had he been, he would have heard Charlie Kroger's voice.

"What time ya' got, Ed?"

He would have seen Ed Lemanski throw a glance at his watch and reply, "Eight forty-five, Charlie."

He would have known that they had but one minute to live.

He would have heard the music: Muzak's *Autumn in New York.* He would have seen Charlie Kroger rise from his desk and say, "How about some coffee?"

There would have been fifty-six seconds remaining.

He would have seen Lemanski nod and smile as he replied, "I could go for that."

He would have seen him organize some papers he was working on; would have seen him stand and walk with Kroger across the office.

There would have been forty-four seconds left.

Down the hallway he would have walked with them, to the employee's lounge.

Thirty-two seconds would have remained.

He would have seen Kroger draw a cup of coffee; would have heard Natalie Forrest remark, "Gonna be a warm one today, Charlie. I can feel it."

There would have been twenty-one seconds left.

Then Kroger would have said, "Yeah, you might be right," and he would have cast a glance at the window's bright expanse of glass as he added, "It's sure a sunny one."

He would have seen Kroger walk to where Natalie was sitting and ask, "Did you catch Leno on *The Tonight Show* last night?"

There would have been twelve seconds left as he heard Natalie's reply, "No, not last night. I went to bed early. I seldom watch that anyway."

And then seven seconds would have remained.

He would have heard Lemanski laugh as he began drawing coffee; would have seen him look over his shoulder and say, "Oh, you should've heard him, Nat. He really had Bush's number. I was …"

He would have seen the coffee fly from Lemanski's cup.

It would have been eight forty-six.

He would then have felt the 93rd floor of the World Trade Center's north tower suddenly tremble, would have felt it shudder as though struck by the very fist of God. In that nanosecond of time, he too would have known their lives had ended; that below them on the 90th floor there was limitless wreckage; that there were fire blood and terror beyond conception; that they were trapped, with no way down save to fall; an immutable truth that would have filled him, and everyone in the room, with a galvanizing dread.

There would have been no alarm. From other offices on the floor he would have heard cries of helpless panic. There would have been weeping. The reality would have been understood. Here he would die. Ed's coffee cup would never be filled.

The war of 1914 — the Great War — was still in progress.

Peace had been taken away from the earth.

ADDENDUM

1914 – A Pivotal Year

In some respects, circumstances regarding this landmark year remind one of the story of the three blind men who went to see the elephant at the zoo. To the man feeling the elephant's side, the animal seemed like a wall. To another, examining the elephant's leg, the creature was as a tree. And to the third, having touched only the trunk, the beast was very much like a snake. They had all experienced the elephant's presence; they had literally reached out and touched it; yet none of them understood it — none of them saw it for what it really was.

And thus is 1914 not fully understood. Yet without doubt, that blood- soaked year and the unnerving, terror-filled decades which have followed, are assuredly like an elephant for their colossal enormity. And like an elephant, they may not — at least by sensible people — be ignored.

Or better perhaps, these past decades may be seen collectively as an insidious cancer in chronology. Yet the world's Illuminati, its knowledgeable leaders — its *Doctors of Delusion* — have thoroughly misdiagnosed the illness. Having exhausted trillions upon trillions of dollars in treating it economically— unsuccessfully it must be said — they have also misdiagnosed it as a military problem; a political problem; a religious problem; or one of a social nature. But none have treated it as the grievous *moral* malady it actually is — Oedipidic in its gravity. Therefore are Bertrand Russell's following words particularly appropriate.

Quoting from the *New York Times Magazine* of September 27, 1953, we may read: "Ever since 1914, everybody conscious of trends in the world have been deeply troubled by what has seemed like a fated and pre-determined march toward ever greater disaster. Many serious people have come to feel that nothing can be done to avert the plunge towards ruin. They see the human race, like the hero [read Oedipus] of a Greek tragedy, driven on by angry gods and no longer the master of fate." How very like Oedipus indeed!

And the honorable Mr. Bertrand Russell is in no way unique in such an opinion. Consider the following observations:

Regarding the historical significance of World War I, the English author J. B. Priestley wrote: "If you were born in 1894, as I was, you suddenly saw a great jagged crack in the looking-glass. After that your mind could not escape from the idea of a world that ended in 1914 and another one that began about 1919, with a wilderness of smoke and fury … lying between them."

From *The Scientific Monthly* of July 1951: "It is indeed the year 1914 rather than that of Hiroshima which marks the turning point in our time." — Rene Albrecht-Carrie, An editorial in *The Seattle Times*, of January 1, 1959, commented: "The modern era … began in 1914, and no one knows when or how it will end. It could end in mass annihilation."

James Cameron, in his 1959 book *1914*, states categorically: "In 1914 the world, as it was known and accepted then, came to an end." Note, please, his last four words as regards the world.

"Thoughts and pictures come to my mind," said German Chancellor Konrad Adenauer in 1965, "thoughts from before the year 1914 when there was real peace, quiet and security on this earth — a time when we didn't know fear …. Security and quiet have disappeared from the lives of men since 1914."

The Economist, of London, England, under date of August 4, 1979 observed: "In 1914 the world lost a coherence which it has not managed to recapture since. … This has been a time of extraordinary disorder and violence, both across national frontiers and within them."

"The whole world really blew up about World War I," wrote novelist Dr. Walker Percy in *American Medical News*, November 21, 1977, "and we still don't know why. ... Utopia was in sight. There was peace and prosperity. Then everything blew up. We've been in a state of suspended animation ever since."

On January 27, 1980, Frank Peters of the *St. Louis Post-Dispatch* wrote that, "Civilization entered on a cruel and perhaps terminal illness in 1914."

"Everything would get better and better," said British statesman Harold Macmillan. "This was the world I was born in. ... Suddenly, unexpectedly, one morning in 1914 the whole thing came to an end." — *New York Times*, November 23, 1980

And we would add one more comment. The publishers of Charles L Mee Jr.'s book *The End of Order – Versailles 1919*, make this comment on the book's jacket: "The first world war and the Versailles Treaty that followed produced the most serious upheaval in the long and stormy course of modern world history; ... Far from restoring the world to order, the diplomats who met in 1919 at Paris and at Versailles plunged the world again, this time irretrievably, into the chaos of the twentieth century. It was the end of order."

In the body of his book, author Mee goes on to explain: "At the end of the Great War, however, the diplomats confronted a world in fragments, a world that seemed to be in the midst of a massive psychic breakdown, of a breakdown of old combinations of states and of empires, of the disintegration of economic orders, of nineteenth-century capitalism, of the eruption of sudden disaster, of riots and assassinations, of tyranny and disorder, of frivolity and despair, exhilaration and dread on such an order of magnitude as to numb the mind. ... The diplomats gathered [at Versailles] —and, far from restoring order to the world, *they took the chaos of the Great War, and, through vengefulness and inadvertence, impotence and design, they sealed it as the permanent condition of our century.*" (Our italics)

What an intellectually provocative consensus of opinion. And more could be said, much more. Thus was Charles Russell correct in 1910, when he told Carlo Perantoni and others in Warsaw that 1914 would be as the end of the world. And James Cameron therefore, in 1959 and as quoted above, does but echo Mr. Russell in his saying, *"In 1914 the world, as it was known and accepted then, came to an end."* (Our italics)

With that thought in mind then — if Mr. Russell and Mr. Cameron are correct — this portion of an article that appeared in the Sunday magazine section of *The New York World* newspaper is more than deserving of our attention. Under date of August 30, 1914; on pages 4 and 17 and addressing Mr. Russell by a title never used by himself or his associates, namely, "Reverend," we would have read what follows:

"According to the Calculations of Rev. Russell's 'International Bible Students,' This is the 'Time of Trouble' Spoken of by the Prophet Daniel, the Year 1914 Predicted in the Book, *'The Time Is at Hand,'* of Which Four Millions Copies Have Been Sold, as the Date of the Downfall of the Kingdoms of the Earth.

"The terrific outbreak in Europe has fulfilled an extraordinary prophecy. For a quarter of a century past, through preachers and through press, the "International Bible Students," best known as 'Millennial Dawners,' have been proclaiming to the world that the Day of Wrath prophesied in the Bible would dawn in 1914. 'Look out for 1914!' has been the cry of the hundreds of traveling evangelists who, representing this strange creed, have gone up and down the country enunciating the doctrine that 'the Kingdom of God is at hand.' ...

"Although millions of people must have listened to these evangelists ... and although their propaganda has been carried on through religious publications and a secular press service involving hundreds of country newspapers, as well as through lectures, debates, study classes, and even moving pictures, the average man does not know that such a movement as the 'Millennial Dawn' exists. ...

"Rev. Charles T. Russell is the man who has been propounding this interpretation of the Scriptures since 1874. ... 'In view of the strong Bible evidence,' Rev. Russell wrote in 1889, 'we consider it an established fact that the final end of the kingdoms of this world and the full establishment of the Kingdom of God will be accomplished by the end of A.D. 1914' ...

"But to say that the trouble must culminate in 1914 – that was peculiar. ... And in 1914 comes war, the war which everybody dreaded but which everybody thought could not really happen. Rev. Russell is not saying, 'I told you so;' and he is not revising the prophecies to suit the current history. He and his students are content to wait — to wait until October [corresponding to the Jewish 7th month of Tishri, 607 B.C.E.], which they figure to be the real end of 1914."

The above article was published when the First World War was still an infant; it had only begun to be organized. Suddenly, like a virus worldwide, declarations of war were proclaimed, treaties were broken and frontiers violated. Invasions began. The first large-scale bloodbath had already taken place the previous week, when more than 27,000 French soldiers were slaughtered in a single day. An event that shocked the world. By the day the article was printed, 250,000 Russian soldiers had been added to the carnage. This was but the beginning, the overture, and in September the infamous war trenches began to appear all along the western front. The war had dug in to stay.

So what did happen in October of 1914? Did Charles Russell and his Bible Students really wait for an "October miracle" to happen, as the August article implied; did they wait until October for a decisive confirmation of their understanding? No. Beyond doubt, by October 1914 it was the World's condition that validated what the Bible Students had been expecting: Namely, that the 2,520 years of Daniel's "seven times" prophecy had been exhausted. Since 1914, human governments are on borrowed time; they exist only due to God's patience; allowing all to clearly see that man can dominate man, only to his injury.

In conclusion then, the writers of *Arrivederci Leopolis - The Lion's War* are hopeful that the World War II experiences of the Perantoni family and their friends may alert others to the critical and historical importance of 1914. For the Greater Lion's War, that of the "Lion that is of the tribe of Judah"— the one whom history knows as the man Jesus

Christ — has yet to be fought; a war that will permanently eliminate all that is deterrent to mankind's happiness.

The 'Good News of that Kingdom' and of its pending warfare is currently being "preached in all the inhabited earth for a witness to all the nations." And the imminence of its Sovereignty is clearly seen in the earth-shattering events of 1914 and thereafter. Truly, we are in what the prophet Daniel called "the time of the end."

May you prove to be a survivor.

www.ingramcontent.com/pod-product-compliance
Lightning Source LLC
Chambersburg PA
CBHW071526120726
47907CB00013B/1084